FIERCE AT HEART

A PINE HARBOUR NOVEL

ZOE YORK

THE KINCAIDS OF PINE HARBOUR

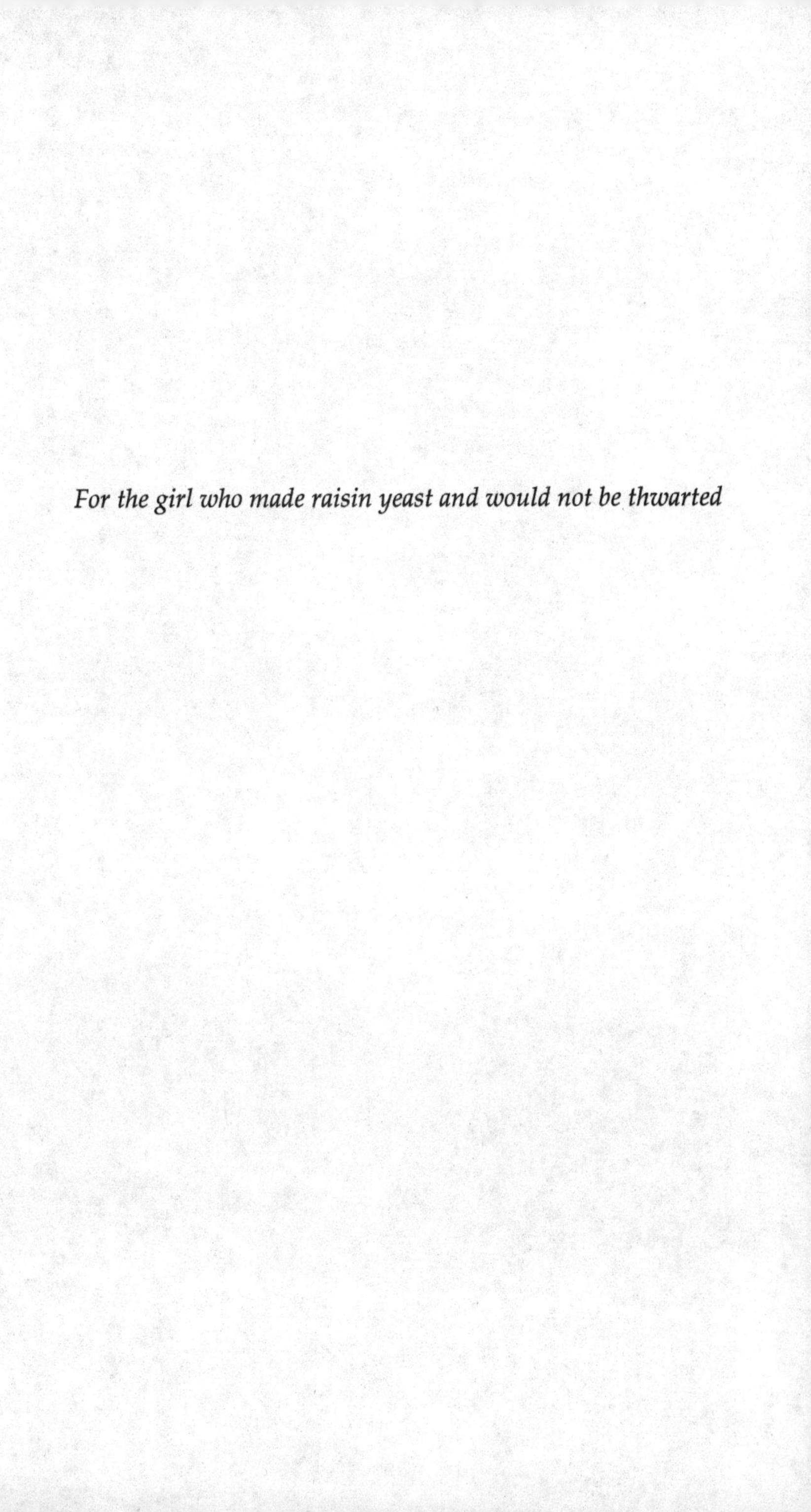

For the girl who made raisin yeast and would not be thwarted

CHAPTER ONE

SOMETHING about the way the man strode through the crowded mezzanine caught Isla Petersen's attention. She had just sold another box of bake sale treats to a customer when the shape of him caught her eye, and for a moment she panicked. But when she swallowed back that fear and took a good look, she knew it wasn't her former husband she had spotted in Toronto's oldest market. Adam Kincaid was taller than her ex, and broader, too. Brawny now, in a way he hadn't been four years earlier when she saw him last—at an airbase a few hours away, both of them having just returned from Afghanistan.

A lifetime ago.

She blinked, ready for him to disappear, be replaced by someone who just looked like him, shared the same thick golden brown hair and square jaw, who walked with a cocky confidence she knew he didn't always feel.

But even after shaking her head, he was still there, and getting closer. His eyes twinkled as he took in the sight of her, and she knew he was having the same moment of *hey,*

I recognize you, but wow, you've changed disconnect. Except in her case, that change wasn't so clearly for the better.

"How much are the cookies?" he asked, pointing to a sign that clearly said *25 cents each*. She'd missed his gentle teasing, the way he followed the question with a smile that warmed his eyes. "No way they're only a quarter."

Laughing, she rounded the table and launched herself into his embrace. He squeezed her back.

"Master Corporal Kincaid," she whispered as she stepped back and bounced.

"Captain Petersen," he echoed, setting his hands on her shoulders and holding her still so he could get another good look at her. "Look at you."

"It's just Isla now." She swallowed hard. "I got out."

He grinned. "Me, too. I bet that's no surprise to you."

She let out a relieved breath, and he laughed with her. "I guess it's been a while."

His gaze raked over her, lingering on her hair, which was loose and wavy now, quite different from the bun she always wore in the army. Then he glanced behind her at her hand-painted sign, the touch of whimsy that hopefully conveyed what her stall was all about. An old-school *Bake Sale!*, just like people remembered from high school. When Adam nodded approvingly, something tight in her chest eased a little. "You're a baker now?"

"It's a long story." She grabbed at his hands and laughed again. "This is such a surprise. Are you living in the city?"

Adam was a self-described country boy, born and bred, from a small town called Pine Harbour on the Bruce Peninsula. "Temporarily. I came here for school. How about you?"

"Same. I just graduated from a culinary academy. This

is part of our segue into the working world. We do these pop-up events at markets to test our wares."

"Then I really do want a cookie. And two of everything else."

She got a white box from behind the table and picked out a selection for him. "Two of everything," she repeated, her curiosity getting the better of her. "Are you sharing these with someone?"

He winked. "Nope. They're going to be my rewards for getting through my final week of training. I'm a few weeks away from finishing firefighter school."

"Oh, Adam. That's amazing. Well done." Her lips twitched in amusement. "I was going to say that you looked good, like you'd put on some muscle, but didn't want to make it sound like..."

"Like the last time you saw me I was verging on malnourished?" He gave her a rueful smile. "You ran us into the ground, and I mean that with all due respect."

Her smile softened, went bittersweet. "That was a hard tour." She thought of his best friend, a fellow reservist from Bruce County who had experienced some of the darkest moments of their time overseas. "You still keep in touch with Stevie?"

Adam nodded. "Yeah. We worked together for a while, as house movers. He's hanging in there. He moved out to B.C. this year to work at a ski resort."

She watched him intently as he talked, wishing the market wasn't quite so noisy, wanting to hear everything about how he'd gotten on after he got out of the army. "Good. I'm glad—"

Another customer approached, and Isla had to cut herself off.

Adam stepped to the side, then came back when she'd

completed that sale. They tried again, but the next lull in traffic didn't last long, either.

Isla's heart sank when he gave her a look that said, *what are you going to do?*

"It was really good to see you—" he started.

"How long are you—"

They both stopped and tried again, at the same time —again.

Adam gestured for Isla to continue.

She hadn't known how much she'd needed to reconnect with someone from her past until this moment— someone not toxic, someone who maybe understood what she was going through in starting a new career from scratch. Someone who was going through it themselves and knew a little bit of where she came from. "We should catch up, if you have time?"

"Absolutely. I'm going to be around the market for a while, so…if you're free when you're done here…give me a shout."

She grabbed a business card from the table. "Text me so I'll have your number."

He pulled out his phone and did just that, then lifted his gaze again. "It was really good seeing you."

It felt like he was studying her face, and something warm and unfamiliar softened in her chest. "Same."

———

After strolling around the downtown market, Adam found a table on a patio a block north of the market, with an oversized umbrella to protect him from the scorching hot summer sun.

He'd been living in the city for a year. A year of living

on ramen and frozen veg, of sharing an apartment with three other college students, most of whom were almost a decade younger than him.

For the first time in his life, Adam had felt like the old man, and he'd loved that part of the experience. The rest had left a lot to be desired. Every weekend he tried to get away from school and the basic, cramped apartment.

He was looking forward to moving home again.

Being away was not for him. This wasn't the first time he'd tested that theory, either. He'd done a tour in Afghanistan with the army, with a full year of training on a base in Petawawa before he'd deployed.

Toronto was better than Pet, that was for sure.

Adam's relatively short career in the army had been generally miserable, but there were a few bright spots. Serving under the brief command of Captain Petersen had been one of those highlights.

The last time he'd seen her, they'd both been in uniform, on a base six hours away.

Now she was a baker.

A student, starting over, just like me.

His phone lit up. Speak of the devil.

Isla: Hey, are you still around?

Adam: I sure am. Just sat down at a patio.

Isla: I'm nearly done here. A big group came through and I sold out! So I'm free.

Adam: Can I buy you a drink?

He texted her the address.

Under the table, his leg bounced. He shoved his heel into the ground to make it stop. It had been a while since he'd talked to anyone from his days in the army, other than his friend Stevie, who would never bring it up—his ghosts being worse than Adam's by a country mile. And Isla wasn't just another buddy. Her leadership had helped him through a miserable, scary time overseas. He didn't feel like that same man at all. He'd grown and matured, and was making different choices now. Following his own dreams instead of those of his brothers. But that didn't mean he didn't still have echoes from the past that affected him to this day, and Isla was one of the few people who knew that about him.

While he waited for her, Adam texted Stevie and told him about bumping into the captain, then he dove into the group chat his brothers were having around visiting the city for Adam's graduation.

Seth: What's the plan for Adam's graduation ceremony? I can fly south and could collect folks on the way, shorten the trip? Let's coordinate.

Adam: Countdown is ON.

Josh: We can't wait. I'm coming down early to party.

Will: Seth, can you pick me up? Unlike Josh, I have a full-time job with responsibilities.

Josh: Hey, I'm an entrepreneur with a million followers on TikTok.

Will: As I was saying...

Adam: Owen, what's your plan?

Seth: Newlyweds don't answer text messages this early on a weekend. We should all be so lucky.

Owen: My wife is still sleeping, thank you very much. I was making her coffee. I think we'll drive down, though. Wouldn't miss it.

Adam: Cool. Hey, do you remember Captain Petersen? We're going to meet up for drinks.
Owen: I'm not sure if I know Petersen.
Adam: You've met her. Tall blonde. She was my boss on tour, worked in Meaford for a while.
Will: Rings a bell.
Adam: She's given up the army life and is a baker now.
Josh: Is she hot?
Adam: Shut up.
Seth: Shut up.
Will: I was going to say, but they beat me to it.
Owen: I'm going to go wake up my wife now. We have a farmer's market to get to.
Josh: Words I never thought I'd hear you say.
Adam: I was just at a farmer's market!
Josh: What is happening to this family? What happened to our core value of being committed bachelors?
Will: I can't tell if he's being serious. Anyone?
Seth: Sorry, I can't hear you guys over the roar of the farmer's market I just arrived at.
Josh: He's joking, right?
Will: We're texting, you idiot. Yes, he's joking. But I have to go, too. Farmer's market single mingle starts in ten minutes.

Adam could have kept ripping on Josh for quite a while, but he didn't like the way his brother had asked if Isla was hot, so he put his phone away just in case Josh looped back to that. He didn't want anything to ruin the good mood he was in right now. It was silly, getting this excited about meeting up with a friend. On the other hand, his whole life for a year had been nothing but school. A real connection, something more than trying to keep in touch with a few people through the miracle of technology, was a gift at this point.

He liked his classmates well enough, but they weren't close. A half-generation divided them. They all liked to party, but Adam was growing out of that—and suddenly.

Deep down, he just wanted to go home, so much that he was secretly counting down the days.

He'd never understood why he disliked being away from home so much—his demons were almost all in Pine Harbour, and it was a place that sometimes made him feel very small. But this time, he was heading back to a real career. His job offer had been confirmed the week before; he was going to be the newest member of the Pine Harbour Fire Department. Which would come with its own set of complications, in the form of over-protective older brothers worried about him stepping down the same career path their late father had followed.

Adam wasn't worried about that, though. He was going into this eyes wide open about the health risks, and knew how to protect himself, both physically and mentally.

"You're deep in thought," a lovely, laughing voice said, dragging him back to the present.

He shook his head and stood up. Isla gave him another hug. The blue apron was gone, but the faint scent of sugar remained. "Good job on selling out of your food today."

"Thanks." She slid onto the chair across from him and flashed him a smile. She'd put lip gloss on, something pink, and it was distracting in a good and unexpected way. "You weren't waiting long?"

"Nope. Got caught up on messages. I texted Stevie,

told him I bumped into you. Then I had to deal with some logistical stuff with my brothers around my graduation. We have a group chat that gets out of control sometimes." His lips twitched. "Do you remember Owen? The oldest?"

She laughed, and her lip gloss glittered in the sun. "Vaguely, yep. Bossy and overprotective?"

Adam told himself to stop noticing her mouth. It was hard, though. Captain Petersen had gone and transformed into a very pretty woman. Of course, she'd always been beautiful, but it used to be in an off-limits, she-could-charge-him kind of way. Now she made cookies and they were both civilians. "That's him. But actually, he's a bit of a work in progress. He got married. She's good for him."

Isla nodded politely. "That's lovely."

But she said it in a way that said she thought otherwise. Adam frowned.

"I'm sorry, that was rude of me. I'm a bit…jaded. How long has it been since we saw each other last?"

"Maybe four years?"

"Yeah." She cleared her throat. "Long enough for me to get married and divorced."

"Holy shit." Adam blinked in surprise. "I missed hearing about that through the grapevine."

Isla shook her head. "It's okay. I'm glad to hear that it wasn't gossip fodder, to be honest. It was a bad idea from the start. My ex was always anti-PDA, including online. Turned out, that's because he had a couple of things going on the side, among other…problems."

A jolt of anger shot through Adam at the injustice of that. Why get married if you weren't all in? "I'm sorry."

She shrugged it off. "I've done my turn in therapy. I know it wasn't about me, and I'm focused on living my best life now. I won't make that mistake again, don't worry."

He was relieved that she hadn't let that asshole get the better of her. He leaned in and braced his forearms on the table, feeling vaguely guilty for thinking too much about her mouth and not enough about what had been going on in her life. "Good. And you look happy now."

"Oh good, that means the stress is all on the inside." She winked. "No, I'm kidding. Mostly."

He could relate to that, and he told her as much. "I know the feeling. Some days are better than others, and some scrape along barely better than survival mode."

She tilted her head to the side, her brows pulling together. "Yeah?"

Adam shrugged. Nodded. Then laughed. "Yeah."

Isla sighed. "Sometimes I think I should have stuck it out with the army, you know?"

"I thought you would have for sure. Woulda bet money you were a lifer."

"That was the plan." She shrugged. "But plans change."

Adam wondered if her ex was in the military. It would track for some of the asshole behaviour he'd seen, but people were dysfunctional all over the place. And before he could ask, while he was still mulling over if he *should* ask, the waiter returned to take Isla's drink order. He had menus in his hand, too. "Do we want food?"

Isla gave him an uncertain look. "Do you have time for lunch?"

"For you, I have all day." And he meant it, too. His plan when he'd come downtown was to do some shopping, because it was one of his last weekends living in the city. It was, in hindsight, a lonely, boring way to spend the day, especially when the alternative was an afternoon on a patio, catching up with an old friend.

There was something else, though. A tiny, whispering thought that if he hadn't headed to the market to get a coffee first, if that hadn't been the only parking garage that had spots big enough for his truck, he might not have seen Isla's bake stand at all. Could have left the city behind and gone back to Pine Harbour without knowing his former commander was out there doing something similar to what Adam was doing—starting life over again in a new career.

———

They took their time eating lunch, and while they didn't order any more drinks—both of them switching to lemonade with their meal—Isla still found herself pleasantly buzzed in a way as they lingered over the last few bites. The conversation had gone in every different direction, from funny to serious and back again, and it felt so effortless after more than a year of feeling very alone in this world.

"Funny that we both went back to school this year, eh?" Adam paused as their plates were cleared away, then nodded that they'd like to see the dessert menu. "How did you find it?"

"A necessary evil."

"Same!" He chuckled. "I worried I was being ungrateful."

"Not at all. It was so hard to start over as a trainee who really didn't know what she was doing," she confessed. "The most humbling thing I've ever done."

He couldn't keep the shock off his face.

She waved her hands. "I know, after Afghanistan, that probably sounds awful."

"Not at all," he said, wiping the corner of his mouth with a napkin, and shoving his empty plate away. "But I worry about who the hell is teaching pastry chefs if it's that traumatic."

"My own stubbornness might have been a part of it." She shuddered. "I forced myself to be the best, even at things I wasn't naturally good at."

"Like what?"

"My knife skills aren't that great."

"You can't do the..." Adam mimed a perfect rapid chop, his fingers curling precisely.

She shook her head. "I like to grab a cleaver and just get it done. *Whack.*"

They both burst out laughing as someone at the next table obviously caught the wrong part of that conversation.

"It's not that hard, it's just muscle memory and practice. I just..." She leaned in conspiratorially. "I don't *care*, you know? And it turns out, that's actually pretty important for me."

"Life is too short for perfection?"

Exactly. And she'd wasted four years on a lying narcissist.

"So can you run a pop-up bake sale with only so-so knife skills that are probably secretly spectacular?" His eyes danced, and she didn't miss how he turned the tease into an unexpected compliment.

A stark contrast to how she'd minimized her own abilities. "They're secretly not *un*spectacular," she admitted. "And I hope so. It's an uphill climb to get the business going, but once I have all the pieces in play, I think it has a pretty profitable business plan."

They were still talking when the bill arrived. Adam grabbed it before she could stop him. She pulled out her wallet anyway, but he shook his head. "This is my treat."

"Thank you. This was really nice." That wasn't the right word at all. It had been so much more than nice. There was something about Adam that set her at ease now, and in a way it felt like a full-circle turn on their friendship in the army. He'd leaned on her experience then; it had been her fourth tour, and his first. But there had always been a goodness to him, and she wasn't surprised he'd turned into this thoughtful, caring man now. Even when he'd been frightened and unsure, he'd had his buddies' backs. As soon as she saw him this morning, all those memories had flooded back.

And then over lunch, she'd discovered a whole new Adam Kincaid. A man on a mission. Unlike her new career, which was fragile and precarious—literally and figuratively, depending on what she was doing with sugar—he had found something deeply meaningful and stable. She was impressed, and found herself wanting to know even more. That aching curiosity inside her, that clawing feeling like she should reach across the table and touch him again and again, was probably more about herself than him. But she couldn't just say goodbye. "When do you move home?"

"End of the month."

"Do you have exams next? What's your schedule like?" She paused, not wanting to overstep, but fuck it. She might never see him again if she didn't say something. "Do you want to catch up again?"

"I'm pretty busy during the week." He hesitated, too,

and she wondered if he'd blow her off. "But I'm free next weekend."

"Me, too." She would have cancelled any plans even if she had them, which she didn't.

He grinned. "Then it's a date."

CHAPTER TWO

THE FOLLOWING SATURDAY, Isla took the subway downtown for dinner. Adam was going dancing that night with his classmates, but he was coming in from the suburbs early to have drinks and a meal with her first.

When she emerged from the station, Adam was waiting for her. He was more dressed up this week, his thick hair tamed and slicked back. Instead of blue jeans and boots, he was wearing polished shoes and dress pants—but ones for clubbing, clearly. His shirt was fitted, tucked in, and the whole outfit left nothing to the imagination.

She whistled when she stopped in front of him. "You look positively virile," she teased.

"Have to look good for my date." He winked. "And then look better than the kids in my class tonight, too."

She laughed and shook her head. "Let's eat and you can tell me more about that."

It was her treat today, and she took Adam to a restaurant owned by one of her teachers, a quiet little space with a tasting menu and an extensive wine list.

Adam took one look at the menu and told her he would eat whatever she wanted to try. "We're supposed to share, right? That's the idea?"

"Yep."

"Then surprise me. You're the chef, you tell me what's going to be great. I'm here for the company."

"Charmer," she muttered, smiling. "Any allergies?"

"Nope."

After ordering, Isla asked Adam about his exams that week. He told her about a vertical obstacle course they had to complete under a time limit. "You start with a hose carry, up a fire escape. It's bundled, over your shoulder, so off-balance, but it's not bad."

"How many storeys?"

"Three. Then you drop the hose, and a partner on the ground tosses you a rope so you can haul up another bundle. Hand over hand. It's a different set of skills from army stuff, but the basic principles are the same. Conserve energy, work smarter, not harder. Pace yourself because the hard stuff is at the end."

"Sounds like fun." And she was serious.

Adam took it as she meant it. He nodded. "It is. The stamina part is really important. And the younger guys have it like crazy."

"You've mentioned the age difference before."

He grinned. "I think it's because I'm the youngest in my family. Back home, people call me The Kincaid Kid. I like that I'm the old man in my class. I think the only time I haven't either been way younger or way older was on our tour in Afghanistan." His face sobered up, his mouth pulling tight. "We were all too young, then. But at least we were in it together."

She reached across the table and squeezed his hand. "Yeah."

They had bonded that tour. All of them. In over their heads. It had been Isla's third roto, and the first one to not be fully, properly staffed at all levels. Her section was more than half reservists, all excellent soldiers, but only Adam had done the full pre-tour work-up training. And the leadership overseas had been in shambles, too. It was the first tour for her where shit went sideways. She'd stepped into a leadership role someone else should have occupied, and they all got through it.

But when they got home, most of the troops under her had returned to their own units. Adam and his friend Stevie had returned to the peninsula. Others had gone to Hamilton, Vancouver, and Calgary.

They'd lost touch.

"I'm sorry I didn't keep tabs on you guys," she said softly.

He gave her a surprised look. "That wasn't necessary."

She disagreed. "In hindsight…"

Now it was he who squeezed her hand. "We're all still hanging in there."

"Tell me about Stevie." She leaned in, hanging on his every word as Adam told her about his friend moving out to B.C., turning into a ski bum. It sounded wonderful.

"We worked as house movers for a while. It was good for him to be home, for a while, but then he got restless. He likes to be alone on the slopes."

When their food arrived, Adam had lots of questions about why she'd ordered each one. The wine was good, the food was great, and the company was best of all. Before she knew it, it was dark outside and both of the desserts they'd ordered had been polished off. A second bottle of wine was nearly finished, too, and she was feeling the effects of that all over. A good kind of buzzy.

"I should get going," she said reluctantly, because she had nowhere else to be that night, but he did. "You have a party to get to."

"I wouldn't call a bunch of drunk kids blowing off steam a party."

She laughed. "You used to."

"Damn, you knew about those?"

That made her laugh even harder. "Young corporals and master corporals are not great at being subtle."

He gave her an aw shucks look that made him look five years younger. Just as charming, but more vulnerable in a most unexpected way. He'd once used that charm to cover up fear. She'd seen it then, and she realized now that was the big difference.

This Adam oozed confidence. He knew he was capable of this new career. The way he talked about his training, with pride and a cocky knowledge, was totally different from how he saw his role in a complicated military campaign. Firefighting felt like a better fit for him, a more direct use of his kindness and compassion. And almost certainly more likely to give him feedback that he was actually making a difference.

That younger man she'd just caught a glimpse of again had seemed unmoored and uncertain. Tonight's Adam was neither. He was intense and earnest, still very charming, but with a new depth—which would be dangerous for her to get too distracted by, but she felt the irresistible tug anyway.

Outside the restaurant, she waved in the direction of the subway. Where she should head to, so she could go home and crawl into bed. "Well, have fun tonight."

"Do you have to get going? We could grab a drink, keep talking."

"What about your classmates?"

"I can blow them off." He paused. "Or you could come with, if you wanted?"

The last time she'd gone clubbing would have been the winter after they returned from Afghanistan. Four years ago.

That woman felt a decade younger than Isla felt lately. She was only thirty-five, but a divorce and a radical career change had taken their toll on her. Except, right now, she felt absolutely up for it. "Are you sure?"

His face lit up. "I'd love to have a friend there."

Why the hell not?

The dance club was a short walk away, and a line snaked down the sidewalk. Isla was relieved that her black skinny jeans and silky grey blouse didn't look out of place against the younger people waiting ahead of them. It didn't hurt that Adam managed to make direct eye contact with the bouncer and, through the magic of his wholesome farm boy charm and "is he a Hemsworth cousin?" good looks, he got them waved to the front of the line.

He clapped the bouncer on the shoulder. "Thanks, man. We've got friends inside."

The bouncer winked at Isla. "We'll let him think it's *his* pretty smile that got you in, yeah? Can I see some ID?"

———

Adam didn't miss how the bouncer flirted with Isla—or how genuinely surprised she looked at the compliment. She blushed as she handed over her driver's license.

That wasn't the Captain Petersen he remembered.

The Isla he had met in Petawawa on work-up training for tour had been a force of nature with a magnetic draw. Everyone wanted to work with her, and everyone had wanted to get in her pants, too, but the two were mutually exclusive. She didn't date NCOs, the rumour mill promised bitterly, so everyone took the consolation prize of getting to be under her command.

It would never have been appropriate back in the day to ask her how she felt about all the hot young kids panting after her, but now he wondered if she'd ever known, or if the Wonder Woman myth they'd spun about her had been one-sided.

Now that he thought about it, it wasn't like Wonder Woman was exactly aware of her impact on men, either.

"What's the game plan?" he murmured as he guided her inside, his hand lightly hovering behind her back. "How long do you want to stay? Do we need a signal if you want me to get scarce if someone buys you a drink?"

She laughed. "This is your thing! How long we stay is up to you. And nobody is going to want to buy me a drink."

He was pretty sure she'd be approached twice before they made it to the bar, but before he could say that, the crowd parted and he caught sight of his classmates, who waved and hollered. The first wave of people who would want to hit on Isla, he was sure. "There they are, let me introduce you."

Over the loud pulse of the music, he made a round of names that probably nobody would remember. It didn't matter. His heart hadn't been set on hanging out with everyone tonight, and after dinner with Isla, he felt that indifference even more keenly. He liked the way she looked at him and listened to his ideas. He loved the way she nodded along as he told her about his dreams for his new job, what he hoped it might turn into—a career in his hometown, something he could be proud of, something that would make a difference.

The way she looked at him was different from how anyone else had ever looked at him. Women liked his muscles and his smile. His brothers saw him as a burden, a worry. Anyone from his parents' generation remembered him as a skinny problem child, too complicated to help.

He hadn't needed help. The Kincaid brothers had survived just fine, and he was going to show everyone that the Kincaid Kid, the youngest of the bunch, finally had his shit together.

It felt like an uphill battle to everyone except Isla, who beamed at him.

No, he didn't want to spend the night with anyone other than his long-lost friend. They didn't have much time left, anyway. He was going home soon.

As predicted, though, he had competition for her company. Less than a minute after he finished making the introductions, the nearest kid—and in that moment, Adam absolutely thought of him as a fucking child, not old enough to ask Isla for the time—offered to buy her a drink.

"Do you want a beer?" he asked, his eyes bright, like he'd already had a few and wanted her to catch up. He didn't know they'd already had more than enough at the restaurant and were already loose and ready to dance.

"I'm sorry?" she asked, moving around Adam to stand close to the infant. Adam resisted the urge to catch her around the waist and haul her back against him. "What was that?"

"I said, lemme buy you a drink." And then he winked.

Isla giggled and glanced back at Adam. She looked

delighted. Then she shook her head. "I'm okay for now." When he moved on to someone else, she leaned in to Adam. "That was nice of him."

Nice had nothing to do with it. "He was hoping to get you drunk."

She shook her head.

Adam wasn't going to argue with her, but his protective side knew what was what.

The music changed, and she swayed. Yeah, that was a better idea. Adam moved his hips too, and that was the end of talking with his classmates. Everyone splintered, but Isla stayed close.

They danced through a couple of songs. At the start of the second one, she rolled her loose sleeves up to her elbows, and by the end of the third, she was playing with the buttons running down the middle of her blouse.

Her skin was slick with sweat. He wanted to lick it off.

Where did that come from?

She threw her hands in the air and laughed, a wild sound of abandon that hit him squarely in the chest.

There. That sound. That was where that feeling came from.

She caught his gaze, then leaned in close enough to talk beneath the music. Her body arched against his as her lips reached for his ear. "Thanks for inviting me to tag along."

He brushed a damp strand of hair off her cheek. "You look like you're having fun."

"I am." She grinned and wiggled her hips. "I needed this."

"Me too." He caught her with his arm, twisting her in the direction of the bar. "Want a drink now?"

"Sure." She undid a button. "My treat."

His attention was locked on her fingers now, on her

neatly trimmed nails and the dark shadow of a bra or a tank top beneath her blouse.

"Adam."

"Yeah." He jerked his head up.

She gave him the same dazzling smile she'd beamed at him a week before, and her lips glistened in the pulsing lights of the dance floor.

A sizzle, a spark. She gave him a curious look. "Are you sure you want a drink?"

He wasn't. Instead, he was thinking he wanted to fuck his former boss and current friend, and he couldn't think of a single reason why he shouldn't indulge that desire if she shared it. "Want to get out of here?"

———

A girl could lose herself in the way Adam was looking at her right now.

Did she want to get out of there?

Isla didn't know what she wanted. But up to this point in her life, she'd been absolutely sure of some very terrible decisions, so maybe she should try something off-script.

Like kissing Adam Kincaid, a man six years younger than her.

A friend.

A bit of a wreck, or at least he had been in the past, but she was hardly one to talk.

She leaned in and pressed her lips against his. Warm, solid. Smiling. She could feel that, too, and when she lingered, he parted for her, welcoming her to taste his mouth. A lovely feeling rushed through her, an easy, low-key arousal. Like this might be what sex would be. Laid-back Adam, up for whatever she wanted.

She crowded closer and wrapped her arms around his neck. His hands skated up and down her back, playing with the nerve endings there, before settling low on her hips and tugging her pelvis up against his.

Oh, hello there. She gasped at the happy press of his erection against her mound.

"No pressure," he whispered against her mouth. "But if you want to have some fun…it's been a while for me, and I'm feeling in a celebratory mood."

She pulled back, her breasts brushing against his chest before an inch of space appeared between their upper bodies.

Adam grinned at her and rolled his hips. "Or we can stay and dance like this for a while. Whatever you want."

"I didn't see this coming." She leaned in for another kiss. "It's nice."

He caught her lower lip gently in his teeth, then released. "Nice?"

She laughed.

He spun her around.

"Is that okay? I could use some nice right now." She whispered the words against his neck as she squeezed him tight.

He cupped the back of her head with one of his hands, big and warm and comforting. "Your wish is my command."

"Where do you want to go?"

He pulled out his phone. "Let's see what hotels around here have vacancies."

A wild thrill danced up her spine. A one-night stand in a hotel room. Booked last minute. Could they be more obvious? She loved it. "Splurge on a nice room. My treat."

"You got dinner." He kissed her again. "This is *my* treat."

She opened her mouth to protest, then changed her mind and pressed her lips to the corded muscles of his neck instead.

Adam tasted *good*. A little bit of salt, a lot of warm man. It had been too long, clearly, because she was suddenly ravenous to devour more of him.

He groaned and yanked her tight against his body. "Give me a second. Okay, got it." He kissed her temple. "The Four Seasons. We'll catch a cab."

When she said *nice*, she hadn't meant that nice.

Adam must have heard her gasp beneath the pulse of the music above them.

"My. Treat," he growled in her ear. "Now let's find the backseat of a cab so you can bite my neck again."

CHAPTER THREE

THE NIGHT before came to Adam in pieces as he woke up the next morning.

He knew exactly where he was—in a hotel room, with Isla, who smelled like sugar and delicate flowers. But once upon a time, she'd been a captain and he'd been a non-commissioned member, and what they ended up doing last night would have been very off-limits.

Even more than that, Isla wasn't just a random hook-up. She was a friend of sorts, a colleague who had also seen him at his worst. At his most scared.

Last night they blurred those lines in a bunch of creative ways.

A cocky grin pulled at the corner of his mouth. Now she'd seen him at his absolute best, too.

"You're awake, right?"

He bolted straight up, yanking the sheet over his naked lower half.

Isla smiled at him from the foot of the bed. Her hair was a tousled, messy version of the day before's waves, and she was half-dressed, already wearing her blouse and underwear. "Hey."

"Hi."

"You started grinning to yourself."

"I was running through the highlight reel." He cleared his throat. Kissing, laughing, business talk. Isla's Bake Sale stall idea. More kissing, sex, and then, as they stretched out in the dark, drowsier chatter about starting over, and how it was never too late to tackle hopes and dreams—an understanding he'd found sorely missing among the other people in his life. "That was fun, right?"

"Best night I've had in a long time." She dropped her hand onto his sheet-covered foot. "I have to get going, though. I didn't want to slide out before you woke."

"That was thoughtful." He paused. "Do you want to catch up again before I move home?"

Did we ruin our friendship?

"Yeah, maybe." But something about how she said it told him this was a onetime event, and he understood.

He shifted gears. "If we don't connect, I want you to keep me posted on how your next pop-up stand goes." He leaned over and grabbed his boxer briefs from the floor.

She turned, giving him a bit of privacy.

He quickly pulled on his underwear, then his jeans.

"Your idea," he said as he pulled his shirt on. "It's a good one."

"We'll see. It's the scaling up that's the real problem." She'd told him all about that the night before as he'd given her a foot rub, while they waited for middle-of-the-night room service. How she would need a business loan to afford commercial baking space, and her divorce had left her with nothing. "But I talked about that enough last night, didn't I?"

"I'm seriously interested, though." He rounded the bed and caught her fingers lightly in his.

"Adam…"

"As a friend. Nothing more. I swear up and down, cross my heart. I think this was kismet." He turned his wrist so their hands were aligned like a formal handshake. "We were meant to hang out again, and now I'm meant to be your cheerleader as you figure this out. Don't overthink it."

She pursed her lips, then shook his hand firmly. "Thanks. I'll keep you posted."

"That's all I ask." He twirled her around, then sent her spinning away from him. "Now put the rest of your clothes on, friend."

———

They didn't meet for dinner again. They didn't stumble into a hotel room, laughing and a little bit drunk, and strip each other's clothes off again, although Adam woke up with an erection more than once imagining that they had.

But they *did* keep in touch, and as quickly as he'd gotten her naked, Adam slid right back into the friend zone.

He added her as a contact on social media and they texted a few times. The boundary was clear, and he wasn't the type of guy to ignore those cues.

The night before his graduation, when his brothers arrived and he met them at the hotel for dinner, Will asked about her out of the blue. "Hey, did you ever meet up for drinks with Captain Petersen?"

"Yeah. And then we had dinner the following week." He didn't elaborate, and Will didn't ask for further details.

But that put her back on his mind. It didn't take a lot for his thoughts to turn to her. Something about her starting over at the same time as him had triggered a kind of kismet between them, and her pop-up bakery stall idea would spring into his thoughts at the strangest times.

He pulled out his phone and fired off a quick hello.

Adam: Will asked about you tonight.
Isla: Have your brothers all arrived?
Adam: Yep. We're having dinner at their hotel.
What are you up to?
Isla: Baking the World's Best Ever Chocolate Chip
Cookies.
Adam: Photos or it never happened.

She sent him a picture of chewy, pillow-y looking morsels of goodness, and he replied with a drooling emoji. Then on a whim he added the address of the college. Just in case she wanted to come and say hi to Owen and Will, he said. She knew his oldest brothers from the army. It was a low-stakes invitation.

Isla: I wouldn't be intruding on a family thing?
Adam: Not at all.
Isla: Then I'll see you tomorrow.
Adam: Can't wait!

He regretted the exclamation mark as soon as he hit send. It wasn't his usual texting style, and it made him seem over-eager. Hitting the tone of his fledgling friendship with Isla just right was important to him.

"Who are you texting?" Owen grinned at him, a little loose from a few beers.

"Isla Petersen. She said she might come tomorrow. I told her I was hanging out with my brothers, and she sent me back a photo of a tray of cookies." When he said it out loud, it sounded weird. "She's a recent grad, too. We're new career buddies."

He was making this worse, he realized, but he couldn't stop talking.

And Owen just shrugged and looked happy.

Fuck, maybe that was part of the problem. He'd been on edge all night, but his brothers were all on their best behaviour. It took an odd combination of brotherly restraint and genuine enthusiasm to buy the Kincaids a night without sparring. Maybe Adam had come into the evening expecting the usual love-laced criticism, especially from Owen, who had essentially raised him after their parents passed away—even while he was raising a toddler, too.

But Owen seemed to just be enjoying his weekend in the city with his new wife, and something inside Adam shifted loose. He changed the subject. "I'm glad you guys are here."

"We wouldn't miss it. This is a big deal for you." Owen's attention slid to the side as his wife Kerry approached. "Right, babe? We're proud of Adam."

Adam just hoped that pride held tight when he moved home and started working in the same building as Owen.

———

Isla was stuck in traffic on the DVP. It more closely resembled a parking lot than a major freeway artery cutting through a city, and she swore under her breath.

She was going to be late for Adam's graduation, and

that sucked, because she wasn't planning to linger after the ceremony.

No dinner, no late night drinks.

She glanced sideways at the two dozen cookies sitting in a travel container on the passenger seat. "We shouldn't do that again."

The cookies didn't respond. They were neutral on the concept of friends with benefits.

But Isla wasn't, not for herself. A one-night stand was one thing. She had the bandwidth for that, because it had clear limits. Anything beyond that, and she could see herself falling for the *idea* of Adam, of an easy relationship, and she knew that would be bad for her tender heart, especially because he would be living hours away.

It would be even worse if he stayed near the city. There was no way any entanglement would end well, basically. Not because of Adam, but because of her past.

And a little bit because of Adam, not through any fault of his own. The sex had been good, but the friendship was better, and that was her singular goal today. Show up, be a good buddy.

And she was already failing on the showing up part. Ahead of her, brake lights blinked off and traffic started rolling again.

Slowly the line of cars crawled north, and when she finally took the exit ramp to the 401 East, she let out the breath she'd been holding. The traffic and parking gods were kind to her, and she slid into a seat at the back of the college auditorium just in time to see Adam's class receive their certificates. When her friend paced across the stage, four large men closer to the front of the audience jumped to their feet and hollered in support.

Isla smothered a laugh. Those would be his brothers, no doubt.

And sure enough, when the ceremony was over, she made her way closer and recognized Owen, Adam's oldest brother. He had his arm wrapped around a pretty woman with dark curly hair, and his other hand was gesturing animatedly at the other Kincaids.

Catching his eye, she waved, and he cut himself off. "Hey there. Adam mentioned you might come. This is my wife, Kerry. Kerry, this is Isla Petersen. She served overseas with Adam."

Isla shook Kerry's hand, then did the same with the others as Owen introduced Will—"We've met, right? Meaford training base? Nice to see you again"—and Seth, a pilot based out of the Sault, and finally Josh.

"I'm a mechanic," he said. "One of these things is not like the other."

"Story of my life," she said with a wink. "I never fit in. And my dad was a mechanic. What do you like to work on the most?"

They talked about the older muscle cars he liked to work on until Adam joined them.

"I promised you chocolate chip cookies." She held up the tin. "Congratulations."

He took the tin with one hand, and looped the other arm around her shoulders, pulling her in for a half-hug. "Thank you for letting my guilt trip work."

She poked him in the side. "This is a big deal. I'm glad I got to see you convocate. It's always good to have cheer-leaders, right?"

He gave her a surprised look, and she gave him a *this works both ways* funny face right back. It was a silent exchange that shifted something inside her.

No, she wasn't going to sleep with Adam again. Their accidental meeting had led to something better than a friends-with-benefits arrangement. It had found her an unexpected ally and a lighthearted friendship.

Seeing him again, being welcomed by him into this celebratory space with his family, it all felt *right*. She was going to do everything she could to hold on to his friendship with both hands.

Without letting go of her, Adam gestured to his family. "There are some picnic tables out back, let's go sit and have a celebratory cookie."

At the edge of the graduation space, there was a table set up with coffee and tea. They stopped there to grab paper cups of hot liquid—quality to be determined—then followed the newly certified firefighter to a quiet circle of trees.

The coffee was mediocre, as Isla expected, but the group response to her cookies promised they were up to her usual high standards.

"These are the best cookies I've ever had," Adam said after inhaling his second.

She beamed. "I know."

All of his brothers laughed at that, but her confidence wasn't misplaced. It was a killer recipe, and it would be the cornerstone of her business model—once she found an investor willing to lend a divorced woman with negative assets the seed money to start a professional bake sale business.

"Will you share your recipe?" Adam waggled his eyebrows at her. "If I bake these at the firehouse, I'll impress the whole team."

"If you try to bake at the station, you better clean up after yourself," Owen growled. "And there are unspoken rules about who gets to cook on what team. You—"

"I'm aware," Adam said evenly. "Took a class on baby firefighter etiquette and everything. Got a C+ on the test, but I think I'll manage."

He wasn't serious, was he?

Seth shoved Will into Owen, who took it like an oak tree so he wouldn't barrel into his much smaller wife, and Josh snickered.

Adam grabbed another cookie and rolled his eyes at Isla.

No, not serious. Adam held her gaze while his brothers moved on from ribbing him to ribbing each other and gave her a smile that said, *what are you going to do?* She didn't know the answer to that. She had one brother who was eight years older than her, but they had never been close, not like this. And even with her own age gap between siblings, she had never been "the baby".

Nobody had ever worried about her the way these men, these big, grown, hulking men, clearly worried about their baby brother. Except he was almost thirty and both big and hulking himself.

He wasn't the young kid she'd once known, either. Not that she was that much older than him, and not that he hadn't always been capable. He had. But when they went to Afghanistan, he had been openly scared at times.

Had his brothers known that? Could they see that he didn't carry that same worry now about being a firefighter?

She returned the private smile and mouthed, *I'll send you the recipe.*

His eyes crinkled and he nodded in acknowledgement.

After he walked Isla out to her car, Adam headed to the hotel where his brothers were staying. He felt wrung out in the best way possible.

Tomorrow, he'd move home.

Tonight…

There was a wild part of him that had wanted to talk Isla into hanging out, but she'd made the boundaries clear. And where would he convince her to stay? His side of a bedroom he shared with another trainee? Would he get a room at the Holiday Inn where his brothers were staying?

It was quite the downgrade from the Four Fucking Seasons.

And it would be more than pushing his luck. It would be blowing up their friendship. He didn't need her to spell that out. He'd seen it all over her face the morning after they'd slept together. He hadn't fully processed it at the time, because he'd been naked and still—frankly—a little horny.

Horny Adam was not the most clever. Sometimes the most creative, but…

He dragged his thoughts to the immediate present. Dinner with his brothers, then back to his apartment to finish packing.

Of course, as soon as he parked and hopped out of his truck, Josh was waiting for him. "Dude. Where's your girl?"

"She's…" Adam huffed a laughing breath. "Definitely not that."

"She made you cookies. She put up with all of us for two whole hours."

"And I am eternally grateful that you didn't refer to

her as *my girl* that entire time. Kudos on that self-restraint, I know that was really hard."

"Agony." Josh didn't miss a beat as they headed inside. The rest of the family was sprawled out in a collection of chairs in the bar in front of the restaurant.

Adam waved and moved to make a beeline for the bartender, but Seth yelled out, "Graduation boy does not buy his own drinks."

"Graduation man, you mean," Adam said, pivoting to join them. "And I'll have a beer, in that case."

The next person to stick into him about Isla wasn't one of his brothers, but Kerry. When Owen got up to get the next round of drinks, his wife slid across the couch and perched herself right in front of Adam. "So…"

"Not you, too."

"She's really nice."

"She was my boss."

Kerry shrugged. "Operative word: was."

"It's not like that. She…" He dropped his voice. He liked Kerry, a lot, and trusted her to parse this information appropriately back to Owen. To shut down the chatter. "She got divorced last year. It was messy. She's not in a place for a relationship, but even if she was, it wouldn't be with a guy like me."

"What does that mean?" Kerry looked genuinely offended on his behalf. "You're a catch."

"I'm a work in progress."

"Aren't we all," she said breezily.

Owen returned carrying four bottles of beer. The bartender followed behind with a shot of tequila for Josh and a gin and tonic for Kerry.

Adam's oldest brother looked at them both suspiciously. "Aren't we all what?"

"Works in progress," Adam and Kerry said simultaneously.

Adam needed to change the subject. "Is it too early to think about dinner? Graduation man wants a steak."

Dinner passed without any more grilling over his friend showing up. But it still took Adam a long time to fall asleep that night. He tossed and turned, consumed by thoughts of his brothers. By the little comments that got under his skin, and the wildly different ways he and Josh had dealt with the older three.

It was like there was a gulf between them, Owen and Will and Seth having raised Adam after their parents died a year apart, their father suffering a catastrophic heart attack when Adam was eleven, their mother dying of what Adam had always thought of as a broken heart a year later. Josh had been a minor, too, but at fourteen, he had escaped the parental triad somehow. Rejected them in that role. Tolerated Owen as his legal guardian until he turned eighteen, and then he popped smoke.

Adam had clung to his brothers instead. He hadn't moved out of Owen's house until he was twenty. He'd relished his role as a young uncle to Owen's daughter Becca, and justified his prolonged presence as in part for her. He was her uncle, sure, but also a de facto older brother.

Which made Owen his father figure.

For every moment that Owen's over-protective instincts grated on Adam, there were just as many moments where Adam had wanted that—wanted all of them at his graduation, needed their help moving him home.

That was always the way it was for Adam. A double-edged sword. He missed his brothers when he was away from them, but as soon as he saw them, his skin itched like he knew their gentle criticisms, their loving criticisms, would inevitably follow. He was always going to be picked on because he was the baby.

They loved him so much it hurt sometimes.

CHAPTER FOUR

THE PINE HARBOUR EMERGENCY SERVICES building was an impressive three-story building, newly built on the edge of town. It backed onto forested snowmobile trails, and on the other side of those woods stood Mac's Diner, which had previously been the "edge of town" landmark. Beyond that stretched the small rural community where Adam had been born and raised, not much more than a Main Street and a dozen blocks of residential buildings before a visitor would hit the hill running down to the harbour.

He loved this town and longed to return to it whenever he left.

And now he was formally charged with protecting it from fire and other unexpected disasters.

This wasn't his first time reporting to work at this building. He spent a year on the volunteer fire brigade before leaving for an accelerated firefighter training program in the city. But this was the first time he would get paid for it, and a thread of doubt was loosely stitched right through his midsection—that he wasn't ready for this, that it was too much responsibility.

That he was still, at twenty-nine, too young for this.

Which was objectively just not true. Most of his classmates had been almost ten years younger than him. Only in Pine Harbour, where he'd gotten into a fair amount of trouble after his parents died, was he still seen as the Kincaid Kid.

It wasn't even like anyone thought he was still a troublemaker. They hadn't even bought him as a troublemaker back then. He'd simply been following his brother Josh around, so it had been excused. Adjusting to being raised by his older brothers. He was a good kid who would eventually grow up.

So he'd joined the army, following in the footsteps of Owen, Will, and Seth.

Josh had gone in a different direction, but now they were both back in town—and both living with Will.

More than a decade had passed, and they were both still figuring their lives out.

Technically, Josh didn't *live* with Will. He'd bought a garage down at the harbour and was restoring it. There was an apartment behind the garage, but it was, well, an apartment behind a mechanic's garage, and hadn't been updated in thirty years. So it wasn't entirely habitable, and more than a year after returning, Josh didn't seem to be in a big rush to make the apartment his proper home. All he cared about was the garage, and his growing clientele for customized muscle cars.

But Josh wasn't Adam's problem.

Adam was Adam's problem. Like figuring out why he was still standing in the parking lot, even though his first shift started in ten minutes and he wanted to be early.

A familiar truck crunched into the gravel parking lot.

Had he been waiting, on some subconscious level, for Owen to arrive? Adam had checked. They would both be at work today, although technically his brother wasn't his supervisor. Owen ran the whole building and managed the paramedics who worked out of it.

The fire department was managed separately. They had one pumper truck stationed here, a single team of four fire-fighters switching out every twenty-four hours. Other teams were stationed at the base of the peninsula, and there were volunteer brigades to the north and south.

Emergency services on the peninsula was a compli-cated quilt, always on the edge of not having enough funding and needing to augment with volunteer services. Pine Harbour had lucked out with getting this building constructed and they all knew it.

And now two Kincaid brothers, the oldest and the youngest, worked here.

"Did you just arrive?" Owen asked, grabbing his coffee and backpack from the passenger seat.

"Yeah, pretty much."

"You nervous?"

"Nope."

Owen chucked him on the shoulder. "Liar. We're all nervous at first."

Adam wasn't sure if he believed his brother. The only thing Owen had ever been outwardly nervous about in his whole life was personal shit. Falling in love with Kerry had done a number on him. Having Becca, and then Becca having Charlie... but work stuff?

Of course, Adam had only been a kid when Owen had started his career in emergency services. Maybe a lifetime ago, Owen *had* been nervous. It better not take Adam two decades to lose the "what the fuck" feeling inside his chest. He rolled his eyes—maybe at himself, maybe at his brother—and followed Owen inside.

He'd met two of the three firefighters he would be working with the other day, when he came in to sign his contract and get his certifications photocopied. Stan and Denise were both twenty years into their careers, contemporaries of Owen's, and Adam had a sneaking suspicion they were going to treat him with kid gloves for a while.

That was fine, he would prove himself in time.

But the real challenge would be winning over Richard, who drove for their team. He'd been a firefighter for thirty-five years, and could retire any time.

The first thing he told Adam was that his retirement wasn't going to happen any time soon. The second was that Richard didn't see anything wrong with the way they'd always been doing things, which Adam took to be a reference to the fact they used to send out a truck with just two or three firefighters, and round out their numbers with volunteers.

If there had been any doubt about what Richard meant, he came back to it again and again over the course of their shift. By the time the four of them sat down to a dinner Stan had made, twelve hours into their day, Adam had run out of ways to say, "I hear you, but I'm glad to be on the team."

He couldn't deny there were people who had been on the volunteer brigade a lot longer than he had. But none of them had taken a year to do the required training to be become a full-time firefighter. None of them had shared a two-bedroom apartment with three other people and counted every last penny so their savings stretched over the entire year in the city.

He'd earned this position, and he would demonstrate his value to the team in time.

Or now, because as soon as dinner ended, the alarm went off. They'd had two callouts earlier in the day for minor problems, but the report coming in over the radio was that this was a three-alarm blaze at a rural home.

Fifteen seconds after the call came in, Adam dropped down the pole and sprinted to where his gear waited next to the fire truck.

After a year of intense training, this drill was unconscious routine. He kicked off his shoes and stepped into his boots, already inside his pants. The straps came up next, over his shoulders. Once the pants were on, the balaclava hood went next. Finally the coat, his thumbs sliding into the protective cuffs. His gloves, helmet, and breathing apparatus would all go on in the truck.

Less than a minute later, they were buckled in, barking the all-clear to Richard so he could get them to the scene.

A ladder truck met them at the farm, both arriving at the same time, and they worked together to account for all members of the family and get the kitchen fire extinguished. They managed to confine the damage to one part of the home, and while it looked devastating, Adam knew they'd saved the structure from complete disaster.

It was late in the night when they were cleared to leave. "Pine Harbour Pumper 2, heading back to station," Richard reported to dispatch.

"Roger Pumper 2."

Back at the station, Richard backed the truck in, then they all unbuckled and climbed out. Their gear needed to be sorted out, scrubbed off, and reset for the next call.

"Kincaid," Richard barked out.

Adam stopped and turned.

"Good job, kid. Welcome to the team."

It was a win. It wasn't the end goal—the *kid* was still there, tagged on as always—but he grabbed onto the praise with both hands. "Thanks. That means a lot."

———

Adam: First shift done.
Isla: How'd it go?
Adam: It was busy. We had a kitchen fire. Saved the house, though.
Isla: Good job.

She didn't call him kid. Maybe she would have once upon a time, but not anymore.

Isla: Are you going to sleep now?
Adam: As soon as Will leaves for school. He's noisy to live with. I need to find my own place. That's on my agenda for tomorrow.

Down the hall, Adam heard Will's shower turn off. His brother had a really nice new-build home that had more than enough space for Adam and Josh to crash, but the bedrooms were all right next to each other.

Maybe he could move into the basement for the days when he had to sleep post-shift.

Or maybe he could just find his own damn home. He was on his second real career. He had sorted his shit out, and knew what he would be doing for the rest of his adult life.

That unexpected realization—that he was now, finally, in the position that Will and Owen had been in for years—

carried him off to sleep, and when he woke up in the midafternoon, his first call was to the local credit union.

"I'd like to make an appointment to speak to a mortgage advisor," he said.

It would be good to do, just to get his ducks in a row. Find out how much money he might need to save up so he could buy his own place.

"Do you want to come in today?"

"I was thinking in a few weeks," he said before he realized how that sounded.

The woman on the other end of the line laughed kindly. "Sure, did you want to make an appointment?"

"You know what? Today is just fine."

He made himself a quick sandwich, using up the last of Will's sliced ham, then made a grocery list and headed out the door.

The bank was his first stop. It turned out the financial advisor had gone through school with Josh, and she knew all about Adam being the new hire on the fire department.

"Based on your salary, you can qualify for a mortgage for this amount," she said, scribbling a figure on a notepad. "Now let me look at your savings account…"

Adam winced. It wasn't significant anymore. He'd had a small inheritance from his parents, and then brought back a decent amount of money from his overseas tour— when other guys had spent their per diem allowance, Adam had socked every cent away. He'd more gradually added to that savings over the last few years. But then he'd gone away to school and spent a good chunk of it to get him back home with a real career. "I may not have enough now for a down payment…"

She grabbed a pamphlet. "There are some programs for

first-time home buyers who want to borrow against their retirement accounts."

Adam had that. It had been the first thing Owen made him do when he turned eighteen, and he'd kept up with the maximum contributions ever since. "I don't want to touch that."

"It wouldn't need to be for long. Let me show you what a repayment plan might also look like."

He frowned. "This seems too easy."

"Home ownership is a big step, but for someone in your position, you have options." More numbers scribbled on the pad. "Basically, you're pre-approved for this amount of lending, and it could be a mortgage or a secure line of credit. And that's my card if you have any questions."

Was this what it was like on the other side of a full-time job? People just gave you access to piles of money so you could buy a house?

Piles of money one would have to pay back, with interest, over twenty-five years. He knew enough not to be stupid about this decision.

Adam's head spun with the realization he could actually get his own place. He thought about it all the way to Wiarton, where he did a big grocery shop, because three grown men sharing a fridge meant it needed to be restocked with shocking regularity.

Becca: Are you awake yet? Dad says your first shift was yesterday. How did it go? Tell me everything!

He grinned and called his niece, who had recently moved to Vancouver with her boyfriend, a rookie in the

NHL, and their baby. His great-nephew, Charlie, babbled in his ear as soon as Becca answered. "Hang on," she shouted from across a room. "I'm just grabbing Charlie a snack. Then I want to hear all about it."

Adam had been nine when his big brother—who looked like a man and had already joined the army reserves—told the family he was getting married and having a baby. Their mother had cried. That was the clearest memory Adam had from that night. Their father had muttered something about "the boy would sort it out", and he'd been so confused, because Owen wasn't a boy, hadn't really been as long as Adam had known him, except for those fuzzy first memories when all of his brothers had been skinny beanpoles of varying heights.

But by the time Adam hit elementary school and memories cemented, Owen was always coming and going, driving four wheelers by himself, and then a car.

And then a baby.

Becca. Who now had a baby herself, because life was funny like that.

When their parents died, Owen sold their family home, divided up their parents' estate into five small nest eggs, and bought a smaller bungalow with his own inheritance —a hell of a tight place to grow up, with a toddler girl running around half the time.

But that toddler girl had imprinted on him. Half-niece, half-the-sister-he-never-had, who understood his complicated relationship with his older brothers in a way nobody else ever could. In some ways, his brothers tied him to Becca's age, not his own. In their mind, he was still nineteen, not twenty-nine going on thirty.

"Okay," Becca said breathlessly, taking the phone away

from her babbling kidlet. "How was your first shift? Did Dad embarrass you?"

That made Adam laugh. "Nah, he was great. Saw him at the start of the day, and then a few times as we passed each other. But there is a guy on my team who is going to be a similar, gotta-prove-myself type of challenge."

"Just ignore them."

Easier said than done. "Yeah."

"Are you happy to be home?"

"Very. How about you? Happy to be away from home?"

"Very. And it's almost time for a Mommy and Me yoga class, so I'm going to pick you up." Adam guessed she was talking to Charlie. "And we'll pick up Uncle Adam, too, and then we'll ask him about the pretty lady who came to his graduation."

Adam grunted a not-surprised laugh under his breath. "Who told you?"

"All of them. Kerry was most excited of all, but Seth snapped a picture, so he won the gossip title."

Curiosity definitely won out over annoyance. "If there's a photo, I want to see it."

"I'll forward it in a minute. Who is she?"

"They didn't tell you that part?"

"Well, sort of. They said you used to work together in the army. But she made you cookies? That's different."

"Her name is Isla, and she's very nice. Very different. And she's getting over a difficult divorce, so don't get any ideas."

"Rebound relationships are—"

"Doomed to fail?"

"Exciting and hot."

He groaned. "I don't need to know what you think is hot."

"Grow up."

"You grow up."

"Already did. Had the baby and everything." She said it lightly, but he still apologized.

"You know I'm just teasing. We're both all the way grown up now."

"I started it, it's all good. Okay, we're ready for yoga. When is your next shift?"

"Day after tomorrow. Are you going to check up on me afterwards?"

"Maybe. If only to make sure that Dad hasn't picked on you."

"He doesn't pick on me."

"He has been better lately," Becca conceded. "Kerry's a good influence on him."

Owen's new wife was a *great* influence. They could all agree on that.

It was only after they hung up that he realized he hadn't told Becca about the mortgage pre-approval. For the best—if he told her, he would have to swear her to secrecy so she didn't start a chain reaction of *are you sure you're ready* texts from his brothers.

His phone vibrated. It was Becca, forwarding the photo Seth had taken of Adam, his arm slung around Isla's shoulders. It looked like he was holding her against him, instead of the split-second hug it had really been.

He smiled. Well, that would distract the rumour mill for a while.

Leaving him wide open to look into some real estate. After dropping the groceries at Will's house, he popped in to Catie Berton's hair salon on Main Street. She had a client in the chair getting foil highlights.

He waved. "Afternoon, ladies. I'm just here to look at the real estate wall."

Catie pointed to a big QR code framed on the wall. "I've gone high tech, if you want to check out the latest listings on my website."

Hell, he could have done that from home. "All right."

"And as soon as I put Donna here under the dryer, I can chat more with you about what you're looking for."

He pulled up her website on his phone, just to have it, then went to the wall as he had intended. Catie was Pine Harbour's only real estate agent, and it wasn't a full-time job, so she kept a mini office in the corner of her salon.

It wasn't long before she joined him. "See anything you like?"

"Any of them would do," he admitted. "I don't have a clear idea of what I want, other than I don't want it to be expensive. I'm done renting, and I'm done living in my brother's house—not that Will isn't a great host," he hastened to add when her eyebrows curved up.

This town and its gossip were both hard to control sometimes.

"It's just time for you to find your place." She filled in the blanks, which Adam appreciated. "How many bedrooms?"

"It's just me, so something small and basic is fine. But the bedroom needs to be quiet."

"Because of shift work, of course. Bathrooms?"

"Same, but if I could have a bathroom attached to a bedroom, that would be even better."

"En suite. Got it. Garage? Does it need to be attached to the house?"

"I'd want one, but no, it doesn't need to be attached."

"How do you feel about a fixer-upper?" She picked up a tablet and brought up a listing. "This one needs some work, but it's empty. And the owner is eager to sell. It hits all of your criteria. It has three bedrooms, one of which has an en suite. The whole house is quiet, because it's set back from the street a fair bit."

As Adam clicked through the digital slideshow, the salon door opened and Anne Minelli came in.

Catie gave her a bright smile. "Afternoon, Anne. What can I help you with?"

"I want to talk about the listing for my cafe."

Adam didn't miss the way Catie almost rolled her eyes before sliding a professional expression of enthusiasm onto her face. "Of course, give me one second to finish up with Adam and check on Donna."

Adam flipped back through the photos. "It looks great. Can we go take a look at it sometime soon?"

"How about later today?"

"I can do that."

"Meet me there at…" She twisted to her client in the stylist's chair. "Donna, do you want a blowout?"

"Yes ma'am, I have a hot date."

Catie nodded affirmatively, then looked back to Adam. "All right. Let's say five o'clock."

After she reminded him of the address, Adam stood and waved Anne into the chair. "Your turn."

"You Kincaid boys have grown up so fast, buying houses now. What will come next? Babies?"

He didn't bother to point out that Owen had been a father for nineteen years. He knew what she meant. Owen was the father figure, and Adam was the "kid", even though there were only ten years between them. He didn't need to stick around for any more of that conversation.

Without missing a beat, Catie took over. "What would you like to do about the cafe, Anne?"

"I want to drop the price."

"Good plan. What were you thinking?"

"A dollar."

Adam froze. He couldn't have heard that correctly.

Catie clearly couldn't believe it either. "Say that again?"

"With certain specific conditions, I want to drop the price of the cafe to a dollar." Anne paused, and Adam felt her attention drift in his direction.

It wasn't his fault that her real estate agent's office had zero privacy, because it was in the corner of a hair salon. But on the other hand, it wasn't polite to be a nosy Kincaid. He lifted his hand and waved goodbye to all three ladies.

Maybe if he was lucky, Catie would fill him in at the showing in two hours.

CHAPTER FIVE

TWO THOUGHTS ROCKETED around Adam's mind as he waited for Catie outside the house he was going to look at. He really wanted to tell Isla about Anne Minelli basically giving away her cafe. It was a de facto bakery—they had homemade muffins and pies. And at the same time, he knew the conditions were a deal-breaker.

He didn't need to wait for Catie to show up and spill the tea. She'd updated the cafe's listing on her website just a few minutes ago.

Looking at the screen again, he shook his head. He couldn't ask Isla if she wanted to…

No.

He flipped over to their text messages.

Adam: What are you doing?

Isla: Chopping pistachios. How about you?

Adam: Waiting to look at a house. I might buy it, although it's not much to look at from the outside.

Isla: Are you there right now?

Adam: Standing across the street

He took a picture of the one-and-a-half-storey cottage with peeling paint and a sagging porch and texted it to her.

Isla: Ooh, I like that! Call me later and tell me if it's cute on the inside, too.

She was way too kind. The house was only cute if he squinted, and inside he expected the same.

He shoved his phone in his pocket and took another hard look at the house. It was a few blocks from Main Street, on the same side of town as Owen and Kerry's place. Will lived on the other side, in the newer build, but everywhere was walkable.

He liked the long driveway and the tall trees. The paint was a long weekend of work to repair, and a new porch was doable. But from the photos, he knew there was work to be done inside as well.

Was he biting off more than he could chew?

And was he really considering buying a house he hadn't yet stepped foot inside?

It's time. He felt that inside like a drumbeat. He had the job, now he needed a home. One big enough for him and a wife, maybe.

He crossed the street just as Catie arrived.

The porch creaked, but the boards held up just fine under his weight. Catie got the key from the lockbox on the screen door as he peered in the windows.

"It's unfurnished," she said as she pushed the door open. "A blank canvas."

The foyer was dark, the doorway they were standing in the only source of light. Catie moved in further and flipped on an overhead light in the wider room beyond the entrance. In that space, a small living room with a fireplace on the left wall, a staircase climbed up the right-hand side of the room. So far, it looked just like the photos in the slideshow, if a bit smaller in real life.

Adam squinted and tried to picture where he might put a couch and a TV. The place had nice wood floors. Easy to keep clean, he figured.

"It's cozy." The brightness in Catie's voice made Adam laugh.

"Your positive spin is noted," he said dryly. "Is the kitchen through there?"

"Yep. And one of the bedrooms." Her expression slid from salesperson to delicate professional. "The former owner lived on the main floor for the, uh, final few years."

"Ah." Adam poked his head into the kitchen. It was as he expected from the listing, small and forgettable. Then he pivoted and went down the small hallway to the bedroom at the end. Unlike the rest of the house, it was large, with a window that overlooked the front garden. But the best part of it was an en suite bathroom built off it, with a tiled walk-in shower. He whistled. This looked bigger and better than in the photos.

"This bathroom is definitely the selling feature for the house. There's another one upstairs that's more...original. There weren't any photos taken of it for the listing."

"Let's go see that, then." He led the way, already feeling at home in the space.

The stairs were narrow, but the landing at the top was big. Off of it were three doors. The aforementioned bathroom, with an original cast iron tub, cracked linoleum flooring, and yellowed wallpaper. At the front of the house was a room that didn't look big enough for a full-sized bed, but it could be an office or a workout space.

The second bedroom, though, was a decent size. And more importantly, as he walked over to the small window overlooking the backyard, he realized it was completely quiet.

He could have a bed up here for when he needed to sleep during the day and avoid any street noise.

"Do you think the price is firm?"

Catie hesitated.

"I need to do something about that bathroom, and the kitchen downstairs. This place needs more than a little work."

"The price reflects the potential. But if you made an offer, they can always counter."

Adam glanced at his watch. It was twenty minutes after five. His brothers should all be available for a quick consult—but he didn't need them to weigh in on this.

He thought about what he'd been pre-approved for at the bank, and the list price. He could easily afford to offer just below the list price and still be able to get a line of credit for the renovation work. Or maybe he'd do it himself, slowly.

It wasn't like he had anything else to do in his downtime.

By five-thirty, they were back at the salon so he could sign the offer. By six, his offer was accepted. And he'd done it all on his own.

"Congratulations," Catie said as she locked up the salon behind them.

"Thanks." Adam thought about asking about the cafe, but then thought better of it—he didn't need to feed a rumour mill that might get back to his brothers, who were already sharing photos of Adam and Isla looking like they were falling in love.

Once Isla's tarts were in the fridge to set, she put on her favourite YouTube workout and poured her frustration into a high-intensity interval training session that left her drenched in sweat and feeling thoroughly wrung out.

Her final bake sale pop-up event organized through the school was a week away, and she had zero prospects for work on the other side of that.

She didn't want to get a job in a restaurant. She'd left that kind of high-pressure alpha environment behind when she left the military. But she had enough money to cover her rent for three more months, and that was only if she didn't spend any extra money on recipe development.

Her phone rang just as her workout ended.

"How was the house?" she gasped as she collapsed on the carpet.

"Are you all right?"

"Never better."

"You sound like you're being chased by a murderer."

"This is how I spend my free time. Practicing for the apocalypse. Don't want to be anyone's prey."

Adam snorted. "Are you in the middle of a workout?"

"You're quite the detective. I just finished. Tell me about the house."

"Well..." He laughed. "I bought it. I take possession in ten days."

"What? That's incredible."

"I think the previous owner may have died in it? I didn't ask. But it's been on the market and empty all summer, so basically, as soon as the mortgage and title transfer can get set up, it's mine." There was a bit of wonder in his voice that made her chest ache. Once upon a time, she'd wanted to buy a house, too. In a different life. "It's not much, but it's mine."

"Congratulations. Are you celebrating tonight?"

"Just waiting for my brothers to get home, then I'll break the news to them."

She knew he was staying at his brother Will's place. *Breaking the news* didn't sound like a celebration, though.

"I didn't even know you were looking." She felt a bit silly saying that, because it wasn't like they were close enough for him to confide a big life decision like that— except he had told her, hadn't he?

"Neither did I until this morning."

That sounded specific, like something had triggered him to go hunting. "What happened?"

"There isn't a ton of privacy at Will's. It's all open concept, so sound carries. When I got home from my shift, he was just getting ready for the day. And I just thought… I'm a grown man. I need my own space, that's nice and quiet, so I can come home and rack out without waiting for someone else to have a shower."

"His shower pushed you over the edge?"

"It was loud."

"And then you went to see a house, and then…done."

"It just felt right." He yawned in her ear, like he'd just stretched. Or like he'd just had a twenty-four-hour shift and only napped a bit.

"You sound tired."

He chuckled. "A little. I'm still adjusting to the sched-ule." Then he groaned. "Speaking of a lack of privacy, my brothers are back from work. Hang on, I have to go tell them I bought groceries." She listened as he moved through his brother's house, as he greeted people and told them there was cold beer in the fridge. "I'm just wrapping up a call with Isla, then I've got some news."

There was a scramble, then a different voice came on the line. "Hey, Isla. This is Will."

"Hi, Will." She laughed. "Can you put Adam back on the phone?"

"He's busy right now. Listen—" He grunted as the phone was grabbed back, and in the background someone shouted about wanting more cookies.

"I gotta go," Adam said, out of breath. Then he hollered something profane back at his brothers as she heard laughing.

"Now you're the one who sounds like they're running from a murderer," she teased.

———

Adam set his phone down after Isla hung up and flipped his brothers a double bird. "Was that necessary?"

Will grabbed his suit jacket from where he'd hung it on the back of a chair. "It was more fun than necessary. The way you got all panicked when I tried to talk to her. Man, you've got it bad."

Shaking his head, Adam went to the fridge, nudging Josh out of the way. He needed a beer. "You don't know what you're talking about."

"She'd be good for you," Josh said.

It wasn't like Adam didn't see what they saw—Isla was smart and beautiful, kind and funny. But he didn't need a woman to improve his life. He was doing just fine on his own. And he'd already told them she was getting over a divorce. So he said nothing, just shrugged and popped the cap off his bottle.

Will made it almost out of the room, then stopped and turned around. "Hey, thanks for grabbing the groceries. What was the total damage? I'll transfer you some money."

Adam waved him off. "Nah, it was my turn."

"You sure? I don't mind covering that while you get your feet under you."

Fucking hell. He loved his brothers, but the concern was misplaced. A worn-out laugh ripped from Adam's chest. "It's all good. Go change, then come back down so I can share my news."

Will frowned. "What's wrong?"

"Why do you assume something is *wrong*?" Adam turned to Josh. "How was your day?" *I bought a house.*

Josh made a not-displeased face and flicked his hair, still damp from a shower, out of his eyes as he pulled a tray of steaks out of the fridge. "Not bad. Started work on a sweet 1970 Firebird. Hey, T-bones!"

I bought those, too. Adam took a long, cold swig of beer.

Will returned quickly. "So, what's your news?"

Adam grinned, took another long slug of beer, and shrugged. "I bought a house."

Josh set the steaks on the counter.

Will crossed his arms over his chest.

And then they both gave each other a look that broadcasted concern clear as day.

"Is that wise?"

"It's not a money pit, is it?" Oh, that was rich, coming from the guy who'd bought a garage that was barely habitable.

Adam blinked at them both. "Thanks, I'm thrilled."

"Right. Of course. We are, too." Will cleared his throat.

Josh took his sweet time nodding. "Totally. Congrats, man."

"Fuck you both."

"Well, it's surprising," Will said. "Why'd you keep it a secret?"

"When do we get to see it?"

He ignored the first question and went straight to the second. "I have a home inspection tomorrow. Middle of the day, though."

As if it were just dawning on him that Will would be at school. Owen had to work tomorrow, too. He'd picked that timing deliberately to minimize Kincaid overload. But he couldn't stop Josh for clearing his schedule.

"I'll be there." Then Josh nodded at Will as if to say, *don't worry, I'll look out for him.*

Adam snorted. "I don't need a babysitter. But you're welcome to come along if you want to see how a grown man buys a property that actually includes a functional kitchen."

Functional was about the only adjective for it, but he was grumpy now.

Will grunted. "Right. Sorry. I channeled Owen a bit too much there."

They all did it. "One of these days, you're going to realize I'm almost thirty and can do things on my own."

"Like buy groceries?" Will had the good grace to look chagrined.

"Exactly."

Josh picked up the T-bone pack. "So are these celebration steaks?"

"Nah, those were just because I'm sick of your obsession with chicken breasts. Get cooking." He waved his beer bottle at his brothers. "And I told you two first because we know Owen will have big opinions, be stubborn in his concern. I'm telling him next, and I expect your support. Baby brother or not, I can take you."

"I'm so scared," Josh drawled, but he grabbed a cast iron pan and set it on the range in Will's island.

CHAPTER SIX

WATERFRONT CENTRE WAS quiet at six in the morning. The arts and community hub in downtown Toronto, right on the edge of Lake Ontario, would be buzzing in an hour.

Isla stood back from her table and took a picture for her nascent Instagram account. She had seventy-two followers, and she loved every single one of them. And one of the most recent followers was a certain firefighter from Pine Harbour.

Her hand-painted bake sale banner made her happy every time she looked at it, and she hoped it sparked in customers the same sweet nostalgia it gave her—of high school fundraising, of picking out treats to take home to family. And maybe one to snack on immediately.

Her offering today was a variation of what she'd tried in the last three pop-up events. Her best ever chocolate chip cookies were only a quarter each, which barely broke even. But that was a part of her marketing plan. Hook them with the twenty-five cent cookies, then earn her profit off the higher-end offerings. Today that was a pistachio and raspberry tart, a sinful Black Forest brownie, huge Rice Krispies squares with visible marshmallows, and apple cider muffins.

Technically, Isla had graduated from culinary school in June, but as part of their supported transition to working in the industry, grads interested in running their own businesses had been invited to participate in four pop-up market events over the summer. This was the final one, and she was excited about it. She was also nervous, because her business plan was still sketchy at best for how to move forward and make the pop-up bake sale a viable job for herself.

Her phone vibrated, and she glanced at the screen.

One like on her newest photo, a selfie with the bake sale sign behind her. The like was from Adam. That made her laugh.

Isla: You're up early.
Adam: At work. One hour left in my shift.
Isla: So I shouldn't call you when I'm done here
and wake you up?
Adam: You could.
Isla: Or you could call me when you wake up, so
I'm not the bad guy.
Adam: You wouldn't be. But okay, I will. Good luck
today. It looks amazing.

That vote of confidence lightened her step, and she finished her setup with enough time to sit down and drink some tea from the thermos she'd brought.

Then it was go time.

Sales were slow to start, but built over the morning. She sold out of chocolate chip cookies at ten-thirty, which was the earliest yet. Making a mental note to up that volume by twenty-five percent for the next sale, she grabbed the brightly coloured sold-out sign and set it on the tray.

Rice Krispies squares were next to sell out, with only a few of the muffins and the brownies remaining when the pop-up event ended in the early afternoon.

But her raspberry tarts...she did some quick visual math. She'd broken even on them, but her optimism had gotten the better of her. Those ingredients were too expensive to not have a higher sales percentage.

She quickly boxed up the remaining tarts, two to a container, then took them around to the classmates who she might want to partner with in the fall.

"Do you have any leftovers you want to trade for tarts?" she asked at each table, grateful to those who said yes. "Do I have your card? Here's mine. Let's keep in touch."

By the time she had everything packed back into her car, she had enough food to eat like a queen for a few days. An excellent save on those expensive ingredients. But her happy mood didn't last long. When she logged into her computer to do her accounting, she saw an email from the coordinator at the college.

Congratulations on completing the summer pop-up program. We wish you all the best in your culinary business. Attached is a flyer on the vendor packages for the different market spaces we used. We have secured a discount for our graduates...

The rest of the email was filler, so Isla scrolled to the attachment and opened it up. All of her fragile hope deflated when she saw the monthly rental fees charged by the locations they'd used—even with the discount offered for the first year, it was more money than her gross revenue had been on any of the bake sales so far.

In the other room, her phone rang.

Shaking, she left the computer behind and dug through her bag. By the time she found it, the call had dropped.

Adam.

Adam, who had just bought a house, who had a career, who was turning his life around.

She couldn't talk to him right now. She wasn't up for cheerleading today.

Her phone slipped from her hand and bounced on her bed before landing, screen up. She stretched out beside it and closed her eyes.

The worst part was that Adam—a random Army acquaintance who she'd had a one-night stand with—was the closest thing she had to a confidant right now.

Isla didn't make friends easily. Not close friends, nobody she could bounce business talk around with. Jackass had ruined those kinds of conversations for her, but even before her marriage, she'd been tight-lipped. A career army officer at that point, she'd been a woman in a man's world, where everyone learned to say what was expected. Opinions had to be pre-filtered against the possible, the preferred.

She was so tired.

Her eyes were hot. Sad.

Something else her marriage had stolen from her—the ability to cry.

Beside her, the phone vibrated again.

Swallowing hard, she forced a smile onto her face, because expression affected tone, and answered it. "Hello."

"How did it go?"

She squeezed her cheeks wide. "Great. Turns out, pistachio raspberry tarts are a bit of a hard sell, but everything else performed better than expected."

"Baking math, how exciting."

That softened her smile into something real. "I like it. It overwhelms me sometimes, but once I figure out the perfect ratio on the other side of the frustration, there's nothing quite like that sense of accomplishment."

"Better than planning a successful reconnaissance mission?" Adam dropped his voice and dug into a memory she'd forgotten.

She closed her eyes and listened to his voice, letting him carry her back to Afghanistan. Just for a second. She didn't want to dwell in the past. "You're very good at bolstering morale, aren't you?"

He narrowed in on the wrong part of the question. "Wait, is your morale low?"

She didn't answer.

"What's wrong?"

She groaned. "Nothing. Toronto's just insanely expensive and I don't know where I'm going to take my business next. It's not important."

"It's critically important. And I say that as your official morale booster."

"Are you everyone's cheerleader, or am I a special sad case?"

"I don't think you're a sad case."

"Clearly I haven't told you enough about my ex-husband."

A choking cough suggested Adam hadn't been expecting her to say that. "Uh, do you want to?"

"I prefer not to think about him."

"Same."

That made her laugh. "Glad we're on the same page. But there's a limit to how much my morale can be boosted when the real damper on everything is the debt I wound up shouldering in the divorce."

"Shit."

"Yeah."

"Can I ask a strange and overly familiar question?"

"Sure." She rolled onto her side, then pushed herself up to sit. Whatever Adam would ask, she trusted on a bone-deep level it wouldn't be too invasive.

"Do you see yourself ever getting married again?"

She barked. Out loud. Sharp and caustic. That wasn't overly familiar, but it was *ridiculous*. "Never."

"Never ever?"

"Love made me exceptionally stupid. I won't ever make that mistake again. I don't even…our night together? That was the first time I had sex in two years. Thank you, by the way. It was a lot of fun."

"I aim to please."

"And I just feel like, okay, that was a good dip of the toe. I'm good for a while. I don't need to do that again for another year."

"I'll make a calendar reminder."

"Adam!" She giggled. Then stopped. "Wait, you're not serious. Right?"

"Of course not."

She exhaled in relief.

"I don't need a calendar reminder to know you want to bang me again in three hundred and thirty-five days. I'm pretty sure that will just stick at the top of my to-do list…" He trailed off. "Yes, I'm kidding. I know you aren't interested in a repeat, and that's fine."

"Thank you."

"Listen, I know that the answer is going to be that you aren't interested, but I've been carrying something around for a few days that I want to tell you about. Not sex related, I promise," he hastened to add. "There's a cafe for sale here."

"In Pine Harbour?"

"Right on Main Street."

Isla opened her mouth to protest that she couldn't move to his town and start a bakery, but it was so ridiculous an idea she didn't even need to counter it. Besides, it was funny, and she didn't have a lot of amusement in her life. So she humoured him instead. "Tell me more."

"It's a nice building, at the end of a block. I haven't been inside it in years. It's not really my type of place. The lady who owns it is known for her pies. She serves breakfast and lunch, and it has a little gift shop. It's where ladies of a certain age meet for tea. But she hasn't had any luck in selling it, because there's a big diner on the other end of town, and Pine Harbour doesn't need two restaurants."

"You're really selling it," Isla said dryly.

"The thing is, the cafe could be converted to a commercial bakery space pretty easily. It has glass cases for your chocolate chip cookies and whatever else you want to have in your daily bake sale. I'm guessing the kitchen is already set up for—"

Guessing. That's exactly what he was doing. He'd gone out and bought a house—on a whim—and now he thought she should do the same with a whole business?

She should never have told him about her struggles in finding the right next step for her business. The worst part was that it was no longer funny, because she could picture it.

A little shop on Main Street. Brightly painted sign in the window. *Bake Sale!* And beneath that in smaller letters, *New Treats Daily.*

She should have been even more brutally honest. Told Adam how her ex destroyed her credit, that she wouldn't qualify for a mortgage or a business loan no matter how good her plan was, and it hurt to even fantasize about the dream of having her own bakery.

That wasn't in the cards.

Maybe she could sell cupcakes on Instagram. That was enough—for now. She would build to the dream, down the road.

"Isla?" Adam's voice broke through her thoughts, and she realized she'd stopped listening. "Do you want me to send you the link for the listing so you can look at it yourself?"

He was so earnest and kind.

She scrubbed her fingertips against the tension in her temple. "Adam—"

"It's a dollar."

"What is?"

"The cafe."

"I don't understand."

"The owner is a grandmother who wants to retire, and can't bear to see her cafe shuttered. It's been for sale for a year with no bites. So she's dropped the price."

"To a dollar."

"Yes."

Isla's heart clawed its way into her throat. "No. It's too good to be true."

He exhaled. "Yeah. There is a not-so-small catch."

"What is it?"

"We would have to get married."

Two days later, Isla could still hear the strain in Adam's voice. He followed it with an apology, and an explanation. He didn't know how to tell her, but also didn't ever want to regret not telling her, because it seemed like a perfect, imperfect opportunity.

She understood.

It was an impossible deal for her to make, though, no matter how tempting the dream might be. And she had dreamt of a little Main Street storefront that night, and the next.

There was a part of her that was making it a little too magical, a little too perfect, she decided, so she searched for Pine Harbour real estate.

She'd declined Adam's offer of the link.

No, she didn't want to look at the listing. She couldn't marry her friend just to be able to buy a cafe for a dollar.

It was absurd.

But here she was, two days later, clicking on the photo gallery. It was a cafe for women of a certain age, that was for sure. Stuffed with tables and floral decorations. But maybe those women of a certain age might like brownies instead of scones.

Her eyes ran over the fine print, the special condition on the listing to encourage someone from within the community to take it over. *Residents of Pine Harbour and their immediate family members are encouraged to apply for an owner-offered rebate. Eligible buyers able to commit to continuing the sale of locally made baked goods to community for a period of no less than three years…*

Three years.

This wasn't just getting married to sign a contract and

then quietly getting a divorce. Her second divorce in as many years, what a record that would be. But no, this contract would mean that she would need to stay married to Adam for three years, running a little shop called *Bake Sale* for three years, and live with him in his new house.

For three—

She grabbed for her phone, pausing only to quickly do a calendar check in her head, but Adam should be awake.

He answered on the first ring, a happy sounding, "Hey."

"Why do you want to marry me? Stay married to me for three years?"

He coughed, then muttered something to someone in the background.

She flushed, biting her lower lip as she listened to him move, as she heard a door open and then close.

"Okay," he said slowly. "I'm alone now. So...hi. Are you looking at the cafe?"

Embarrassed heat swirled through her lower belly. "Yes."

"I didn't mention the three-year part because we didn't get past the *do we want to get married* part, which seemed to nullify all that followed."

"It's a long time to pretend to be married."

"I wasn't planning on pretending anything."

She gripped her phone, confusion mingling with the embarrassment now. A riot of uncomfortable emotions, and she still clung to an undefined something that drove her deeper into the conversation. "I don't understand."

"You need a bakery for cheap. And an official morale booster, I'd like to point out, which is built right into the job description of a husband."

Not in her experience. "But that's why I should want to marry you. What do you get out of it? For *three years*."

"At least three years," he corrected. "Are you already planning on leaving me?"

"I'm not planning on marrying you!"

"But you're looking at pictures of the cafe, right?"

"No," she muttered. "I was. Now I'm on the Pine Harbour website."

He laughed, and it was so warm and soft it made her insides quiver. What a sweet, naïve summer child he was, that he thought two friends could just get married and all their problems would go away. Except he still hadn't answered her.

"I don't understand. If you want to get married, why not...start dating with that goal in mind? I'm sure there are no shortage of nice girls who are more local to you and willing to, you know, actually fall in love with you."

He didn't answer right away.

She waited. She wasn't going to let him off the hook. It was a fair question.

"I don't want to get married," he finally said. "Not to just anyone. But I've been carrying around the idea of being married to you for a few days, and I like that just fine. In fact, just the other day, I had a very clear personal realization that my brothers think I need to find a wife who will be a good influence on me, change me, and I don't want to be changed. I'm happy with what my life is turning into. I have a job, I'm getting a house. For a long time, I didn't have either of those things, and I did that all by myself. Frankly, it's all I want to focus on for the next few years. What better way to ensure I can focus on that than skip to the good stuff with you?"

"What's the good stuff?" Her mind unhelpfully offered

up a flash of his mouth on her body, his head buried between her legs. Lovely, but not on the table. "I don't...I can't get romantically involved again."

"I know. This isn't about sex. The good stuff is having a partner in crime. I realized that my brothers are thirty percent right. They look at me and they worry. I bristle at it, bark that I'm just fine, and we go in this cycle. It's not the end of the world, and I know it comes from a place of love. But even though you have seen me at my worst, you don't look at me and worry. That's...Isla, if you married me, I would finally shake the whole *Kincaid Kid* reputation I haven't deserved in a decade. And a pretty nice roommate—who is both pretty and nice."

"You're laying it on thick."

"I mean it. You said you would never get married again, married for love. But that's not what I'm asking—or offering. I'm offering transparency and friendship and mutual support."

Everything that had been missing in her first marriage.

"You're still young," she whispered into the phone. "What if you..."

"So are you. You know what you want in your future, right? So do I. And I don't...I haven't dated a lot since I came home from overseas. That's four years of not getting laid that often. I'm not giving up some wild social life. I like to go dancing. If we got married, you could come with me. The nearest club is an hour away and it's kind of gross compared to the place we went in the city, but it's got pulsing lights and loud music. If you ever change your mind about wanting some intimacy, I'd be up for that, too. But I'm fine without it. God gave me two hands for a variety of experiences and—"

She laughed in shocked relief. "Is your marriage

proposal really including a detailed breakdown of how you jerk off?"

"I wasn't going to be that explicit."

Sighing, she clicked to a new tab on her browser. A map, to see just how far away Pine Harbour was. "When is your next weekend off?"

"This coming one. I get possession of the house on Thursday, so I'll be unpacking."

"Can I come up and visit you? I can help."

"You want to see the bakery?"

It wasn't just the bakery. She wanted—needed—to see Adam again, too. Spend a weekend in his house and figure out if she could actually pretend to be his wife. *Nothing pretend about it.* Actually *be* his wife, for his sake and for hers. A mutually beneficial agreement.

It was wildly unrealistic—but also, intensely practical.

A bakery for a dollar.

Or she could spend the next five years working as a pastry chef in a restaurant, hoping to meet the right investor for her idea, which someone else would surely have taken and run with in the meantime.

Who did she trust more? Some random future potential investor, or Adam Kincaid, the nicest man in NATO? When she put it like that, testing his harebrained scheme out for a weekend was the least she could do. "I do. And I want to hang out with you, too. See if you might do as a husband number two."

"Husband number two. That rhymes."

Isla thought she might faint. "I was going for levity."

"Levity achieved." His voice softened, going feathery light. "I'll text you the address. See you on Friday."

CHAPTER SEVEN

ON THURSDAY, Adam got the keys to his house. His brothers came with him to do the first wave of unpacking. They called Seth on video chat after carrying in the biggest pieces.

"How many beds do you have?"

"One for upstairs, one for the main floor. I like to have sleeping options." Adam spread his arms wide. "In my kingdom."

Seth leaned in to the screen, squinting. "Your kingdom looks like it needs a new coat of paint."

Adam shrugged. "It needs more than that, but it'll be a fun project. Let me show you the new bathroom, though."

When he got back to the living room after giving Seth a virtual tour, Josh and Will had carried one of the two beds upstairs. He'd ordered them both online, to be delivered to Will's house, and they were identical. Basic black wood frames, good quality mattresses.

Owen picked up the memory foam mattress, vacuum packed in a giant tube. "This one is ours to set up."

Adam got out of his way, grabbing the headboard.

They made quick work of it, setting up the frame first, then carefully cutting the plastic wrapping open so the mattress could expand into its full size.

"You got bedding for this?"

Adam rolled his eyes. "Nah, I was planning on sleeping on it just like that. Minimalist style. This isn't a frat house, Owen. Yes, I have bedding. But we have to let the mattress air out for a few hours first. Let's go get more shit from my truck."

After they unloaded everything, the thought of scrubbing down the kitchen was exhausting, so he took his brothers to Mac's for burgers.

"This is on me," he insisted when Owen and Will both tried to grab the bill. "Thanks for your help tonight."

"We'll help this weekend, too," Will said.

Adam shook his head. "Actually, I'd rather you didn't. I'm having a visitor come up tomorrow."

"Who?"

He forced his face to stay nonchalant, even though he was pretty damn excited. But that warm swell of energy that he felt when he thought about Isla coming up to stay with him was complicated and layered and none of his brothers' business, really, so he'd put off telling them for days.

He didn't want to hear their opinions about her, in any direction. His friendship with her was private and special and none of their business. But it would be worse if they caught wind of her visiting, or dropped by and she was helping him put his kitchen to rights.

So he shrugged like it was no big deal. "Isla."

Josh pretended to search his memory. "The woman with the cookies?"

"Shut up, I know you guys have been talking about her and me for weeks."

Owen looked at Will in exasperation. "Who snitched?"

Adam wouldn't rat out Becca. "No snitching required. Whenever I talk to her, Will gets this matchmaking gleam in his eye."

Now it was Will's turn to flip him off. "Fuck you."

But that wasn't a denial.

"Look, we're just friends." He took a deep breath, setting the stage for what might come next. "But if—*if*—anything develops between me and Isla, that's about us. She's slowly sorting her life out, and frankly, so am I. Neither of us need meddling in our lives, got it?"

Will looked far too fucking proud of himself.

But nobody suggested Adam needed help with the house again, and that was a small miracle.

That night, he crawled into the upstairs bed and lay wide-awake wondering what Isla might think of the house, the town, and most importantly, the cafe.

She was a grown woman. If she didn't like any part of his wild idea, that would be fine. She could wish him good luck with his family, his house, and his job, and be on her way after what he would do his best to make sure was a fun weekend either way.

That was the official line in his head. It would be fine. But as he lay sprawled on his bed, alone in his own house for the first time, it wasn't hard for him to admit how much he was looking forward to seeing her again and spending extended time together.

Some of his feelings didn't quite make sense, even when he looked at them real hard. He couldn't put his finger on why he was drawn to her or why she made him feel so sure of an outlandish plan.

But as he drifted off to sleep, he knew he would be disappointed if she passed on the opportunity. He'd spent a lot of time in his life scraping by with "fine". He wanted more than fine, he wanted great and awesome. He wanted a cheerleader just as much as he wanted to be someone's cheerleader, and Isla was the first person who had ever inspired that in him.

He couldn't wait to show her just what that life together could be like.

———

Isla left the city early and arrived in Pine Harbour in the middle of the day. She knew the area a bit—there was an army training base on the other side of Georgian Bay, in Meaford, that she'd worked at many times. But she had never driven onto the peninsula before, and she marvelled at how suddenly the landscape changed. Farmland gave way to rocky outcrops and dense forest, and the highway narrowed. Nothing but road and wilderness for quite some time, until she saw the turnoff for Pine Harbour. She didn't miss the emergency services building at the highway, and smiled to herself. That was where Adam worked, and she was proud of him for it.

And then, when she pulled into town, Lake Huron glittered at the end of Main Street. It was a quiet, quaint little village, but something about it made her pulse quiver.

She had to—got to—drive past the cafe to get to Adam's house, and her breath hitched in her throat when she finally caught sight of it. She imagined the striped awnings vanishing, leaving the big windows open for her bake sale painted letters on the glass.

If she wasn't careful, she would find herself falling hopelessly in love with the fantasy of it all.

She turned at the next block and drove deep into the residential neighbourhood, past neat bungalows and larger Victorian-era homes. Adam's street was nearly at the edge of town, and the houses here had more space between them, the landscaping a little wilder.

Then she saw him, close to the road, pushing a shiny red lawnmower.

Slowing, she waved through her window before turning into the long driveway.

Adam had sent her a photo, but it didn't capture the fairytale magic of his little cottage. It was tucked back into a dense grove of trees, and overgrown vines crawled up the front of the porch.

When she got out of her car, her legs aching from the long drive, he had mowed to where she was and turned off the engine. He held out his arms and she folded in against him for an easy hug.

He smelled like fresh-cut grass and gasoline, and when she pulled back, he had a ready smile for her.

"I'm here," she announced. *Ready to discuss the wildest plan.*

He squeezed her hand. "I'm glad. Let me show you inside."

That same wild, fluttery feeling she'd had on Main Street rioted in her chest as he pushed the door open. There was a small foyer, which was dark, and a living room immediately to the left. Also dark. But to the right was a staircase, and a window high on the wall flooded that with light. The whole place smelled like wood cleaner and fresh laundry.

"I've been cleaning all morning," Adam said apologetically. "But there's still a lot to be done. I have a room for you, though. This way."

He led her past the very small but cozy living room, then stopped again. "The kitchen needs the most work. Well, other than the bathroom upstairs. That does, too. Just—"

She realized she hadn't said anything, and she grabbed his hand. "It's beautiful, Adam. I love it. And I can tell that you've been getting it ready. It's a lovely work in progress."

His brows pulled together, and then he shook his head, laughing. "Just like me."

"Me, too."

His mouth curved in a slow smile. "Bit of a theme, then."

As he'd warned, the kitchen was dated, with rough-looking appliances and no furniture. Boxes were stacked beside a back door that looked out onto a private backyard.

Then he led her down a short hallway that also had a door back to the living room on it. "And here is your room," he said, leading her into what had probably been the rest of the living room at some point.

It was now a beautiful suite, with what looked like a modern, classy bathroom at the back of the house and a bed under a big window that overlooked the front yard. "There's lots of space in here to make this your own…you know, should you decide to…"

The elephant in the room. If she wanted to marry Adam, this would be where she would live. This would be her room.

He'd called it that, but it hadn't sunk in.

A wild, wobbly laugh bubbled in her chest. She rubbed

that spot, hoping to keep it inside, but it didn't work. It burst out, and she shook her head as she laughed again and again. She doubled over, blindly grabbing for Adam, who found her and put his hands on her shoulders, righting her.

"You okay?" He chuckled. "It wasn't that funny."

"It's just so absurd." She wiped her eyes. "This would be my room? Who are you, and why don't..." She stepped into the bathroom, which was stunning and didn't match the rest of the house. "Surely this should be your room."

"I'll sleep upstairs. Do you want to see that, too?"

"Of course." Her head was spinning. They should keep moving so she didn't stop and think or have random fits of the giggles again.

"Before I told you about the cafe being for sale, I planned to sleep in both rooms," Adam said as he led her up the stairs. "Downstairs most of the time, because of that bathroom—you'll understand in a minute—but when I'm sleeping during the day, nothing will beat the quiet of up here. This room is at the back of the house and..."

She followed him across the landing and stopped just inside the door to his room. Sure, he didn't have a walk-in shower, but he was right. His room was the quietest in the house, by far. And out the window was nothing but trees. It was serene and peaceful. The perfect place to sleep after a twenty-four-hour shift.

"So I'll make renovating this bathroom a priority, and we'll both be set."

There was that elephant in the room again. She gave him a nervous smile.

Adam sat down on his bed. "Shall we talk about it now?"

"Oh, I don't..."

He patted the bedding beside him. He had nice sheets, dark purple up here, light grey downstairs. Solid colours, easy to add her own touches to if she…if they…

"Come here," he said softly. "You look like you're going to faint."

"This is mortifying." She plonked herself down next to him, then fell backwards, tossing her arms over her head. If they were going to talk seriously about being married and sharing this house, the least she could do is get used to stretching out on her husband's bed. "I was a captain in the army. I shouldn't be all freaked out over what is simply a tactical decision."

He laughed. "Sure. But you're also a human being faced with a scenario that seems surreal, right? I've been a bit freaked out this week, too. Nervous and excited."

"Excited?"

He lay down next to her. "Of course. I've been looking forward to your visit all week."

That made her feel better. "What do you want to do first? What do you want to show me about your town?"

"Are you hungry? We could go to the cafe for lunch. Scope out of the place. Or did you see the diner on the way in? That's always good. High likelihood of running into my family, of course."

"I like your family."

"That's a relief. They're kind of all around us."

"Where do they all live?" She didn't really have a map of the town in her head, so where Adam pointed didn't make a ton of sense, but she liked listening to his voice.

"Owen and Kerry aren't far from here, a little closer to the highway, but still on this side of town. Will is on the other side—that's the newer build area. Josh doesn't actually have a house, he lives with Will sometimes, and pretends the apartment over his garage is habitable some of the time, too."

"Can you show me?" She didn't want to go to the cafe just yet. Couldn't finish falling in love with it just yet. She needed to see more of Adam's life here first. "Can we go for a drive together, so I can see your town through your eyes?"

He helped her up, then they went downstairs. While he put the lawn mower away, she unpacked and refreshed from her drive. Then they headed out in Adam's truck.

He headed down to the harbour first, where she was expecting to see a ramshackle mechanic shack from the way he'd described it, but Josh's garage was Instagram perfect against the backdrop of the glittering lake. A white-washed two-storey building with bright teal letters and a bright red muscle car parked out front, it was beautiful.

"On the outside," Adam said. "But his apartment is…it makes my kitchen look down right fancy." He gestured to the marina across the road. "That's where Seth docks when he flies in."

"He has a float plane?"

"Yep."

"And where does he live?"

Adam pointed northwest. "A hundred and fifty clicks that way. Spends all summer ferrying people to fly-in fishing and hunting lodges. He'll pick up charters from here, too, but there's more traffic out of the Sault and Sudbury, so his base is halfway between the two."

"Do you ever go up there?"

"I did once." Adam put the truck in gear and headed back up the hill, away from the harbour. This time he drove up Main Street, and Isla tried not to crane her neck to look at the cafe as they drove past.

Adam didn't say anything if he noticed her eagerness.

"We didn't have a lot of money growing up. My parents did okay, but they invested everything they had in a house big enough for five boys." He stopped in front of a large Victorian house on a corner lot. "That's where I grew up."

"It's beautiful." Isla glanced over at him, but his expression was unreadable.

"Owen had to sell it after they died because he couldn't afford the property tax and upkeep. He put the money in trust for each of us, and used his portion to buy a smaller place two blocks that way."

"Show me."

The small post-war bungalow was neat and tidy, but nothing like the first house. "How old were you when you moved here?"

"Thirteen. A year after my mom died."

"You were so young."

He made a face. "Yeah."

It would have been a big transition for a teenage boy to go from all that space to cramped quarters. "And Owen had his daughter then?"

"Becca was three, yeah. Bossy and loud." This time Adam's expression was clear. She could tell that he loved his niece and enjoyed everything about her. "Still is, which is awesome."

He put the truck back in drive and headed across town. "You know, I was raised by teenage boys, basically. It could have been Lord of the Flies territory. "

"But it wasn't?"

"No. That was all Owen. He went from twenty to forty overnight. Mature and responsible before his time."

"You all seem pretty responsible. Maybe it was a group

effort." She squeezed his fingers. "Where are we going now?"

"Will's place. The thing I want you to know, I guess, is none of us take anything for granted. Our family stuck together, but it was hard. All of us came out of the years after my parents died with a painful awareness of just how precarious life is, how precarious it is to have a roof over one's head. You can probably trace all of our current living situations back to that time of uncertainty, when Owen realized just how expensive it was to own the house we'd all grown up in. How he'd have to take that away from us, or it would be ripped away at some point." He was still holding her hand as he turned the truck down a very different-looking street. This part of town was newly built in the last ten or twenty years, Isla could tell. The houses were all modern, the streets neat and the sidewalks wide. "This is where Will lives."

"He's the second oldest? And he's a teacher?" She thought she was seeing what Adam was showing her. Both of his oldest brothers had established themselves in town in a permanent, responsible citizen way. Josh was at least trying, in his own way, too. She didn't know Seth's whole story, but this was what Kincaids did. They put down roots.

"A school principal now. Yep. And he's in the army reserves, too."

"Responsible, good with money. And he bought the modern version of a house big enough for the whole family?"

"He really doesn't mind having Josh and me there. It would drive me batty." Adam gestured at the wide garage. "And then Seth and Josh are all about their businesses. They don't even own homes."

"But you do."

"I guess I do." He grinned at her. "Surprised myself there. So, what do you want to do next?"

It was time. "The cafe."

His grin grew. "Yeah?"

She rubbed her palms on her thighs. She was shaking. "Yep."

They parked in a lot behind the main drag, then walked around the block. Adam pointed out Kerry's midwifery clinic, down the street, then gestured across the road. "That's the hair salon slash real estate office where I first heard about the sale price."

"Catie's Cuts? I'm guessing Catie is the…"

"Real estate agent slash hair stylist? That would be correct." Adam pushed open the door of the cafe, and a little bell chimed overhead.

The cafe wasn't busy. There were two tables with customers, but Adam steered her away from them to the counter. The glass display case had takeaway food in it, sandwiches and salads on the bottom two levels, and some sweet treats on the top shelf. She could picture it full of baked goods.

He leaned on the counter and gave the middle-aged woman behind the counter a flirty smile. "Anne, nice to see you again."

"Adam. How did the house hunting go?"

"Quite successfully. Moved in yesterday." He told her the address, and she said something about the previous owner Isla didn't quite follow. She couldn't concentrate on the conversation, she was trying to see the kitchen, too busy visualizing— "And this is Isla."

"Pleasure," she said, holding out her hand. What had she missed?

"Are you new in town?" Anne asked.

Adam fielded it. "Isla's visiting me for the weekend. I'm giving her the grand tour. We were hoping to grab some lunch."

"Takeout or a table?"

He glanced at Isla. "We'll take it to go?"

She nodded. "The sandwiches look great. Two of those?"

Back at his truck, takeout bag clutched firmly in her grip, Isla finally exhaled fully for the first time since she walked into the cafe.

"I thought I was ready to see it," she said to Adam, a sort of apology, because he was looking at her with concern. "But it's just so much. Your idea...and that I could have..."

He opened the passenger door for her, and after she climbed up, he stood in the open door and leaned against the frame of his truck. "This is why you're here. To consider if we might want to do this. Nothing's set in stone."

"I know." She felt wildly out of control, though, because she didn't know. Not really. Not enough.

Everything she might want in life was so close she could taste it, and yet the hurdle to get there seemed ridiculous to even consider for real.

Marriage.

"I know you explained this before, but..." Even though they were alone in the parking lot, she dropped her voice to a whisper. "Are you sure you want to do this?"

"Yes."

"Why? It has to be more than just being my cheer-leader, Adam. That's not a reason people get married. I've been there, done that. I...this doesn't make any sense."

He exhaled roughly. "I don't know how to make it make sense. It just feels right."

Her throat was closing up as she gazed up at him. "You know, you could break my heart and yank this all away. So I'm going to assume that you're being serious here. But I have to know more about your reason why."

"Okay." He nodded. "That's fair. Can we go back to the house?"

The short drive back was quiet. Not tense. He kept giving her reassuring smiles, but his gaze was a million miles away, like he was deep in thought.

Inside, Adam paced ahead of her into the kitchen. She followed with the sandwiches.

"I'm going to say something," he started. "And it's going to sound more extreme than it really is. Because I'm fine. I'm happy, even. But when you say, *that's not a reason people get married*, I know that. Intellectually. I know people get married for love. And I didn't say this before, because I think it makes me sound like a monster, but deep down? I'm broken. Maybe I always have been, but it definitely got sharper when I was overseas."

He paused there, and she waited. Sometimes, talking about the barbed realizations learned on tour took time. She had all the patience in the world here, especially if he was opening up about what this meant for them.

That didn't make it any easier to hear what he said next.

"I don't believe in love. There's no part of me that wants to marry a soul mate or anything like that. I remember my parents being in love. I see how my brother fell in love, how my niece fell in love… I don't have that inside me. It doesn't exist." He made an anguished face. "That's the raw truth. Then we reconnected. And in you, I see something, I see someone I could build a partnership with. We have a real bond, I think. Don't we? And you said yourself that you never want to get married for love. Maybe I latched on to that too much. But it's hard living alone. I don't like that either. So…"

He was silent for a long time. Isla stood stock-still as she watched him think about it—really think about it. Tension rippled across his face. His hands clenched in front of him, his knuckles white. And when he looked up at her again, his eyes big, his mouth tight, his face sombre, he said, "I don't know. I wish I could give you a better answer. I never wanted to get married and lose myself in someone else. But being side-by-side with you? That sounds nice. I don't know why that sounds so nice, but it does."

She knew that that was the truth. It was true that he didn't know and she took some comfort in that admission. She took comfort in his ability to tell her that he was not sure but he wanted to go on this adventure with her anyway.

It was the opposite of romantic but it was deeply kind. It spoke to a rare kind of friendship, one maybe she had never experienced before in her life but she recognized it as that. No, more than friendship, she recognized it as a kinship. She might not love Adam, but she felt a familial bond with him. Deep, and if she was sure of it, abiding too. "Sometimes 'I don't know' is the right answer. I just needed to hear it again. And maybe more than once, but… I believe you."

"Thank Christ. I was worried there that I wasn't smart enough to convince you, and that would be a damn shame, because the look on your face in the cafe…"

"Yeah?"

"It was pretty awesome, seeing you dream like that. It looked like how it felt for me when I started going to the volunteer fire brigade training. And my brother was dead set against me becoming a firefighter. In that moment, all I wanted was someone in my corner."

That knocked the wind out of her, and she set the sandwiches down. All of Adam's talk about wanting to be her cheerleader was coming from a place of earnest want himself. She moved to him and gave him a hug. "I'm in your corner." She stepped back. "You know, when I arrived in town, I saw the fire station and knew you worked there. I was proud of you."

His face transformed, softened. "Thanks."

"Should we eat our sandwiches, or were they just subterfuge for reconnaissance?"

"Leave perfectly good sandwiches?" He snorted. "Bring them to the living room."

"If I'm going to move in, we'll need a kitchen table."

"On it."

They settled on the couch, and ate together in companionable silence. Once they finished, Isla asked the next question on her mind.

"Is it going to be weird, sleeping in separate rooms?" She waved her hands around. "Is this going to get awkward?"

"I don't think so. Should we test it out?" He stood up and picked up their plates. "All right, I'll wash these up, then I'm off to bed."

She laughed, because it was early afternoon. "See you in the morning, I guess."

He bowed slightly. "See? Not awkward."

She stood and followed him to the kitchen. "And what

about how we act in front of your family? I don't want to be surprised with any awkwardness."

"Like if there's a situation where we have to kiss?" He made a face as he crossed the room to stand in front of her. "Ew."

She pushed at him. "Yes."

"I think we can kiss without getting carried away." He wiggled one eyebrow. "You worried you can't resist all this?"

She laughed and then sighed, leaning against his chest, wild remnants of laughter rippling through her.

"Isla thinks I'm irresistible," he sang against her hair. Then he gave her a tight hug. "Come on. Give me a kiss."

She leaned back, took his face in her hands, and pressed her lips against his. Happy warmth tingled inside her, but that was it. No fireworks, no desperate need. And Adam didn't deepen the kiss, but she knew if he did, it would be more of the same.

He was a sexy, handsome friend, and they could absolutely live together without it getting complicated.

After they broke apart, Adam dropped to one knee. Isla laughed. "What are you doing?"

"Asking you to marry me, properly this time." His grin was both confident and endearing. He held out his hand, offering her a firm handshake. "Isla Petersen, will you be my wife? Will you let me help you make your bakery dreams come true? Will you make cookies for me, and come to my family Christmas parties, and just generally help me look like the grown-up I am to my family?"

She took his offered hand and shook it.

He didn't let go.

"Yes," she whispered. "I will marry you. I will share

this house with you, and bake you cookies, and kiss you in public whenever you need me to."

His eyes twinkled. "Lucky me."

"Adam…"

"And only in public," he added hastily. Then he stood up. "At home, we're a strictly hugs-only marriage."

She leaned into him. "Thank you."

"This will be good for both of us," he promised.

CHAPTER EIGHT

"WHAT THE FUCK is wrong with you?"

Adam had a strange relationship with confidence. Most of the time, he had it in spades. He'd graduated top of his class. He knew he was a good firefighter, and he knew his place on the team. He had lots to learn still, but he was capable.

And then there were moments like this, when his restless energy converted in the wrong direction to overstepping. He knew his riding position was to support his crew. He knew he wasn't supposed to be the first off the truck. But they'd arrived at a medical distress call, a child couldn't breathe, and frankly, Adam ran faster than everyone else on his team.

"It wasn't a fire. We can all do CPR," he muttered. Which hadn't even been necessary. The toddler had a febrile seizure and had started breathing again on his own as they arrived. But what he had known in that moment was resuscitation might be needed, and he could be the quickest one there.

Which was the wrong answer, even though it was the

right instinct. The *correct* answer was that they had systems for a reason, that crew discipline mattered, and he would communicate better next time.

He didn't say any of that.

And it didn't help that they'd had two volunteers with them for the call, newer trainees who just happened to be in the station at the time.

They were upstairs now, and the volunteers were downstairs. So instead of making lunch, Richard was tearing a strip off Adam that the younger firefighter was pretty sure everyone in the building could hear. The thin veneer of rank was a farce.

Denise got in between them. "Okay, let's take a pause—"

Richard wasn't pausing. "You have a lot to learn about being a part of a real team."

Adam forced himself not to roll his eyes. He wasn't going to react at all. If having four older brothers had taught him anything, it was that another storm was always on the horizon. Something else would sweep in soon enough to piss Richard off, and until then, Adam would just live in the doghouse.

Instead, he just nodded.

And after another blustery grumble, Richard let it go. They only had one more call that night, a car fire that meant significant cleanup at the site, and Adam took extra care to follow both procedure and the team routines he'd learned in his short time with them.

It was a by-the-book call out with no room for Richard to criticize him.

He didn't get a "good job, kid" after, but he wasn't yelled at again, either. Not by his teammates, anyway. And not while he was on shift.

The next morning, after they'd handed over to the next crew, and he was dragging his weary ass to his truck, he saw Owen waiting for him.

A concerned older brother ambush.

Just fucking great.

"I'm tired," he said as he tossed his bag in the passenger door.

Owen followed him around to the driver's side. "What happened last night?"

Adam frowned. "Were you even in the building then?"

"News travels fast."

"It wasn't fucking news." Adam scrubbed the heel of his hand into his eye socket. He was so tired. Sighing, he leaned against the side of his truck and rolled his neck. "Come on. You know how it is with rookies and senior crew members. There's an adjustment process."

"You don't want to get a reputation as being hard to work with."

"I'm not hard to work with. I'm as easygoing as it comes. I just…" Adam laughed. "Never mind. It doesn't matter. You don't need to worry about me."

"I always worry about you."

"I am aware, and it is exhausting. Please stop."

Owen scowled.

Adam gave him an exasperated look. "Come on."

"All right. You're okay?"

"I'm fine."

Owen gave him a half-smile. "Is Richard in one piece?"

"I said nothing. I let him tear into me."

"I don't like that, either."

"He was right on a technicality, so I let it go."

Owen clapped him on the shoulder and headed inside.

Adam waited until his brother had disappeared before

he climbed into the driver's seat, and it was another minute before he started the truck. It would be hard to make this transition anywhere, to any fire service. Doing it in his home town, in a building his brother managed—that wasn't better or worse, he figured. Just complicated.

And exhausting.

He'd said that out loud to Owen, and he felt it in his bones.

All he wanted to do was go home and rack out. But when he walked into his kitchen and smelled something bad, he knew sleep wasn't going to happen immediately.

At first he worried the breaker had blown and the fridge had been without power for twenty-four hours, but that wasn't it.

Holding his hand over his nose, he took a deep breath and thought about where else a noxious odour could be coming from. It was likely a dead animal that had gotten into the ceiling or the wall before expiring.

His only ladder was pretty flimsy, but he managed to get it braced against the wall in the hallway beneath the access door to the crawlspace above the kitchen. It wasn't a full attic, just a place to store boxes. Adam didn't have anything up there, but they might need to use it once Isla moved in.

He nudged the door open, bracing himself in case there was a whole family of raccoons mourning their dearly departed buddy or something like that, but the space was quiet—and scent-free, so whatever the source was, it wasn't here.

Shining his flashlight around over the space, he verified for himself that it was critter-free, and he was about to head back down when he caught sight of something shiny. It looked like a small toolbox, and he'd missed it when he'd looked in here last. Hoisting himself up onto the bare beams, he crab-walked toward it, and snagged it with his fingertips.

Then he sneezed and dropped it.

Swearing under his breath, he reached down to grab it again and lost his balance. Fucking clumsy, he thought, his tired brain not moving fast enough to stop himself from putting his foot down—and through the ceiling of his kitchen.

"Oh, fuck."

He stared down at the gaping hole he'd just created. At the ugly-ass kitchen, the tired linoleum floor.

The house he had just bought cockily, without thinking it through, and to which he was going to bring a bride back soon, was falling apart.

Another string of curse words echoed around in the small space before he climbed out the access door and down the ladder.

He was so mad at himself, he didn't even go into the kitchen to look at the damage. He stripped off his dusty clothes right there and stalked into the shower in Isla's room and turned the water on as hot as it would go.

Fucking hell.

He stood under the steam until the water temperature started to fade, then he gave his house the finger as he stalked upstairs.

But after he crawled into bed, he didn't go to sleep. Instead, he called his secret fiancée.

Her voice was full of sleep as she answered. "Morning."

He smiled at the mumble. "Sorry to wake you."

"It's okay." She slurred the two words together, and the

tension band around his head eased at the softness. "What's wrong?"

"Bah. Stuff. Nothing. Just wanted to say hi before I went to bed."

"No no, back up. What stuff?"

He screwed up his face, closed his eyes, and unloaded the whole story. She listened without interrupting. When he finished, he sighed. "That's it. Then I called you because I didn't know what to do next."

"Go to bed. That's what you do next. The hole will still be there when you wake up, and you'll have more capacity to deal with it. I always need sleep before I fix things."

"Do you?"

"Fuck yeah."

He laughed out loud at the unexpected emphatic curse. "Fuck yeah," he repeated quietly. "Thanks."

"Adam?"

"Yeah?"

"Is anything else wrong? Are you getting cold feet?"

"I think that's supposed to be the bride," he muttered, his hand clenching hard on the phone. "Why? Are you?"

"No." But the silence that followed told him she had been thinking about it. Wondering if it was a mistake, maybe.

Fatigue clawed at the inside of his eyelids, but this couldn't be left half-addressed. "We have other options. I was thinking, because the offer is for any Pine Harbour resident or their immediate family, we don't need to get married. I could buy it as a silent partner."

"And then I would work for you? And we'd be room-mates? What would your brothers say about you buying a business at the same time as buying a house and starting a new career?"

He groaned. Fuck. "That would be a disaster."

"I appreciate you giving me an out. But I don't want one. Unless—"

"No. I don't want one, either. I'm looking forward to you getting here. I really am." This morning it felt like Isla was the only person in the entire world who understood him. He felt like that a lot. She believed in him just as much as he believed in her.

The next week felt like a year. A disaster year that made Adam second-guess himself at every turn—and reinforced how grateful he was going to be when Isla came back to Pine Harbour with him.

Isla texted him that she'd picked up a marriage license and booked an appointment to get married at Toronto City Hall, and a not-unexpected but still surprising relief washed over him. This plan was going to work.

He checked the bakery sales listing every day, to make sure it was still available, and he thought about contacting Anne Minelli, telling her he was marrying a baker who would want to take over her cafe, but something held him back.

His brothers hearing about it. That was what was holding him back. He didn't want their opinions. He didn't want to hear that he was rushing into this, that it was a mistake to get married quickly or at all. Or might be even worse if they would be relieved, which was wild, because that was what he wanted. He wanted them to know he had a partner and didn't need them anymore.

And yet, he didn't want them to be the ones to say it.

He was doing this himself. For his own reasons. For Isla. For them, and their unconventional bond.

It was private and didn't need outside justification or support.

What Adam really wanted—what he needed—was space.

And a wife, he found himself realizing more and more each day.

So when Isla texted him in the middle of another rough shift, he tuned out the pointed "helpful tips" Richard was lobbing his way and checked the message. He was glad he did, because it made his day.

Isla: I got the marriage license!

It was exactly what he needed to hear. It didn't matter that he couldn't do everything himself, all on his own, because soon he wouldn't need to. He'd have a partner who would carry some of the load with him. He didn't even need Isla to carry anything, just to be there and believe in him.

Adam: That's awesome. Hey, should I buy you a ring?
Isla: We can get something simple.
Adam: I'll take care of it.
Isla: You should have one, too. I'll get that.
Isla: What size ring do you wear?
Adam: I have no idea.

Then he sent a grinning emoji, which matched his face.

From across the table, Stan cleared his throat. "You either won the lottery or that's someone special."

Adam thought it might be possibly both. "Yep. Her name is Isla."

"She from around here?"

He put his phone in his pocket. "No. But she's moving here soon."

"Sounds serious."

"Yeah. It is." He swallowed the rest of the explanation. He couldn't tell anyone in this building—or in this town—about the elopement until after it was over, or there would be hell to pay.

His brothers would understand him and Isla doing something quiet. They would never understand hearing about it secondhand.

CHAPTER NINE

FOR HER SECOND WEDDING, Isla wore a yellow sundress. Adam wore a black suit, and after he picked her up, he stopped at a flower shop. "Wait here."

When he came out, he was carrying a small cardboard box. Blue and white flowers peaked out the top. He climbed back into the truck, looking a little nervous and a lot cute. "Okay, so…" He shoved the box at her, making her laugh.

"What are these?"

"Random wedding flowers they had inside. I was going to buy you a sunflower or something, and the clerk was working on these. I asked if she could make an extra one, and she sold me this." He lifted it up. "A bridesmaid bouquet, apparently."

Maybe that would be more luck. Her hands shook as she took it. And nestled beneath it was a boutonniere for his jacket, in matching blue and white.

"I'm probably never going to do this again," he said. "Thought we might as well do it right."

She set her flowers down in her lap and reached across to pick it up. "Can I put it on you?"

He grinned at her, his gaze a warm invitation. "Please do."

"You still feel okay about not telling anyone we're doing this? You don't want your family here?"

He shook his head. "Eloping feels like the right fit for what we're doing. I don't want to make this anything it isn't." Covering her hand with his, he pressed her fingers into his chest. "I never want to lie to you. You know my real vow here is to be your steadfast friend, right?"

She nodded slowly. "Same."

"All right, then let's do this."

When they arrived, they didn't have to wait long. Another couple didn't have witnesses, either, so they observed each other's ceremonies. The other couple went first, then it was their turn.

Before they went to the front of the small room, Adam pulled out his phone and propped it on a ledge on the wall.

"Recording this for posterity." He grinned again. "It's my first time getting hitched, it's kind of exciting."

She slid her hand against his and squeezed his fingers, then told him the same thing he'd said outside the flower shop. "Let's do this."

The ceremony was simple and short.

Do you? He did.

And you? She did, too.

They exchanged their rings. The simple gold band around Isla's finger felt strange but not wrong, and she clung to that feeling. It described what they were doing perfectly.

"You may seal your vows with a kiss." The justice of

the peace beamed at them, and Adam pulled her close, his scent enveloping her. She breathed in the solid dependability of him, the warm trustworthiness, and closed her eyes as his lips met hers.

His kiss was perfect, too. Chaste but lingering, and when he pulled away, he leaned in again to press his forehead against hers. His dark eyes sparkled and he held her gaze until she smiled at him. It didn't take long. She knew that this time would be different. This time, she had a husband who wanted the same things she wanted out of their relationship. So what if it wasn't some super romantic ideal? A true partnership with a friend was better than that any day of the week.

Plus when he kissed her, or slid his hand around her waist like he was doing right now, she knew it wasn't transactional. Ironic, that the most tit-for-tat relationship of her life would be the one where she didn't stress about what a touch meant or if someone was keeping score.

"Good luck to the both of you," the JP said.

They wouldn't need it. They had something better than luck. They had a plan.

She had spent the last week packing up her apartment, so when they finished at the courthouse, they went straight to her place. She got changed first, her sundress being swapped out for yoga pants and a t-shirt. Then Adam ditched his suit and emerged from her bathroom in jeans.

"What do you think we should do with these?" Isla gestured to the flowers. "It's probably bad luck to toss them, right?"

"We'll take them with us." He lifted the lid off a box from her kitchen. It was full of mixing bowls and utensils, and the bouquet fit perfectly inside the top bowl. "There."

It didn't take long to pack her entire life into the back of Adam's truck, and then they convoyed north. It was dark by the time they arrived in Pine Harbour.

Her second wedding night was going to be spent unpacking.

You need to stop comparing the two marriages. Jackass is in the past now. She made a silent promise to herself that for the rest of the night, she would only think about what was to come.

The bakery.

Her plans.

That was her future, and all she needed to think about.

———

As Adam had promised, it wasn't awkward for Isla to wake up on her first full day as his wife and have no idea where her husband was. She had the house to herself, it seemed, so she put on a pot of coffee and happily had a long shower while that brewed.

When she returned to the kitchen, he was back. "Morning," he said with an easy smile. "You were sound asleep when I got up, so I went to Mac's to grab some breakfast sandwiches, and then swung past the hair salon to check Catie's business hours today. She'll be open in an hour."

Butterflies swarmed inside her as she peeked inside the takeout bag. "Wow. You've been busy."

"I don't want to impose at all, but I figured…food is always good. And time spent on reconnaissance—"

"—is seldom wasted." Isla grinned after finishing the thought. "Excellent recce job."

"Happy to be your scout as needed. Do you want me to come with you to talk to her about putting in an offer?"

"It might be easier to do it on my own." She thought about what she would say. *So I married a Kincaid brother just so I could show up and ask about buying a building.* Not that, that was for sure. "Or it might be easier to have you there as the bonafide local? I dunno. I'm nervous either way."

"I'm a phone call away. And Catie is nice." He came to stand next to her and dug out a sandwich. "Want to eat and think on it?"

In the end, fortified with greasy goodness from the diner, she decided to go on her own. She walked, wanting to absorb as much of the town as possible on her way to stake a claim on a part of it.

Would the people who lived in these houses want cookies and tarts? She'd run a number of projections. She knew the population for the area, for the entire peninsula, and how many tourists came up on the weekends from the cities further south. She didn't need the town of Pine Harbour to support her business for it to be a success. She could focus her production toward weekend events, and she had a line on two local markets as well—and stalls there were a fraction of what they cost in the city.

She had options. She just needed a kitchen.

When she turned onto Main Street, she saw the cafe ahead on the next block. It was a corner building, very pretty, and she wanted it with an intensity that surprised her. Adam had been keeping tabs on it covertly, and they knew there weren't any other interested buyers.

Now she just needed to brass it out while she introduced herself to the realtor.

She stopped in front of *Catie's Cuts*, which was conveniently located across the street from the cafe. She could keep her eye on the prize and say whatever needed to be said here.

A sign in the window declared the salon open, and it didn't look like there were any customers inside yet. She pulled the door open and stepped inside. It smelled nice, like a fancy salon in the city, and the faintest strains of spa music played. Just enough to set a mood, but quietly. Unobtrusive.

From the back, a woman's voice called out. "Be right there!"

That gave Isla another minute to look around. There was a single stylist chair on one side of the room, and two hair dryer chairs at the back. On the other side of the room was a desk clearly dedicated to the real estate business, although it looked like that was where hair clients probably settled up, too. It left a lot of open space, and the proprietor hadn't tried to fill it. Despite the folksy feel of two businesses in one, the whole aesthetic was quite modern, like a city loft.

It gave Isla some hope that her plans for the cafe might work. A spare, bright, modern take on a bakery.

That dream grew a little more when the stylist slash realtor appeared, and she was the human version of her salon. Orange eye shadow, blunt blonde bob, and wide, welcoming smile. "How can I help you?"

"I have questions about the cafe for sale?"

"You've come to the right place. I'm Catie Berton. Have a seat."

"Isla Petersen. I just moved here. I married Adam Kincaid." There. She did it. She said the ridiculous thing.

"Oh, wow! Congratulations!" Catie's gaze dropped to Isla's bare hand.

Rings. Right. She'd done this before. She needed to actually wear the ring Adam had bought her.

But then the realtor lifted her gaze, and her smile was

just as big as it had been before. "When did you get married?"

"Well, that's the thing. About the bakery, and the… offer. For Pine Harbour residents and their families. Adam and I started dating in the summer. And we eloped so I would be eligible to buy the bakery." It sounded so obviously a scam, Isla's pulse ratcheted up. But she wasn't going to lie, other than the fib about dating. They'd had dinner. Twice. Went dancing. *Slept together*. That counted. "I'm here to find out more about that offer."

Catie pulled a printed information sheet out of a file folder and slid it across. "Here's the listing. There are some addendums to the discounted listing price for Pine Harbour residents that you should know about. The bakery cannot be sold again for five years, so there is a commitment there to keep it open. It must operate at least five days a week for at least partial food service. A temporary closure for renovations is allowed."

"Is there any requirement that a marriage…" Isla's tongue felt thick in her mouth. *Be real?*

Catie didn't seem to notice. "There is no requirement that a marriage needs to have lasted any length of time." She pointed to another line. "It is simply any long-term (five years or more) Pine Harbour resident, or any member of their immediate family (children, spouses, or legal dependents)."

"I meet all of those requirements." Five days a week of partial food service would be a challenge, but she could do it. She would find a way. It was too good to turn down. She took a deep breath. "Do you need more information from me? I would like to make an offer."

"Here is the paperwork for that. Your spouse will need

to sign it, as the long-term resident, and the seller is asking for a business plan to be attached as well."

That Isla could do, and not even feel a little bit like a fraud while she did it. She handed over her business card. "I'll get this to you by the end of the day. Thank you. And in the meantime, you can check out my Instagram account. I did pop-up bake sales in Toronto all summer." Four of them, supported by her school. Minor details. "That's how I plan to use the cafe. As a daily bake sale."

Catie picked up her phone, and Isla knew the minute she'd won the realtor over. "You make these Rice Krispies squares?"

"I sure do."

"Wow. They look amazing." The other woman beamed. "I look forward to presenting your offer to the seller. Good luck. And welcome to Pine Harbour."

———

She nearly ran all the way back to Adam's house. Their house, now, because this was actually going to happen.

He was in the front yard, cutting back overgrown bushes, when she skipped up the driveway. "That looks like it went well," he called out.

She pulled the papers from her satchel. "We have work to do!"

He immediately set down the chainsaw he'd been holding. "Awesome."

"You can finish—"

"Later." He pulled off his work gloves. "Show me what you need."

"I already have business plans. They want to see that. The offer is basically a forgivable loan, without any payments. So I can buy the cafe for a dollar, on the understanding that I operate it for five years. I need to…" She read the exact language. "Have consistent, regular food service, five days a week. Holiday and seasonal reduction is allowed, but year round partial service is expected."

"That's detailed."

"She wants her cafe to still serve the community, and I…" Isla clutched the papers to her chest and spun around in a circle. "I get it. Oh, Adam. This is really happening."

"What do you need from me?"

"You need to sign it as my spouse. And we need to get it notarized. I told Catie that we eloped so I could make this offer. So it's time to tell your brothers, if you're ready?"

He pulled out his phone. "Me? How about you? Are you ready for a Kincaid family gathering?"

She didn't think it was possible for her pulse to jump even more, but at the thought of facing his brothers again, this time with a *surprise, we're married* announcement made her feel faint. "Yep," she whispered. "Bring it on."

He fired off a group text, then picked up the chainsaw. "Might as well put this away if we're going to have company."

"Do I have time to bake cookies?"

She did, because Josh was in the middle of something at the garage, so the brothers didn't come over until late afternoon. And she didn't just make two kinds of cookies, she also finished unpacking some of her things that would make the living room feel like home—her basket of throws for curling up on the couch at night and her small bookcase with her favourite books about baking and business.

Adam stashed the rest of her moving boxes neatly in her bedroom and closed the door just as Will and Josh pulled into the drive. He came into the kitchen to give her the heads up, then pulled out his phone and video-called Seth.

Isla was keeping herself busy with putting on coffee and assembling trays of cookies, but she was keenly aware of how it played out in the living room. It was a small house, so it wasn't hard to eavesdrop.

"Who else is here? There's a strange car in your driveway." That was Josh.

Isla bit her lower lip to keep from laughing.

From Adam's phone, Seth—who had already seen her briefly, when Adam initiated the call—broke that part of the news. "It's Isla. She's in the kitchen."

"How do you know that from the other side of the lake?" That was Will.

"Because I'm smarter than you," the pilot said.

She couldn't keep a chuckle in at that. *Brothers.* "I'm in the kitchen," she called out. "Making cookies."

It was a thin attempt at distraction, but it worked for the five minutes before Owen and Kerry walked in, and they had bonus family members with them. Adam's niece, Becca and her toddler son, Charlie. "Surprise!"

"What are you doing in town?" Adam asked as Josh and Will abandoned the cookies to descend on Charlie, who Isla hadn't met before, but Adam had told her all about.

He was pretty cute. Definitely worth picking over the cookies.

As Becca explained they'd come home for a week while her boyfriend was in hockey training camp, Adam and Isla had a tiny moment of eye contact. He gave her a confident smile, and nodded.

It's going to be okay, his eyes said.

She nodded back. And then as one, the entire family turned to Adam. "So what's the problem?"

Isla didn't catch who said that, but she'd seen the text message he had sent them earlier that day. He'd asked them if they could come over together because he had something he wanted to tell them. No mention of there being a problem. She stepped closer to Adam, so he could feel her presence beside him.

Owen gave her a half-smile. "Is that why you're here? Moral support because it's been a rough couple of weeks?" He gestured to Adam, who still hadn't answered the original question. "This one has a lot to prove."

"Not to me." It slipped out before she could catch it, but Isla didn't regret being straight with Adam's brother. This was the whole point—might as well not mince around it. So what if she'd originally planned to show it more than just lay it out in three sharp words?

Owen curved an eyebrow high in surprise.

But she wasn't done. She slid her fingers around Adam's hand, hoping nobody noticed that she was shaking. She squeezed tight.

He squeezed back. "Actually, Isla and I have news. We eloped yesterday. We got married at Toronto City Hall, and—"

"Oh my *God*," shrieked Becca, who hadn't even yet been properly introduced to Isla. That didn't stop the younger woman from shoving her way through the group of her uncles and wrapping her arms around both Isla and Adam at once. "That's so wild, you guys. You *eloped*?"

Isla laughed. "Yep."

"We haven't even met, and we're family now?" Becca shifted her attention fully to Isla. "Hi. I'm Becca."

"I'm familiar," Isla murmured. "Your uncle is a big fan of yours."

"The feeling is mutual, so if you break his heart, I'll have to kill you."

Isla blinked. "I'm not planning on that…"

Becca grinned. "Excellent. Welcome to the family."

Behind her, Owen rolled his eyes. "Well, if my daughter has deemed this unexpected news to have her approval, then…"

"We aren't asking for anyone's approval," Adam pointed out. And then he pulled Isla away from Becca, and wrapped his arm around her as if to say, *watch what you say around my bride.*

That's what Isla imagined it meant, anyway. She liked the idea of that. "We're really happy," she said to everyone, trying to be reassuring. She didn't know any of them well enough to read their expressions, except Owen's concern was projected loud and clear. So she locked her gaze on him as she leaned into Adam. "I know this is a surprise, but we have our reasons."

Adam nodded. "The thing is, we've been talking since the summer about what it might be like for Isla to come here and open a bakery. It's been a bit of a whirlwind, but that's exactly what she's going to do, and we decided to get married to make it easier." He beamed down at her, playing the part of an adoring husband to perfection. "And I couldn't be prouder."

"The cafe." Josh pumped his arm. "Called it."

Adam laughed and glanced at his brother. "You did nothing of the sort!"

"I totally did. I told you about it when you mentioned she was a baker the first time."

"I don't remember that."

"It was in a group text!" The mechanic looked to the other brothers, but they all shrugged in unison.

On Adam's phone, which Kerry was holding now, Seth shook his head. "Doesn't ring a bell."

"You're all jerks," Josh muttered. "But that's not going to stop me from welcoming Isla to the Pine Harbour Small Business Association."

Will leaned in and mock-whispered, "That's not a real thing."

Isla had whiplash from the conversation. "Uh…"

Josh didn't seem perturbed. "I'm trying to get it going."

Will rubbed his chin. "And how is that going so far?"

"We've had some challenges."

"Nobody wants to be associated with the random guy who lives above his garage?"

"I'm a social media celebrity."

"You keep saying that like it means something."

Isla grabbed her phone. "Do I search for you by your name or by the garage?"

Josh winked at her. "She knows it means something."

"Well, I have seventy-nine people who follow my Instagram account, so anything more than that is…" She trailed off as his Instagram account loaded. And looked back at the Kincaid clan. "He actually *is* a social media celebrity, you guys."

"I keep telling them. They aren't impressed."

"I'm impressed. Count me in as part of the Small Business Association."

He grabbed a cookie. "Excellent. We accept dues in the form of bartered goods. Bring cookies to our next meeting."

It was barely dinner time by the time they all left, but

Adam sagged against the front door after closing it. "I don't know about you, but I'm ready for bed after that."

Isla collapsed on the couch in the living room, which she'd made as pretty as she could, and they hadn't even sat in there. They'd just all crowded into the kitchen and talked over each other for two straight hours. "They're a lot."

He followed her onto the couch, sprawling in the other corner. "And how. But that went okay, didn't it?"

She laughed out loud. "We survived?"

"Well, yeah. That's my standard for okay."

It wasn't her place to criticize his family—and she saw how much they loved him. She just… Well, what she could do was be positive with Adam. "I think we both deserve more than survival as the bare minimum. It's why I'm here. It's why we're doing this, right?"

"Absolutely." He gave her a tired smile.

She pulled two afghans from her basket and tossed him one. "Do you want to watch something on TV? Veg out and be brainless for a bit?"

"That sounds perfect." He closed his eyes. "And if I fall asleep, you can just leave me here."

She watched him for a long moment, then turned on the TV.

He didn't open his eyes again, and she let him sleep, because he was right. It was perfect.

CHAPTER TEN

TWO WEEKS LATER, Isla woke long before dawn. Her phone told her it was half past four in the morning, and she was foolish to lie there in the dark, grinning to herself. She'd be dragging by the end of the day, and in the weeks to come there would be enough early mornings like this that she should sleep in while she still could.

But she couldn't, not today. Today was the day she got the keys to her very own bakery. She had so much work to do, and she was so excited.

An ugly whisper of doubt tried to intrude, that it would be hard, maybe too hard. Maybe she couldn't do it. But she wasn't making any room for that voice in her mind. Not now. Not ever again, but especially not today.

The house was quiet and dark, but as soon as she flipped the light on in the kitchen, she heard footsteps above.

"Did I wake you?" she asked when Adam shuffled in, rubbing sleep from his eyes.

"Nope." He scrunched up his face. "Yep. But only

because I was sleeping lightly, apparently. I can sense the excitement. So what's on our agenda for today?"

Our agenda. Not hers. Theirs, shared, together.

"You don't need to come with me," she said. To be polite.

He accepted the mug of coffee she handed him, then leaned against the counter. "When I bought this place, I didn't tell anyone until it was a done deal. So if you want to do it all on your own, that's cool. But it's a really big deal, and I can...I dunno, take pictures for your Instagram?"

An excited grin split her face wide open. "Maybe you can come with me to get the keys, and then I'll hang out in the cafe by myself for a while?"

That's exactly what they did. When Catie texted to say the keys were ready to be picked up, they walked over to the salon together, travel mugs full of coffee, and bundled up against the early morning frost.

Then they crossed the street and she let herself in.

It had been thoroughly cleaned and left in turnkey condition. Anne Minelli had been eager to hand it over, and then she did it with a lot of care. Her heart ached a little, for reasons hard to name. Part of it was that this had been someone's dream for a long time, and nobody else had wanted it.

Isla wanted to honour the spirit of her agreement in buying this place, because she did want it. Desperately.

This *was* her dream, although she would change it radically. Most of the tables and chairs would go to make room for longer lines and display tables of packaged cookies.

Silently, she walked through to the kitchen, Adam close behind. She checked out the ovens, the walk-in fridge, the stainless steel work counters. All as they had been when she'd walked through it when her offer had been accepted.

When she turned around, Adam was looking at the fire alarm system, because of course he was. "This is a bit outdated," he said, pulling out his phone. "I want to upgrade you to a different system that better integrates with local emergency services."

Those complicated feelings inside her rose and lodged in her throat. She nodded. "Thanks," she managed to get out.

"I'll leave you to it. How long do you think you'll be?"

"A few hours."

"Text me if you need anything."

And just like that, she was alone in the future *Bake Sale!* to make purchase order lists, to estimate baking capacity, and dream for the future. What purchases she might be able to afford in six months and a year, to make the business even better.

It had been a long time since she'd been in charge of anything.

She liked it a lot.

She'd missed it.

It was early October now. Just over two months until Christmas. She sketched out a calendar. If she opened around Halloween, that would be an obvious treat-oriented event to theme a bake sale around. But could she get the storefront up and ready by then, with the necessary inspections and business licenses?

She would try.

And in the meantime, she could use the kitchen for her back-up plan, something Isla already knew how to do.

———

The first official appearance of *Bake Sale!* on the Bruce Peninsula was planned with three days' notice and announced to nobody. It was the Saturday of the long weekend for Canadian Thanksgiving, the final holiday of the year for many cottagers in the area, and Isla had secured a table at the Pine Harbour farmer's market.

Adam had to work, so she couldn't even be sure to have a friendly face appear. It didn't matter, she told herself. This was research and product testing, and both of those were done on a cold audience.

She started small. Her table at the market featured her 25-cent chocolate chip cookies and her oversized, extra gooey Rice Krispies squares, as well as two seasonal offerings, apple raspberry cupcakes and a pumpkin lace cookie. Nothing too fancy. None of the higher priced tarts she loved to make but hadn't figured out how to make profitable in the city.

Business was slow at the start of the day. Her signs grabbed eyeballs, but she was surrounded by home-baked goods. Traffic picked up mid-morning with a couple of families returning for more cookies, because their children had eaten them all before they left the market. And those customers were also the first to ask her when her shop was opening.

"I'm not sure yet," she admitted as she handed over business cards. "Please follow me on Instagram and I'll announce it soon."

But at the end of the day, she didn't have any new followers.

So much for that being an easy way to connect with the community. By the time lunch rolled around, she realized it would be much more effective if she had an actual opening day planned that she could promote. Live and learn. Instead of being disheartened, she booked her table again for the following weekend, and left, determined to have flyers for an actual opening day when she returned.

Which meant she had to pick a date and stick with it. Nothing like pressure.

The next week passed in a flurry of inspections and eighteen-hour days. She barely saw Adam, who worked and slept and then worked again, until he came home Friday morning looking exhausted after yet another twenty-four-hour shift.

She was about to head out the door to start prepping for her second kick at the local farmer's market, but that wasn't pressing. "Are you going to crawl right into bed, or do you want some breakfast?"

He sat heavily at the secondhand table they'd found for the kitchen and waved off a cup of coffee. "But if you're making something to eat, I wouldn't say no to that."

She put some mushrooms on in one pan, then whipped up some eggs in another. "You want to know the real secret to being a chef?"

He gave her a tired smile. "What?"

"Butter."

That made him laugh, as she'd intended.

A few minutes later, she slid an omelette in front of him. "Can you talk about your shift? And do you want to?"

"Yeah. And maybe. It was…" He took a big bite of mushrooms and made a pleased face as he chewed and swallowed. "This is great."

"Thanks."

"It was a night of a lot of callouts. That's all. Nothing more to really talk about, but there wasn't any time to rest. I'll sleep well today."

"I'll be quiet when I come back."

"You never bother me. You're fine. How long will you be at the bakery today?"

"Probably most of the day."

"Can I have dinner waiting for you when you get home?"

Now it was her turn to look pleased. "Sure. Text me when you wake up and I'll come home then. We can cook together if you want."

————

By late morning, she had her chocolate chip cookie dough in the fridge, her cupcake icing was done and in piping bags, and the Rice Krispies squares were made and cooling in trays. She took a break from the kitchen to sit in the front of the store with her Thermos of coffee and go through the deliveries that had just arrived.

She was most excited about the brightly coloured acrylic paint she'd ordered to paint the *Bake Sale!* sign on the front window. To make it easy on herself, she hung up her travel banner sign on the inside of the window, so all she needed to do was take a chair outside and trace the exact same lettering on the glass.

As she was assembling her painting supplies, two women knocked on the front door. Isla recognized one of them from across the road.

"Can we come in?" Catie Berton asked as she opened the door and they stepped inside. "Oh wow, look at how bright and open it is in here now!"

The other woman held out a bouquet of flowers. "These are for you, a welcome to the neighbourhood, if you will. I'm Olivia Minelli."

Isla extended her hand. "Isla Petersen. Nice to meet you. Are you related to the previous owner of the cafe?"

"Daughter-in-law. But I'm here in the capacity of an enthusiastic community member. I have two little kids and having a new bakery in Grandma's old shop is very exciting to them. Do you have an opening date planned?"

Isla's hands shook as she waved them over to her pile of deliveries. "One of these boxes has my flyers in it…" She dug it out. "There's been so much to do, but I've decided to just go for it. Here, you get the very first hand-out. I'm opening at the end of the month, and this weekend and next weekend, I'll be at the farmer's market on Saturdays."

"Oh, that's interesting that you're starting at the market," Catie said. "Smart, too."

"It's what I know, and there's a built-in audience there. I don't know what to expect for foot traffic here."

"Well, we'll be here on opening day." Olivia pointed to the box. "Can I take a few of those to distribute around?"

CHAPTER ELEVEN

ADAM HAD a shift the night before Isla's second weekend at the farmer's market, but he managed a decent amount of sleep overnight. They hadn't had a single call between ten last night and six this morning, so he racked out and got plenty of unexpected rest. He'd missed her first day at the market, but he wasn't going to miss today, so once they were finished handing over to the next crew on Saturday morning, he drove over to the market instead of heading home.

He saw her as soon as he headed down the main aisle. She was alone, standing ram-rod straight behind her table. He smiled at the sight of her blue apron, and then grinned even more broadly when a family stopped at her table before he did.

She caught sight of him as she sold them an assortment of treats.

Would he ever tire of the way her face lit up? Probably not.

"I wasn't expecting to see you," she breathed when they were alone. "How was your shift?"

"Quiet." He made a face, surprising himself. In his pocket, his phone vibrated, but he ignored it. It wasn't going to be work.

"Isn't that good?"

"Yeah. No, it was a decent shift. Still getting used to the new team, that's all." His phone vibrated again, and again, so he excused himself and pulled it out of his pocket, only to laugh at the long string of messages he'd apparently just missed from his brothers.

Seth: Remember when we used to all do Saturday breakfast at Mac's?

Will: Nope, because you refuse to move home.

Seth: Oh right. We could start a new tradition. I just landed at the marina.

Josh: Dude, some of us have lives.

Seth: You're on a lounge chair in front of the garage. I can see you. Do you even work?

Josh: It's eight in the morning. I'm enjoying my coffee.

Seth: Enjoy another one at the diner, let's go.

Owen: Kerry is sleeping in, but I can meet people at the diner. Seth, are you going to get a ride with lazybones, or should I come down and pick you up.

Josh: I'll drive him.

Will: Adam, are you reading these messages, or have you put us on mute because you're sleeping, too?

He turned the phone around and showed it to Isla. "So apparently Seth flew down this morning. My brothers are all meeting at the diner for breakfast. I'll head over there now."

"Have fun! I'll be quiet when I get home, in case you're sleeping."

"I'll probably try to stay up all day and hit the hay early tonight." He took a few steps towards the entrance as a woman paused to look at the cookies. "Those are delicious, by the way," he said loudly.

The customer glanced at him and he winked at her. She blushed and told Isla she would take a half dozen. Isla bit back a laugh and waved goodbye to Adam.

At the diner, he parked next to Josh's car and headed inside. His brothers had commandeered the corner booth, which normally sat six people. The four of them took up all the space, and Adam had to grab a chair to sit at the end.

"You made it," Seth said, grabbing him in a bear hug before he could sit.

"I was at the farmer's market when you arrived." Adam nudged Josh. "It was hopping."

Owen laughed. "We'll be heading there later. Does Isla have a table there today?"

"She sure does."

As Josh muttered under his breath, Seth handed Adam a menu. "How's the job treating you?"

He didn't want to admit it was whooping his ass.

"And how's married life?"

Fuck, he didn't want to answer that question, either. As long as it was just the two of them, Adam didn't spend a lot of time thinking about how fucked up his brothers would think he was if they ever found out he couldn't bring himself to fall in love, that he'd found an alternative of a sort. So he made a non-committal shrug and smiled. It was great, but not in a way they'd understand.

"How's your new bride adjusting to life in Pine Harbour?"

Now there was a topic he could sink into. "Isla's a force of nature. She's going to have the cafe ready to be re-opened as her dream bakery in a few weeks. She already has an opening day picked out." He went into great detail on the process, and the updated alarm system he'd installed himself, until Seth's eyes glazed over. "How about you? What sparked the unexpected trip home?"

"Had a charter cancel at the last minute and thought I'd spend the day with my favourite people."

Just a day, though. That was almost always the limit with Seth. He might come down for two or three around a holiday, if they were lucky. Like he kept one foot away at all times.

When breakfast ended, he went home and had a power nap, then met Isla at the bakery as she unloaded and cleaned up from the market.

"I thought I'd just check in, see what else needed to be done around here. Are you almost ready for opening day?"

"Nope." She gave him a wide-eyed, terrified look. Then she laughed. "Yes?"

He had no doubt. "Yes."

"Maybe." She ran through her to-do list, then locked up the front, turned out the lights, and followed him out the back door.

Back at the house, he had some training material to read through, which ended up taking more of the after-noon than he expected. While he studied, Isla worked on her computer, both of them quiet and productive in the living room.

When she stretched and talked about dinner, Adam was startled to realize it was already that time of night.

"Do you want to keep working?" She pointed to the kitchen. "I can make something and bring plates in here."

He got up. "Let's eat in here, but I'll take a break and help you cook."

"Sandwiches?" Isla poked around in the fridge. "Or there's some chilli we could re-heat."

"Do you mind sandwiches? Easy to eat while I study."

"Not at all." She pulled out the fixings, and they worked side by side to make a couple of different kinds.

Then they went back to their work, food at hand.

When he finally finished his reading, he collected their plates and washed them up. She'd put her computer away and curled up under a blanket when he returned.

"I'm done for the day."

"Me too." He knew he should go up to bed. Instead, he sat down on the couch near her feet.

"Hey, you didn't say how breakfast went with your brothers."

He made a face. "They asked me how married life is going."

She laughed gently. "And what did you say?"

He repeated the shrug and smile he'd given Seth instead of answering. "Just that. I didn't elaborate. Let them draw their own conclusions."

"Works for me." She sighed and leaned back on the couch. "It honestly didn't occur to me that they would be curious. Nobody ever asked me about my first marriage." She made a face. "Maybe that was a sign everyone thought it wasn't good. And they weren't wrong. But even growing up, my parents never talked about other families. I'm a pretty closed person in that regard. You can always say something like that if it comes up again. 'Isla's private.' It would be true."

He gave her a tired smile. "I don't need to push it off on you. *I'm* private, too. It's none of their business. It's just an adjustment, because I used to go clubbing with them, we'd be each other's wingmen. But I was always playing a game there. They just don't know that."

She frowned. "I'm sorry. That must be lonely."

He exhaled roughly. "It is what it is. We all came out of the loss of our mom with baggage. Josh rebelled, Owen and Will mainlined responsibility like it was cocaine, Seth…" He trailed off. "I dunno. Maybe Seth is a combination of them all. He was career driven but also wanted to get out of town. And then there was me."

"You were how old?"

"Twelve." Just saying it seared something in his chest, sharp and ugly. He shook it off. "I'm tired, I should hit the hay."

"Yeah." She stood up and folded her blanket, neatly putting it back in her basket. "I'm sorry I brought it up."

He stood too. "No, it's fine. It's just hard to talk about."

"I understand." She moved closer, and Adam thought for a moment that she might hug him.

He wanted her to, and he didn't at the same time.

She gave him a soft smile, grabbed his arm, and turned him, pointing him to the stairs. "To bed, mister. Off you go."

———

After two more successful Saturdays at the market, where Isla handed out all of her flyers and collected a whole jar full of "Favourite Bake Sale Item Suggestions!", she was ready for opening day.

She had no idea how many people to expect. When she walked over to the bakery with Adam, who insisted on coming along for moral support, it was still dark, still quiet. She braced herself for absolutely nobody showing up. Not intentionally. Eventually *some* people would come in from street foot traffic. If she sold a dozen cookies over the course of the day, she would be happy.

Anything more than that would be a bonus.

So by that metric, the day was a success as soon as the doors opened at seven in the morning, because there were three people waiting, and one of them bought a dozen cookies in the first minute. As she boxed them up, she asked how they heard about her shop and was thrilled to hear they'd picked up a flyer at the library.

All in all, she had ten customers in that first hour, ten people who had made it a point in their day to wake up early and come to *Bake Sale!* as soon as it opened. And they were ten people she hadn't met before.

It was a small victory, but a monumental one.

Over the course of the morning, the same questions kept coming up. People asked her about how often she would be open. How often her menu changed, and more than one person asked her if she sold coffee. That's all coming soon, she told them, her cheeks hurting from grinning so much.

When Catie and Olivia arrived mid-morning, she gave them an excited wave, happy to see somewhat familiar faces. They hung back until there was a gap in traffic.

"It looks like it's going well," Olivia said, perusing the

glass case. "I was going to say I'd take a dozen cookies, but it looks like you're running low."

"I have more in the back. I can get you a fresh dozen." She grabbed a cardboard box and collected those from the back, along with a new tray for the display. "Hey, I should thank you. Which one of you put the flyers at the library?"

Catie glanced at Olivia, who shrugged. "Wasn't me."

"Not me." Catie's eyes lit up. "Wait, do you know where the library is?"

Isla shook her head. "I've been so head down focused on getting the store ready, I haven't explored the town at all."

The realtor practically swooned. "It must have been Adam. You got a good one there, girl. The library is upstairs from the fire station, on the top floor of the emergency services building."

"Oh!" Heat rushed to Isla's face. "That's lovely. He didn't say anything."

"How's the morning going?"

"Really well. I still have so much work ahead of me, though. I didn't anticipate how many people would want coffee and tea with their treats. It makes sense because this used to be a cafe. Even if I only offer to-go service, I really need to find a commercial espresso machine."

Catie glanced at Olivia. "Did Frank ever sell the one in the back room?"

"I don't think so. It was there the last time I popped in to say hi." Olivia already had her phone out. "Let's go over there after you close up. Could we do a late lunch? He'll want to meet you, Isla."

"He?"

"Frank." Catie pointed in the general direction of the highway. "He owns the diner on the edge of town, Mac's.

We both worked there in the past, and it's the only place in town to get a cup of coffee right now—don't worry, he never minded the competition from Anne, and he'll love you. Well, in his own gruff, barking way."

Isla generally didn't care for gruff barking. "Uh…"

Olivia stopped typing on her phone. "Too much?"

"Little bit." Isla took a deep breath. "Thanks for the tip. One thing at a time, though. And I like his breakfast sandwiches. Adam gets them for me sometimes."

Catie sighed. "Seriously jealous of that newlywed bliss."

Isla didn't know what to say to that. Maybe the secret to a happy marriage was to fake it with a friend?

The door opened, and she didn't need to reply because she had yet another customer, a younger South Asian woman, and right behind her was Kerry.

Both of them greeted Catie and Olivia warmly, then Kerry gestured for the younger woman to order first. "Isla, this is Bailey Patel. We play soccer together."

"Nice to meet you, Bailey. What can I get you today?"

"One of everything," the other woman joked. "Actually, just one of every other thing. I'll take a six-pack of assorted treats, please." As Isla packaged that up, Bailey picked up one of the cards on the counter, then pulled out her phone. "Oh, your Instagram is so pretty!"

"Thanks. I'm working on it. It's hard to get people to follow the account, though. I'm quickly learning that word of mouth is more important than online marketing up here."

"Are you from the city?"

"Sort of. I've moved all over. But I love it here." She handed over the box of goodies and rang up the total. Then she glanced at Kerry. "And for you?"

"I'll take the baker's dozen. Owen wants to take some to work tonight."

Isla was touched by the support.

And by the time she closed up at noon, she was run off her feet. She had sold out almost everything. The bake sale model worked in a storefront just as well as it worked at a stall.

After flipping the lock, she went back into the kitchen and jumped as high as she could so she could click her heels together.

It worked.

She was exhausted. She had to do it again the next day. But it had actually worked. And she had Adam to thank in part for that, with his secret flyer distribution to the library. Who knew that was the real hub of the town?

———

Scaling up, as she had promised her customers she would, proved harder than Isla thought it would be.

Once she opened, just staying open was a full-time job. She was the only baker and the front of house employee, too. She was months away from being able to hire someone, but that was on her radar. Until then, she needed to be careful not to bite off more than she could chew.

She got to work at five in the morning most days, which she loved. She savoured the quiet order of unfolding the bakery and getting the first batches of cookies and cupcakes in the oven, before she flipped the open sign.

It was the end of her day, after the bakery closed at noon, that she found wearying. She would do her books, check stock, place orders, and play the guessing game about what might sell the following week.

One Wednesday afternoon in mid-November was extra frustrating, so she went home and had a nap, then returned to the bakery in the evening to get her work done. There was so much math involved, and Isla's eyes were crossing. She scrubbed the heel of her hand against her twitching right eyeball, and tried to sort out her ordering plans again. If she thought she could sell ten dozen—

"Knock knock, am I interrupting?" Adam's voice called out from the front of the house. She must have forgotten to lock the front door.

"I'm back here," she hollered.

He appeared in the kitchen doorway like an absolute angel, holding a Thermos in his hand.

"Is that coffee?" She jumped up, her pen skittering across the steel counter.

"Soup."

"That sounds like a good, nutritious choice," she muttered through a small smile.

He frowned, his eyebrows tugging together. "What's wrong?"

"Nothing." She stood and grabbed the second stool from under the other counter. "Here, sit. Thank you for bringing me some food."

He'd been asleep when she went home. They were like two ships passing in the night with their competing schedules.

"I can't stay, I'm leading the training for the volunteer fire brigade tonight. But I don't work again until Monday, so I'm your personal chef for the next four days."

She twisted the lid off the thermos and immediately

leaned in. It was chicken soup, savoury and rich, and it had a beautiful colour.

"I added some ginger and turmeric."

"I'm impressed," she murmured. "You're hired."

He snagged a spoon for her from the canister by the sink, and she dug in. It was absolutely delicious, and she told him so.

"Are you going to be here late?" He looked concerned.

She shook her head. "No, I can finish this tomorrow. I just don't like to get behind. You know, in the army, I always had a second-in-command to help me keep track of everything."

"Do you feel like this is hard to keep up with? You're so organized."

"On the surface. Deep down, I feel like pure chaos."

"Can I help?"

He didn't assume. Didn't try to take over. Just asked straight up.

She took a deep breath. "Maybe? You have to get going, though."

"How about I come in tomorrow after you close up? Sometimes it's just nice to talk everything through with another human. Even if my primary expertise here is eating the cookies."

That made her laugh. "Hey, do you want to take some to the training tonight? I have some…" She got up and looked at her day old rack for tomorrow. "Caramel pecan? Those didn't sell as well as I thought they would."

"Our volunteers will devour them." He took the box from her, and then casually picked up some of her business cards from the box by the back door.

"Hey," she said just before he opened the door.

"Thanks. For everything. You've been the best support through all of this."

He gave her a mock salute. "Just doing my duty."

But it wasn't *just* anything. And the next day he was back in the kitchen, with more soup, fortifying her in more ways than one.

She wasn't as cranky as she'd been the day before, the numbers didn't swim quite as much before her eyes, so when he sat across from her and said, "Run me through everything", she took a deep breath and did exactly that.

It wasn't just the ordering math, it was keeping track of dates in weeks to come, because as the holidays approached, her suppliers' calendars would shift, and if she didn't stay on top of what she needed, she could run short.

As she talked, he set calendar reminders in his phone, and they buzzed on hers as well.

By the time she finished her soup, they had a calendar gridded out until February, and Adam looked justifiably proud of himself. "I'm good at keeping track of moving parts. You be the genius baker I know you are. I'll keep an eye on the boring admin stuff."

"I like the admin," she protested.

"I know. And I like making that admin a little easier for you. I helped in the office at the moving company sometimes."

"Thank you." She sighed. "I needed help and I didn't know how to ask."

He wrapped his arm around her. "Or you didn't know who to ask."

"Maybe that, too."

He brushed his lips against her temple. It was friendly

and kind, and he'd done the same gesture more than a few times over the last few weeks.

Maybe it was the lack of sleep. Or the profound appreciation she felt toward him. Or maybe the stars were in the right-wrong position, but the brief contact of his mouth on her skin felt different today.

It felt *right* in a deeply disturbing way. Way too right. Definitely also very wrong.

That talented, kind, good mouth. On her bare, sensitive skin.

She twisted away and busied herself in tidying up the papers. "I think we've got it all sorted now," she said brightly.

She wasn't allowed to have feelings for her husband. That wouldn't do at all.

———

Adam liked having a woman as a roommate. His house smelled instantly better, for one thing. There were more vegetables in the fridge. And every so often, Isla laughed in a full-throated way that filled him with a curious lightness. Having grown up in a house full of boys, all moody and struggling at the best of the times, it was a startling change of pace.

And privately, at home, Isla was nothing like the tough Captain Petersen who had befriended him years earlier. She had more make-up and home spa things than he ever thought possible, for one. And she loved curling up on the couch and watching television with big reactions. Horror movies terrified her, but she kept watching them with only one eye open. Reality shows made her mad enough she would yell at the screen—but not turn them off, no matter what.

It was all just a lot of fun. When he wasn't working, he found himself joining her on the couch, each of them under their own blanket. He knew that when he was at the station overnight, Isla often worked late, revising her business plans over and over again, planning ahead to the next summer. She wanted to be ready for the tourists with a social media campaign—and the perfect lineup of treats to maximize on that visibility.

She told him all about it, often while they made dinner together.

One of his favourite things about living with Isla was the way she gravitated to working with him on something. When he lived with his brothers or Stevie, they'd always taken turns cooking. It was a chore none of them minded, but a chore nonetheless.

But Isla loved being in the kitchen, made it joyous, and that was infectious.

And she made dishes he would never have considered himself—like a vegetable tart.

"I thought it would be good with a salad. Is that okay? Do you want me to cook up some chicken breasts?" He made a face, and she laughed. "Okay, no chicken."

"Josh is going through a weight-lifting phase—nothing wrong with that—but it was nothing but plain chicken breasts over at Will's place. I'm chickened out for a while. A veggie tart sounds great."

"I never got into the chicken and spinach routine," Isla said as she dug out the peppers and asparagus. "And giving up bread has never been an option for me. But my intense weight training days are behind me, anyway."

"You lifted?"

"Doesn't everyone in the army? We all go through the Crossfit phase, the heavy lifting phase, the running phase."

"Guilty on all three counts."

"It's utterly fascinating when you're in the midst of it, and horribly boring when someone else is doing it." She tossed him a package of goat's cheese. "Do you want to chop veggies or make the dough?"

She liked to give him the choice, even though they both knew he would chop. It was an in-joke that had developed, that he was intent on getting his knife skills down pat, something she didn't even care about.

"Show me again how you do the onion."

She rolled her eyes. "You can do it however you want."

But he wanted to do it right. He knew his way around a kitchen, and he wanted to improve.

She quickly peeled the outer skin off the onion, then made slices in it, from one end almost to the other. "Hold here," she instructed. "When you curl your fingers, create a lot of tension. That will pin the onion down. Give it a go. Quarter turn, then slice again, and you'll get diced onion, or minced, depending on how close together your slices are."

He chopped into it, and she leaned closer, her voice soft. "Keep it consistent. Good. You're a natural. Stop asking me for guidance when you know exactly what you're doing."

"Maybe I do it just so you'll praise me."

She laughed, and he'd been joking, but maybe there was something to it.

He'd had more compliments in a few weeks of living with Isla than he'd ever had in decades of living with his brothers.

She pulled a bowl from the fridge and lifted out a ball of dough. Just as she started kneading it, her phone vibrated on the counter next to Adam.

He did a double take at the name on the screen. "Are you expecting a call from someone named Jackass?"

She whipped around, "What?"

He held up the screen.

"No." She sighed. "Ignore it. That's, uh…my ex."

"Ah."

"I haven't heard from him in almost a year." She turned and returned to her kneading with extra vigour.

Adam wouldn't want to be that dough right now.

Smack. Whack.

"You don't need to call him back."

"I'm not going to."

"Do you want to talk about it?"

"No." The answer was swift. But it was followed by another sigh. "I dunno. Sorry."

He squeezed her shoulder. "Don't be sorry. It's fine." He paused a beat. "If we ever break up, can I request a nickname?"

She snorted. "Like what?"

Laughing was better than sighing. He put an extra flirty spin on his first suggestion. "The One Who Got Away?"

"That's a little long," she said, playing along.

"How about, The Best I Ever Had?"

"Five-word compliments are not nicknames. Also, we want it to appear on the screen so my third husband can ask me who it is, right?"

She was joking, and he had started it, but that landed differently. A little too close to his feelings, when yes, that is exactly what could happen at some point. Their relationship had started out as transactional, sure, fake or pretend, although he didn't like either of those words to describe a very real friendship. But he'd gotten used to her being in his life and sharing a home together. Building a life together. The thought of her *not* being his wife one day was unfathomable. And yet he had no right to get tangled up in those feelings, he knew that. Evidence A for that fact was that Isla had no idea how her joke felt in his chest.

Now she rolled her eyes. "Come on, Adam. You know it'll be something sweet. Like, I'd put you in there as The Rock."

He pushed away his swirling thoughts and smirked at the sweetly funny name. He had to keep it light. "Let the next guy think you have a secret past with Dwayne Johnson."

She winked. "You are my rock, though."

Now he was grinning for real. "That's really nice."

"I'm really nice." She nodded her head towards his bowl of chopped veggies. "Bring that over here. And put my phone on silent so we aren't interrupted again."

CHAPTER TWELVE

THE BAKERY WAS CLOSED on Mondays, the one day of the week that Isla got to sleep in, and she loved waking up leisurely. She checked her messages as she lay in bed. Her Instagram account was up to a hundred followers.

A skittering at the window caught her attention, and she turned her head just in time to see a mouse duck out of view on the other side of the pane of glass.

She climbed out of bed and caught sight of Adam in the driveway. It was cold out now, but he wasn't wearing a coat. He had a heavy sweater on, and work gloves and a wool toque on his head. He was unloading drywall from the back of his truck.

She drew the blinds closed and quickly got dressed in equally warm clothes. When she emerged from her bedroom, two sheets of drywall were stacked in the hallway, and the door was open for Adam to carry in the last sheet.

"What's all this?" she asked when she stepped outside.

He turned and waved. "I didn't wake you up, did I?"

"Nope." She crossed the lawn. "I think we have a mouse, by the way. He tried to get in my window."

"This place is a shithole. We probably have more than just mice."

"Hey," she protested. "I love this house."

"And I love that you love it." He flipped the bird at the second storey. "But I'm not feeling that charitable towards it at the moment. My shower this morning was the final straw for the wall in the upstairs bathroom. It crumbled on me."

"Oh, no!" She looked at the drywall. "Another emergency repair?"

"Yeah. And I bought new tile because it was on clearance. I guess I'm spending my days off this week doing an impromptu renovation."

"We can share the downstairs bathroom," she offered. "And I can help with the repair."

"It's your day off, I've got it."

"Will it go faster with a second pair of hands?" She propped her hands on her hips. "You helped me at work. Let me at least carry stuff."

He stopped and gave her a slow, appraising look. "I can't argue with that, I guess. Grab that box of tile."

She followed him all the way upstairs, and after setting the tile down on the landing, she peaked into the bathroom.

The tile wall behind the tub had a gaping hole in it, and grout and shattered ceramic chunks littered the floor. "Oh, damn."

He leaned against the doorframe and crossed his arms over his chest. A crowbar in his hands made him look fearsome, very capable of bringing the bathroom to heel. "I'm going to start demolition. There's another pair of work gloves in my truck. Can you grab those, and bring up the plastic garbage can from the back?"

She nodded and slid past him. "RIP, old bathroom."

His laughter echoed around her as she dashed down the stairs, and then she heard a shattering crunch just before she hit the porch. He wasn't fooling around.

His truck was unlocked, and she hopped up into the driver's side. She saw the gloves on the dashboard, and when she reached for them, she noticed a couple of her flyers sitting on the passenger side, neatly paper clipped together with a note. *Drop off at the long-term care centre.*

She sat down and picked them up, her fingers tracing his neat handwriting.

He was helping her in more ways than she knew. Why wasn't he telling her about where he was leaving the flyers? Had she given him the impression she didn't want help?

Maybe there was a part of her that had really wanted to do it all herself, but that was human nature. Same as Adam's first instinct to waive her offer with the bathroom.

She put the flyers down, grabbed the gloves again, and got out of his truck.

But those thoughts kept swirling through her head as they knocked down the walls, as Josh arrived with a trailer for Adam to put the construction rubble in, as they demolished and swept and vacuumed.

By the end of the day, they had the bathroom back to studs and ready to be re-built.

"We make a good team," Adam said as he brushed dust out of his hair outside after dumping the final bin of rubble into the trailer. His breath puffed in front of him.

"You did most of the hard work. You get the first hot shower." She beamed at him. "And I'll put the kettle on.

Do you want tea? Hot chocolate? I've been practicing making these hot chocolate bombs that melt in the cup."

"Yep, that. Sold. But you can have the first shower if you want."

She pushed him back into the house. "Go. I'll get one later before bed."

He kicked off his boots, then headed down the hall into her bedroom. The shower hissed to life, then the bathroom door clicked closed.

She heated up some leftovers for dinner at the same time as she made the hot chocolate, and when she heard Adam reappear in the hallway, she turned to tell him that she had food on as well. She caught the curve of his bare back, broad and muscled, naked down to a low-slung towel wrapped around his hips. He disappeared into the shadows at the front of the house, and an unexpected memory slid to the front of her mind. Adam, sprawled naked in an overpriced hotel room, a sheet barely covering what that towel covered now. How beautiful he had been as she watched him sleep, how young and sweet he looked that morning. She hadn't known then that he would become her best friend. She'd only known he'd been very good for a lonely part of her soul, and she couldn't want too much of that goodness.

Now she turned back to the stove.

It wasn't news to her that her husband was hot. It was just unexpected that she noticed in a blushing, strange kind of way.

———

Her alarm was so freaking annoying. She smacked her phone twice before she found the snooze button.

After the sleep-in the day before, and a thought-disrupted night of tossing and turning, Isla had to drag herself out of bed and into the bathroom. She blinked blearily at her reflection, then washed up. She braided her hair, then pinned up all the loose strands. Quickly and efficiently she transformed herself from a grumpy sleepyhead to a professional-looking baker.

It had snowed overnight, and she pulled on her winter coat and heavy boots for the short walk. Even as the weather turned, she still loved this part of her day.

At the bakery, she traded her coat and boots for the chef's jacket and clogs she kept there.

Chocolate chip cookies in first. They were the fastest, and she needed more of them than anything else. Then cupcakes.

Fifteen minutes before she needed to open up, she took a quick break to eat a bit of breakfast herself, then washed her hands and headed out front to flip the sign.

Weekdays weren't nearly as busy as weekends. There was a pattern to the day. Steady drop-ins for the first two hours, almost always wanting a dozen of something to take to a workplace. And then it was quiet for the next three hours. She would get better traffic here if she served coffee, she knew that, and she thought back to the point Adam had made about knowing who to ask for help.

Her own confession that she didn't like to ask for help grated. She didn't find any pride in that, so she packed up a to-go tray featuring her newest treat addition, marshmallow dream squares.

She put up a *back in fifteen minutes* sign, locked up, and marched across the street. Catie was alone in the salon, working on her computer in her real estate corner.

"Hey neighbour," Isla said, holding the treats up. "I come bearing gifts for a favour."

Catie's face lit up. "I just made a pot of tea, can I interest you in a cup?"

The tension Isla had been carrying between her shoulder blades eased, and she sat down across from the other woman. "That would be great. So, uh, you mentioned something when you brought Olivia in the first time. You thought the owner of the diner might have an espresso machine he's not using?"

"Oh yeah, almost certainly. Frank never throws anything out."

"And he doesn't want to use it?"

"Frank hates latte culture. He thinks it's a waste of time for his employees to make fancy coffee when a drip machine makes a whole pot at the press of a button."

"But people want fancy coffee," Isla protested.

Catie shrugged. "And he'll be happy to send them your way if you want to serve it. Do you want me to introduce you? We could go there for lunch later."

"I would be eternally grateful." Isla took the cup of tea the other woman handed over. "Thank you."

"Milk or sugar?"

"Neither, I'm good with it like this." She nudged the box across the desk. "A token of appreciation."

Catie opened the box and snatched out a marshmallow square. "You can bribe me for introductions to anyone in this town any day of the week."

Isla didn't know what to expect of Frank, who she had yet to meet. She was prepared for the request to be met with reluctance, or for his price to be too high, but what she wasn't going to do was leave the question unasked.

She returned to the salon later, after closing the bakery

for the day. Catie was finishing up with a hair client, so Isla sat in one of the waiting area chairs and picked up a magazine. It had been weeks since she'd last done her hair in anything other than braids and ponytails.

Maybe she'd get Catie to give her a blow out one of these days and surprise... Isla frowned at herself and pushed that thought away. She didn't need to worry about her hair, or looking good for anyone.

She put the magazine down and picked up a newspaper instead.

"How do you feel about walking?" Catie asked when she was finished with her client. "It's not that far, and it's nice to stretch the legs. Even when I get tired from standing all day, it's different to walk."

"Sure. I haven't been doing any regular exercise since I moved here." They stepped outside and Catie locked up. Isla pointed across the street, where her hand painted sign cheerily decorated her front window. "I've been so focused on the bakery, everything else has fallen to the wayside. But if you want company on walks or anything else, let me know."

"You used to be in the army, right?"

"Yep. For almost fifteen years."

"Did you ever do any search and rescue activity?"

"Some. Sure, why?"

"I've been thinking about volunteering for the local search and rescue team, but I'm intimidated by their physical requirements entrance test. Do you know Tom Minelli?"

"Is he related to Olivia?"

"Her brother-in-law, yeah. He's a park ranger, and he runs the team. He put out a call for women to join, specifically because they want to enter a provincial contest but their teams need to be mixed-gender. Would you be interested?"

Dark, wet rain slashed through Isla's mind. She shivered. "I don't know. I'm not really the competitive type anymore. Not like that. Now I just compete against myself."

"Oh, sorry."

"No, it's fine. But if you have the requirements to join the team, I'd be happy to train with you."

"That would be amazing. It's stuff like rope climbing and chin-ups."

"I can do that. Maybe not as fast or as easily as I used to, but it sounds like fun." An excited, bubbly energy built inside Isla. "Are you thinking of starting this soon? Do you want to book something?"

"Could we maybe have a standing date? I'm closed on Monday, and you are, too, right? Or is that your time off with Adam?"

"He won't mind," she said with a smile. "Although this coming Monday I might need to help him with the bathroom if he's not done by then." She spent the rest of the walk to Mac's telling Catie about the necessary renovations. "But it's all for the best. This way he'll—"

She cut herself off. She'd been about to say, *he'll have as nice a bathroom as I have*, but that wasn't a statement she could make out loud.

Luckily, they were at the restaurant. "Oh, we're here."

Inside, Catie waved at the waitress behind the counter and the cook visible through the pass-through window. They both waved back.

"When did you work here?"

"Twelve years ago," Catie said breezily. "Before I moved away for school."

"And then you came back?"

"I did."

"And became a real estate agent and a hair stylist."

"Well, the hair thing came first. The real estate gig…I'm still sort of searching for my true passion in life. Should we eat first? I can ask Frank to join us when he has some time."

Isla took a seat at a booth while Catie disappeared briefly into the kitchen, then returned with two menus. "Is this place usually this self-service?"

Her new friend smiled. "No. You haven't been in here yet?"

She shook her head. "Adam's gotten takeout a few times. We're both pretty busy with work. And the house."

"Everyone loves the burgers, but personally, I'm a big fan of the loaded grilled cheese and tomato soup combo."

"Yep, I want that now." Isla's stomach growled in agreement.

It didn't take long for their lunch to arrive, and the cook himself came out to clear their empty plates when they finished.

"Frank, this is Isla Petersen."

"The new owner of Anne's cafe."

"That's right, sir, nice to meet you." She stood up to shake his hand.

"Catie says you're interested in that espresso machine that does me no good."

"I am. Yep."

"What's your offer?"

She wasn't going to name a price first. "What do you want for it?"

"Pie."

"I'm sorry?"

"Right now, I buy pies from a couple of different places, but the quality is variable. People really like pecan. Can you manage that?"

"I sure can." She wondered how the people of Pine Harbour would feel about a bit of bourbon in their pecan pie. Cranberries for the holidays. Or maybe no cranberries until she'd paid off her pie debt. "A fair exchange of pie for machinery?"

"Three kinds of pie, twice a week. Apple, pecan, and a seasonal one of your choice."

"Deal."

————

When Adam texted Isla and asked if she was going to be home for dinner, and he didn't get a response right away —and then when she did, it was the digital equivalent of muttering about a problem—he knew he needed to take food to her.

Isla managed problems just fine as long as she was well fed. He'd figured that out quickly, and made it a private mission to ensure there was a regular supply of easy to grab and consume soups and sandwiches in the house— and at the bakery, as needed.

For a woman who spent all day making food for others, she wasn't always great at remembering to fuel herself.

Enter, the husband delivery service. He made a couple of sandwiches and a double Thermos of coffee and headed to the bakery, where he found the lights on and the front door open.

Inside he saw Isla's chef's jacket slung over one of the

two small tables she had for customers, and audible swearing was coming from the other side of the counter.

He set down his packed picnic dinner and peered around the side.

"What are you doing?" he asked her legs, which was all he could see.

"Installing my new espresso machine."

He glanced back up, and sure enough, there was a big, shiny machine at the far end of the counter.

"It requires attaching a water line. Which meant drilling some holes and running some pipe."

"So what you're saying is, I could have had you do the plumbing at home?" He chuckled as she swore again.

"I thought it would be simple! You made it look simple, and apparently...I should have called you, yes. That is the takeaway lesson here." She shimmied out from under the counter and stood up. Her braid was coming undone and blond wisps of hair framed her face. They made her scowl almost angelic. "The two pieces of pipe should fit together tightly. They don't. What am I doing wrong?"

He came around to have a look. "You need some plumbing tape. It'll make that seal watertight. We have some at home, I'll go get it. In the meantime, I brought you food."

"Oh." The scowl dropped away and a tired smile replaced it. She lifted one bare arm to swipe a strand of hair off her forehead, which made her breasts jiggle, which in turn made him realize she was only wearing a thin tank top.

Eyes up, Kincaid.

"That's really sweet, thank you."

He was feeling anything but sweet at the moment.

"Can we make a deal? You sit and eat, I'll go and get more supplies."

"Or we can eat and walk? I'll come with you. I could use some fresh air and a break from this place."

She swapped her clogs for boots and pulled her parka on, then locked up.

As they walked home, she asked him about his day—his plumbing forays had gone better than hers, but he downplayed that fact—and devoured both of the sandwiches he'd made. That made him happy.

At home, he grabbed everything he thought they might need, and then they drove back in his truck.

"Apparently Catie's going to sign up for the search and rescue team," Isla said as she unlocked the bakery and turned the lights back on. "She wants my help to train for the physical entrance exam."

"That sounds like fun. Did you know that Will is on the search and rescue team?"

"Nope. But it doesn't surprise me. It's the Kincaid way." She frowned in the direction of the espresso machine. "All right, you beast. Let's get you tamed."

"Where did you get this thing?"

"I got it from Frank, who has had it for at least fifteen years. He won it in some restauranteur event. So it's old, but it's never been used, and it's a good brand."

"And how did you get it here?" Adam really wanted to ask why she hadn't asked him for help. Wasn't it his job to be the big, strong husband?

But apparently that wasn't necessary in Pine Harbour. Isla shrugged. "Frank asked some of his customers to bring it over. And he had a bunch of volunteers."

"Were you there?"

"Yep. Catie and I were having lunch."

He could just imagine Frank asking for volunteers to help carry something for two beautiful women. Adam swallowed back against a wave of misplaced jealousy.

She shrugged out of her coat, then bumped her shoulder against his. "I would have called you, but I knew you were working on the bathroom."

That mollified him a bit. What he liked even more was that she could see he wanted to help. Well, he could still help now. He took off his coat as well, then opened up his toolbox and found the thread sealing tape for the joint, and a couple of different connectors for flexible water lines.

"Is the water turned off?" he asked Isla as they crawled under the counter together.

"Yep."

He looked at the connection she had been working on first, and wrapped the tape around one end before re-threading them together. Then he moved on to the hose, which looked good. It was time to test. "Okay. Where's the main water supply for the bakery?"

"In the back. Next to the alarm."

"Hold tight." He crawled out and jogged to the back. All the plumbing in this place was old and backwards. He turned the knob, then went back to the sink. Nothing came out.

"It's not dripping down there, is it?"

"Nope."

He tried the espresso machine, but it wasn't drawing any water either. "Hang on."

He went back into the kitchen and turned the water supply knob the other way again. Maybe she hadn't actually turned it off. But just as he reached for the sink tap, Isla said, "Oh, wait—"

And he should have waited, but it landed in his brain a

second too late, because she squeaked out a horrified gasp as he let the water run. He hit the tap off fast, but that wasn't the problem.

Water sprayed in all directions from below the counter as Isla's body twisted and thrashed, and then—with more cursing—it stopped, and she dragged herself out from beneath the counter.

"I turned it off here. The water. I turned it off here, and I should have realized why you were going to the main supply," she gasped as she stood up.

The gloriously angelic strands of her hair were now plastered to her face, and fat wet drops of water dripped off her chin and landed on a very see-through tank top. She was laughing as she wrapped her arms around her body, laughing and shivering at the same time, and Adam was an absolute pervert for taking a split-second lusty look before he whipped off his sweater and handed it over. "Here, put this on."

He growled it out, a demand as much as an offer, but she didn't seem to notice.

She needed him to figure out where that line wasn't tight. He couldn't lose himself in how fucking touchable she was in that moment.

"I knew it seemed too easy," she said as her head popped out the top of his sweater.

Even wrapped in heavy cable knit, she looked irresistible, and like a punch in the face he didn't see coming, Adam suddenly couldn't turn off the arousal he felt for his wife.

He thought he'd be able to control it. He *could* control it. But it would take a hell of a lot more effort than he thought it would a month ago.

Well, too late now. He'd convinced her to legally tie

herself to this bakery for five years. He'd promised her it was no big deal that they had slept together.

It *hadn't* been a big deal.

Past tense.

Now?

Now it was a big fucking deal, and he was in big fucking trouble.

CHAPTER THIRTEEN

"DID DAD EVER HAVE A MUSCLE CAR?"

Owen frowned in concentration, thinking about Adam's question. "Not that I remember. Will?"

Their brother lifted his head from under the hood of his beater. "Nope."

"He didn't own one, but he always read car magazines," Josh said, crossing the bar of his garage with a tray of coffees from Isla's shop. "Your wife asked why you sent me, by the way. She misses you."

Adam felt his face heat up. Isla wouldn't have meant it like that, but she'd accidentally sent him an indirect message: she'd noticed that he'd been dodging her. Crap.

He didn't feel great about the distance, either. No, he downright missed her. But when Will had put out the bat call that he wanted to work on his car this weekend, and Adam happened to be off, he jumped at the reasonable excuse to get out of the house. His bathroom renovation was done, and he needed something, anything, to do with his hands that wasn't touching his off-limits wife.

"I'll see her in a couple of hours," he muttered.

Owen took a coffee, and a marshmallow dream bar, too. "How's she liking the new bathroom? Spending a lot of time having bubble baths now that it's all nice in there?"

Jesus, his brothers were killing him in a hundred different ways. Now he was picturing Isla partially covered by pillowy white clouds of— "She's more of a shower person."

Because that was her bathroom and his was the one with the soaker tub. Their two wings of the house, and apparently she had noticed he'd started retreating to his corner a little too often.

It wasn't fair. That wasn't their deal, and he would stop it immediately. The grown-up thing to do would be to lock it down. He waved off the coffee from Josh. "You know what? I'm going up there right now. Will's going to be tinkering for a bit. I'll see you guys later."

At the bakery, he waited his turn in line, watching Isla do her thing. She was charming with her customers, and observant, too. When Olivia Minelli's toddler son demanded a cookie—loudly, and rudely, although Adam understood the tot's urgency, the cookies did look amazing—Isla fetched two of them from the glass case, but didn't hand them over. She gave his older sister a conspiratorial look, softened her tone, and asked the little girl if she would like a cookie as well.

"Yes, please," Sofia said.

"Excellent manners," praised Olivia.

Isla looked at the little boy. "Can you say, *Please, may I have a cookie?*"

He pouted. "Please."

She held it almost all the way out to him. "Of course. Can you say *thank you*?"

Jesus, Adam's insides pulled tight. It was not appropriate for him to imagine her perched on top of him, her tits dangling just out of reach of his mouth, making him be *very polite* before he could suck on her nipples.

She'd been having that effect on him lately, through no fault of her own. Whole scenes would pop into his head like that, from completely benign things she would say. Playful, teasing, courteous Isla, just going about her life in Pine Harbour, turned Adam on in ways that went completely against their deal.

The crush he was developing on his wife was layered, complicated, and entirely one-sided.

This was going to be harder than he thought.

When the Minellis were sorted, their cookies in hand and the rest of Olivia's order boxed up, it was Adam's turn.

"Hey stranger." Isla beamed at him as he leaned against the counter. There wasn't anyone behind him in line, so he didn't need to rush. "Did you finish up with your brothers early? I thought you said you were going to be hanging out with them all day."

"I changed my mind."

"Can I make you a coffee?"

"That's why I'm here." *Not to perv on you, that would be wrong.* "Double espresso?"

"Coming right up." She gave him another wholesome smile that his brain immediately turned into sin. "Is everything okay with your brothers? They didn't chase you away, did they?"

He shook his head. "I just realized I'd rather pop over here and say hi than sit around and wait for Will to finish whatever it was he was doing."

"What was he doing?"

Adam laughed, because he hadn't been paying attention. "I honestly couldn't tell you."

He'd been thinking about Isla instead.

Her smile softened as her gaze lingered on his face. "You've been juggling a lot lately. And it feels like we've been two ships in the night. Our schedules sometimes synch up nicely, and then sometimes..." She mimed an explosion. Then she passed him a perfectly pulled espresso.

He reached across the counter to grab her hand. "I'll make a point to drop in more often, then."

"Good. Because I miss you, you know?" She twisted her fingers around his and squeezed.

Fuck, the things her touch did to him now...

He dragged in a rough breath. "I miss you, too."

———

Over the next few days, Isla noticed that Adam went out of his way to spend time with her, and as they settled into a new routine, she found she was sleeping better and working smarter. From his own accounting, it seemed the same was true for Adam, too, and in hindsight, she realized she'd been worried by his temporary retreat.

She had felt far too lonely in her first marriage, and didn't like it in her second, either, no matter how unconventional their arrangement might be. On the other hand, she didn't feel right asking too much of Adam, or projecting her baggage onto their unique situation, so she was grateful she didn't need to spell any of that out.

But the peace in her heart didn't last long, because one morning mid-week, out the front window of her shop, she caught sight of the last person she wanted to see: her ex-husband.

Before she could pop smoke and disappear, Jackass was pulling her front door open and stepping inside.

Into her space.

Isla's breath caught in her throat, a tangle of fear and anger. What the fuck was he doing there? He looked the same as he had the last time she saw him, slick and handsome and an absolute snake.

She didn't greet him politely. She didn't greet him at all. She went straight for the obvious what the fuck question. "What are you doing here?"

"I've been trying to get in touch with you."

She'd noticed, and ignored. She didn't owe him her time anymore. "Why?"

He dragged out the pause before he told her, going for maximum effect. "I've recently moved to the area."

"You have to be kidding me."

"You know how the Army is." He shrugged. "They move you unexpectedly."

They hadn't moved her, even after she begged. If he was telling the truth, and she had no reason to think he was being honest with her—he never had been before—it was an ironic twist that he'd ended up here.

Had she known the army would move Jackass to Meaford, she would have stayed put in Pet. And then she never would have tapped out, never would have gone to culinary school and become a baker. Probably wouldn't have ever reconnected with Adam and landed here in Pine Harbour, only to end up face to face with her ex all over again.

But even so, it wasn't like Meaford was the next town over. "How did you find me?"

"Someone sent me the link to your Instagram account when I moved to Meaford. Thought it was a small world we landed in the same part of the province again. I thought I'd come check it out."

The way the answer rolled off his tongue, all slick and practiced, she had a gross feeling the *someone* was himself, but she didn't want to accuse him of something she couldn't prove. "You drove an hour out of your way to check out my bakery?"

"It just…" He looked around. Snake snake snake. "This seems like an odd place for you to land."

Her heart pounded in her chest. "What would you know about that? You don't know anything about me. You never did."

That wasn't exactly true. He had known enough about her to push all of her buttons. He had known what got under her skin. What made her doubt herself. What made her feel weak and scared and vulnerable. And maybe he still did, because the gleam in his eye and the knowing smirk on his face said he *did* have her number.

He knew she was here for her own selfish reasons.

At that moment, the back door to the bakery slammed open.

She glanced behind her, grateful to be saved by the dairy delivery. "Excuse me a minute," she said as professionally as she could muster. Then she turned around and stomped into the kitchen, only to come face to face with Adam, wearing his uniform t-shirt and pants.

"You are a sight for sore eyes," she whispered, her heart pounding.

"Hey. I was hoping to grab—"

She threw her arms around him before he could finish

that statement. Right now she needed him to grab *her*, and she'd have to explain later.

Without waiting for him to catch up, she kissed him full on the mouth.

He froze, then slowly wrapped his arms around her, his hands spreading wide across her back. "Well, this is a nice greeting."

"My ex is here," she whispered urgently and for his ears only.

That immediately changed the feel of his hands on her. He tightened his grip on her waist and kissed her right back, deeper this time.

This kiss felt different, possessive. It was an act, she knew that. But one that Adam was very good at. And for a moment, that scared woman who had just been confronted with her absolute worst fears gave into it and let him take her away from the threat of her ex and the worry about what might happen should the truth of her own selfishness be known.

None of that mattered. Not when Adam had her in his arms, with his mouth playing against hers, sure and firm and warm and loving. In her fantasy, this was what a loving, protective spouse did. Adam was as close to that as she was ever going to get. He was head and shoulders above her ex on the other side of the archway. She wanted Adam to know that, too. How much she truly valued him as her partner.

So she kissed him back. Trying to say with her body that they were in this together and she appreciated him. Oh boy, did she appreciate him in this particular moment.

She got a little breathless, the way he smiled when he finally pulled back and gave her a secret, little nod. Every single time he looked at her like they were in this together, like they shared these valuable secrets, she felt absolutely invincible.

She raised her voice. "I thought you were the delivery driver bringing me more butter."

He laughed. "I thought I'd bring you some sugar instead."

It was absolutely cheesy. And it made her laugh. Which made her feel like she could do anything. So she turned and tugged him into the front of the store, where Jackass stood looking a little less slick than before—or at least she wanted to believe that to be true.

"Adam, this is my ex-husband. Apparently he's moved to the area." She took a deep breath. "Brett Jackson, this is Adam Kincaid. My husband."

She felt Adam react, physically, to the revelation of Brett's last name. Jackass had been a fitting nickname in her phone for more than one reason.

Brett narrowed his eyes, and didn't say anything.

Adam gave him a smile colder than anything she'd ever seen before. "Welcome to Pine Harbour. I didn't catch where you were living now?"

"I'm in Owen Sound. I'm working at the base in Meaford."

"That's a decent drive from here. But I guess it's understandable you wanted to check in on Isla. She's doing great. She's loved by this community." He put his arm around her shoulder. Another possessive act Isla appreciated with all of her heart. "Was that the only reason you popped in here?"

It was a clear peacock-y posturing. *Time for you to leave.*

"I'm looking at land in the area," Brett said slowly, and Isla's heart sank.

It wasn't true. It couldn't be true. He had spent all of

their money—his, hers, and a lot of the bank's, too—so he had to be in the same rough financial position she was.

But just the thought of him crowding into her new town made her skin crawl. She couldn't respond to that.

Luckily, Adam was there, so she didn't have to. He squeezed her tight against him. "Might be hard. Won't it, babe?" He looked down at Isla, and she was grateful for the excuse to look away from her ex. "Lots of restrictions on purchasing land up here. Buyer beware. Something to keep in mind."

———

Adam tried and failed to unclench his jaw as they watched Isla's ex stroll across the street to *Catie's Cuts*.

He had to get back at the station soon. He only left to come and pick up some of Isla's day old cookies to take back for his crew. Now he wanted to stay firmly rooted at the bakery. Unless his radio went off, he wasn't leaving until this fucking asshole was on his way out of town.

But where he felt impotent rage, his beautiful wife suddenly kicked into action. She grabbed her phone and, as he watched on with wonder, she texted Catie.

Isla: ALERT. The slimey fucker who's walking in now is my ex-husband. Don't sell him land.

Catie: Roger. I only have swamp land available for one million dollars. I'm guessing he doesn't want that?

Isla laughed, but it had an edge to it that cut Adam to the quick.

"I'm sorry," he muttered. A part of him was still reeling

from the way she'd thrown herself at him—*all* of him had enjoyed the hell out of that until he realized why she needed him to kiss her—but mostly he just wanted her to feel better for real. Hug, kiss, or kicking someone's ass. He was up for whatever would achieve that. "Do you want me to follow him to the town limit in the firetruck?"

She patted him on the chest. "No. But thank you for that. I appreciate it."

He wanted to talk to her about the kiss. To tell her it was okay, he knew it didn't mean anything.

But there wasn't time to talk about that properly. So instead, he gave her another hug, a gentle one, and then he asked her if he could take cookies with him back to work.

It killed him that he couldn't be at home with her that night, to make sure that she was safe and that the guy didn't come back. But when she texted him at the end of her workday to say she wasn't going back to the house, but was going to Catie's for a workout and dinner instead, he breathed a little easier.

———

"I think you misrepresented yourself as a fitness newbie," Isla gasped as she lay on the floor in Catie's basement. All of her muscles burned, and they still had one more tabata on her planned workout.

"Endurance has never been my problem." Catie laughed. "That sounds wrong. But I've been an off-and-on runner my whole life. I can keep going. It's the heavy lifting stuff I worry about."

"A lot of lifting is working smarter, not harder. You won't be rescuing someone alone, you'll be part of a team, and a group of people working together can easily accomplish what seems impossible for just one."

"When you say it like that, I believe you."

Isla smiled at the ceiling above her. "I spent a long time being paid to motivate people with words like that."

Catie didn't reply right away, and then the timer went off. They dragged themselves through the last set of exercises, then collapsed again.

"My shoulders," Catie moaned.

"That's where the change happens."

"The pain? The burning?"

Isla chuckled. "Yep."

"Great. I'm changing like a mofo, then." Catie sighed. "All right. Food next."

They dragged themselves upstairs and Isla offered to help cook.

Catie waved her to sit at the island in the middle of the kitchen. "You're my guest. Sit." She poured them each a glass of water. "Can I ask about being in the army?"

"Sure. It was my entire life for a long time. And a good part of my life. I was really proud of my work, but all it takes is one bad experience for things to go sideways, and I had a couple in a row. So it was time to move on."

"Your ex…" Catie held up her hands. "And feel free to tell me if I'm being too nosy. But he said he's in the army today. Did you serve together?"

"Sort of. We didn't work in the same unit, but we served on the same base. We met there, after my last tour overseas. I came home, and I was at a vulnerable place—in hindsight—so he moved in. Literally and figuratively. We were living together two months after we met, and he convinced me to buy a house three months after that. I thought it was a whirlwind romance. I fell head over heels in love with a promise, not a man, if that makes sense."

"He seemed like he makes promises easily."

Catie was a better reader of people than Isla. "I didn't see that at all, but yes, exactly. Things started to fall apart just before our first anniversary. Well, they had never actually been good, but I didn't know that. I baked him a cake, a really fancy one, and a handmade card. And he told me I was a disappointment as a wife. He told me I should be more like one of his colleagues—and that was when I realized he was sleeping with her already. On our anniversary, everything clicked into place, and I realized what a mistake I'd made."

That was the briefest slice off the surface, but Isla wasn't going to dig into the past any deeper than that. The repeated infidelities she discovered, the gambling, the credit card bills that didn't make any sense. She'd locked away that part of her life forever. She blinked quickly, not interested in hot, sad eyes tonight. Brett didn't get to have that effect anymore.

Catie was gripping her spatula like it was an eight-inch cleaver she wanted to whack into Brett's neck. "And Adam didn't lay him flat out when he saw him today?"

"Adam doesn't know that part. He knows the broadest strokes," she hastened to add. "But I've never told him the details. It doesn't matter anymore."

Or at least it hadn't until Brett showed up.

And Isla still didn't know the real reason he had come to Pine Harbour looking for her, which meant he might be back.

CHAPTER FOURTEEN

THAT NIGHT'S shift stretched on forever. All Adam wanted was to be at home with Isla. He settled for texting with her before she went to bed. He made sure that she was locked up tight for the night, that she was feeling okay. And he told her to call him in the morning before she headed to the bakery. As soon as he got off shift the next morning, that was where he went. He headed back in that same door he had headed in the day before.

This time she didn't kiss him on the mouth with any kind of urgency, but she gave him a sweet kiss on the cheek when he told her he just needed to see her again before he went to sleep.

"I'm feeling better about what happened," she said. "You can go home. Get some rest."

He searched her face, then nodded. "Hey, how about I have a bubble bath waiting for you when you get home this afternoon?"

"Oh, yes." Her eyes lit up. "I was actually going to ask you if I could use your bathroom. I ordered some fancy bath stuff. It's sitting in a box in my office."

Something about how she said that hit him squarely in the chest. She didn't need to ask him if she could use the upstairs bathroom. They needed to revisit the terms of how they shared the house. The only reason he didn't use her shower was because it was actually inside her bedroom. The bathroom upstairs didn't have that same privacy limitation, and he wouldn't care if it did.

He didn't want to invade her personal space. She was welcome to twirl through his all she wanted, but he could hardly say that. It didn't feel right, some murky boundary that felt dangerous and forbidden. He wasn't sure what would be worse, if she started to spend more time in his space and things stayed platonic between them, or if he invited her to tromp on those boundaries and she politely declined. Those were the two options. It wasn't like she was going to magically fall head-over-tits in lust with him after all this time. He didn't do it for her, and the deal they had was that he accepted that in order to have the rest of her, which was pretty fucking wonderful.

The door opened and a customer came in. Isla nodded her head to the back. "Can you grab the bath stuff on your way out? It's sitting in a Sephora box on my desk."

"Yep." He headed through the open archway that led to the kitchen. Because Isla preferred her customers to be able to see the baking magic in progress—and smell it, too—she kept the kitchen absolutely pristine, but her little cubbyhole of an office was jammed full of papers and plans, a bit of a rabbit's warren of long-ranging plans that may or may not ever happen.

Adam liked the way Isla thought of everything, mapping out many different potential outcomes. She planned way down the road, nothing left to chance, because there was always another plan to pivot towards.

The more he got to know her, the more he realized just how deeply her divorce rocked her—in part because she would have had long-term plans with her husband, too.

He groaned to himself at the obviousness of the thought. Of course she did. That was what marriage was. Nothing but long-term plans with the love of one's life. It would have rocked anyone to realize that wasn't a mutual feeling.

But he would bet that Isla had had it all planned out. Kids, maybe. Little blond toddlers with homemade cookies in their fists, saying thank you ever so politely before shoving the crumbly perfection into their sweet little mouths. How many would she have wanted?

She'd never said a word about that.

He wouldn't ask. It seemed off limits—for now. Down the road, though, he wanted to know. He hoped they were building the kind of relationship where they might share confidences like that.

The door chimed, another customer coming in, and he grabbed the brown cardboard box.

At home, he had a quick shower, then cleaned up the bathroom so his stuff wasn't all over the counter, and then he fell into a deep, dream-filled sleep.

When his alarm went off six hours later, he sent Isla a text letting her know he was up, and asked her to give him a heads up when she was coming home so he could run the bath for her.

In the meantime, he assembled everything she might need to pamper herself. Her fancy bath items, two fresh towels, a candle for mood lighting, and a waterproof speaker that hooked up to his iPad, which he set on the counter.

As soon as she texted back, he put the plug in the tub

and started running the water, only to realize he didn't know her preferred temperature. So he called her.

"I'm just leaving the store now," she said to a backdrop of street noise.

"Great. Uh, how hot do you like your baths?"

"Super hot. Boil me like a lobster hot."

Good thing he had asked, because that sounded painful, and wouldn't be what he'd have done by default. "Got it."

"You don't need to do this," she said, her breath chopping a bit like she was walking quickly.

"I want to. You've been working hard."

"Well, I'm lucky then. And I'm two blocks away now."

He adjusted the water temperature, then let it keep filling while he went downstairs.

When she came in, she gave him a tired smile. "You're a gem."

I want to be more than a gem. But there was no point in thinking like that, so he shoved that thought deep down where it belonged. "The tub is filling. I've set out everything you need."

He felt awkward following her upstairs, so instead of retreating to his own room, he grabbed a book and stretched out on the couch. He was well into chapter two when suddenly the quiet of the house was pierced by a panicked shriek from upstairs.

He was halfway up the stairs when she screamed his name, and he skidded to a stop outside the bathroom door.

"Are you okay?"

"The *mouse!* It's back!"

He grabbed the door handle, then paused. "Do you want me to come in?"

"Adam!"

He took that as a yes. Throwing the door open, he tried desperately not to look at Isla, curled up at one end of the tub, her breasts barely covered by one arm and her knees pulled up to her chest.

Her hair was piled on her head, wet tendrils sliding down her neck.

And he would have popped a hard-on right there if she didn't have a look of panic on her face. No, not panic, exactly. Something else. Wild exasperation.

"I'm fucking naked," she exclaimed.

He was very aware. "Yep."

She threw her non-breast-protecting arm in the direction of the toilet. "Get it! I'm not chasing a mouse naked!"

He grabbed a towel and lunged for the little rodent, but it was faster than his arousal-dulled reflexes. Each toss of the towel fell short, and then the mouse was gone, a flash of brown zooming under the tub.

He dropped to his knees in a desperate attempt to follow it, but there was no point.

"What is wrong with you?" She laughed. "You suddenly have two left-feet and are all thumbs."

He reared up, desperate to get out of the bathroom suddenly, but all he could see was her flushed face and her swollen breasts pressed against her arm. "What's wrong with me? You're not wearing anything. All I can think about is following those drops of water as they slide over your skin, chasing them with my fingertips and my, my…" He trailed off, realizing what he'd just said.

What he had just admitted to.

Her eyes went wide.

The tap dripped, and suddenly there wasn't enough oxygen in the room.

She called his name as he spun out of the room, as he stomped down the hall and slammed his bedroom door.

Then he threw his back against it with a heavy thud and sank to the floor.

———

Isla couldn't breathe.

She needed to follow him.

She needed to get out of the tub, go downstairs, get dressed, and then they could talk.

Or not get dressed. Just go down the hall and let him chase water droplets all over her skin. That option made her pulse sizzle dangerously.

But she couldn't do that, because she couldn't handle what would come next. The fallout, the mess. The inevitable dissolution of her second marriage because she wouldn't be enough.

Adam *wanted* her? What had happened to their agreement that their relationship was platonic?

She pulled the plug to drain the tub and climbed out, her legs shaking. She grabbed the towel without really seeing it, dried off as much as she could, then wrapped it tightly around her torso.

In hindsight, she should have brought her clothes up here to change.

She shouldn't have screamed when she saw the mouse, and she should not have called for Adam.

That was mortifying on so many levels.

When she opened the bathroom door, the hallway was dark. So was Adam's bedroom. No light appeared under his door. She hadn't heard him go downstairs, but he could have crept out. He had skills.

Her heart sank and she quickly padded downstairs, dashing to the safety of her own room. No more baths. Only showers for her.

She pulled on a pair of sweatpants and a tank top, and then for good measure layered a long-sleeved tee on top of that and pulled on a hoodie. Layers were good. Layers were protection. Then she put on her face cream, combed her damp hair, and gave herself a stern look in the mirror.

Go and find him.

She peeked out the front window. His truck was still in the driveway, so chances are he was upstairs in his bedroom with the lights out, hoping the dark would erase what had just happened.

Heart pounding, she climbed the stairs again and knocked on his door.

He didn't answer.

"Adam," she said softly. "Can I come in?"

"Nope," he growled. It sounded like he was right there.

"Why not?"

"Because I'm sitting against the door and I'm not moving."

"Okay." She sat down, too. "Can we talk like this?"

"I don't know if we should."

"Because you'd rather keep things from me?" She winced as soon as she said it. She didn't want him to think she felt antagonistic about this situation. They were in this together—or so she hoped. "I *want* to talk. About anything."

And everything.

She hated the idea that Adam was keeping things from her, but not for the same reason she hated secrets in her first marriage. She knew deep down, with intense clarity, that if he was hiding attraction to her, it was for her own good.

Because she'd told him they could only be friends.

He had selflessly given her everything she wanted at every turn.

A long, terrifying silence stretched on the other side of the door, then she heard him move. The door swung open, and a trapdoor in her belly dropped away, too.

Adam loomed over her, his expression unreadable. She scrambled to her feet. "Hi."

"Come here," he said gruffly, and she threw her arms around his torso.

Both of them exhaled at the same time.

"Do we have anything to drink?" Isla asked. Neither of them had bought wine or beer since they'd moved in together. The last time she'd had anything to drink had been the night they'd slept together, in fact, and that felt far too long ago right now.

Adam chuckled, a low rumble against her body. "As a matter of fact, I bought a bottle of something for Christmas. Let's go downstairs."

She hadn't noticed the bottle of Marsala in the kitchen cupboard. And if she had seen it, she'd have thought it was cooking wine, an assumption Adam clearly expected.

"It's a long story," he said as he grabbed two mismatched juice glasses.

They didn't even have the right glassware for emotional drinking. Or maybe what they had was exactly right. She gratefully took the tawny liquid and breathed in the sweet scent. "I love long stories."

"My dad used to drink this every Christmas. I thought we could get a tree, maybe throw a party or something…"

He shifted nervously, his glass still in his hand. "But today is as good as any to share the tradition with you."

"It's nice," she said. A weak response. "Tell me more. Do you drink it every year?"

He shook his head. "Something about being back home, in my own house…it sparked a memory. My parents would have a party every year, and it would basically be adults on the ground floor, drinking and eating, and kids of all ages would crowd upstairs. Our house was huge, with a full attic—that was Will and Owen's space, no little brothers allowed. When they moved out, I had big plans to claim it over Josh, who was already car obsessed."

His face tightened, a slash of pain reminding her he wouldn't get that chance.

She took another big slug of wine. It was very drinkable, which was good and bad, but she was focusing on the good right now. "I'm sorry," she muttered.

He tapped the edge of his glass against hers. "Thanks for sharing this with me. Hey, guess who introduced my father to Marsala? Mr. Minelli."

"Anne's husband?"

"Yep. Our families used to hang out all the time. After Mom died, there was talk of Josh and I maybe going and living with them, but Owen shut that down."

"Oh." Isla pressed her hand to her chest. And she took another slug of wine. "Wow."

"How about you? Any holiday traditions? Or emotional sob stories?"

"All of my emotional trauma is more recent," she muttered. "I wish I had something specific like this as a memory from childhood. We did all the usual things around the holidays, I guess, but nothing stands out. I wasn't raised to make a big deal about anything. It was a bone of contention with…"

Adam grabbed the bottle. "Let's take this to the couch."

She followed. "I didn't mean to make it all about me."

"Hey, if I haven't been crystal clear about this—I'm very into you. Make it all about you, that's just fine by me."

I'm very into you. The elephant in the room. She sank onto the couch. "We talked about how we both have bruises. I'm still learning how to separate sex from love, because my marriage—my *first* marriage—was pretty toxic. I guess my parents were pretty uptight, although I didn't think of it like that. I didn't have a lot of experience before I joined the army, so *that* was a bit of a shock." She laughed nervously.

"Did you date a lot of army guys before you got married?"

"Almost exclusively. Nobody else understood the schedule. It was just easier. But present company excluded, I didn't really find any good ones. At least not in hindsight. I thought my dating life was okay?" She shrugged. "I had to try pretty hard to not be one of the guys, though. And most of the time, I actually preferred being invisible like that."

He poured himself another glass, and took a big swallow as he raked his eyes over her.

His expression was too hard to read, so she didn't even try. She held out her glass and he topped her up.

Then he leaned back, his gaze still inscrutable. "You're not invisible to me."

The only response she had to that was to take a big slug of wine.

One of his eyebrows arched. "Too much information?"

She laughed weakly. "Aren't we way past that point today?" She shook her head. Nothing in her life had felt as hollow as standing on the wrong side of a closed door, knowing he was torturing himself on the other side. "I wanted to talk. That's talking. Thank you."

She might not have wanted to have this conversation before, but even worse than having it would be to *not* have it. Or something like that. *Drink.*

Adam licked a drop of wine off his lip, then leaned further into the couch cushions. "You're beautiful. That's an objective statement. I see people falling all over themselves for you, way more than you notice."

"No." She frowned and shook her head.

He shrugged. "It's true."

"When?"

"Bouncer at the club I took you dancing at. My fucking classmates, even though you walked in on my arm. Sure, we were just friends, but they didn't know that." He laughed under his breath. "Jerks."

"I was dressed up that night." And she still didn't remember it the way he was describing, but she wasn't going to argue with him. She cleaned up all right, she wasn't in denial about that. But it wasn't enough to be a—

"Nah, you're irresistible all the time. Every inch of you. I thought that in the summer, and I still think so now. More now, even, with the way you look in sweatpants?" He paused, like he was thinking if he should say more.

Say more. Did she really want that? *Yes.* And yet she wasn't ready when he gave her more.

"You're fucking *hot*, Isla."

"But—" She cut herself off.

"But what?" He suddenly glowered. "Would it be

better if I banged you even though I thought you were only okay?"

Her head was spinning, but no, that wouldn't be better. "That was...different."

"Not for me."

"We agreed it was a onetime only thing."

"Yep."

"Did you want it to be more than that?"

"I—" His frown tightened. Another pause. So many of his thoughts about her required filtering, apparently.

"Just tell me," she whispered.

"At the time, I thought I didn't. I swear to you, I accepted that it wasn't going to happen again. But I thought about how good a repeat would be. And then I stuffed those desires away, because they didn't matter." He made a strangled sound. "And no, I haven't been frustrated since the summer. Something has changed recently. I like the way you look asleep on the couch. I like the way you look in a t-shirt. And I really like the way you look in absolutely nothing at all, which until tonight had been relegated strictly to my non-waking hours."

Wait, what? "You've been dreaming about..."

"Don't finish that question. I can't be held responsible for where my dreams go."

She drained her glass and shoved it at him. "Top me up."

One corner of his mouth quirked up. "Is this a good idea?"

"It's not a bad idea," she muttered.

He did as she asked, then set the bottle down. "Can I ask you a question?"

"Of course."

"Why can't we see where a physical relationship would go?"

Hot tears pricked at the back of her eyelids. Hands shaking, she set down her glass. How did she begin to explain the layers of complication in her answer? Answers, because there wasn't just one thing. Except none of it came out when she opened her mouth. Was it Brett? Sure. The thought of losing herself again? Absolutely. But there was something else, something she didn't want to look at or think about, and definitely didn't want to get into with Adam.

She winced and simplified it to three words that felt true, three words she could actually voice out loud. "Because I'm scared."

"Well, that's a pretty good reason." He put his glass down as well, then held out his arm, and she folded in against his chest. She felt his lips brush the top of her hair, just for a second, and it broke something loose inside her. Something big and sad and rough, and it pushed her feelings all the way to the surface. Frustrated tears slid down her face for the first time in far too long.

She tried to hide her face in his shirt, but that was getting wet, and this wasn't fair. She couldn't sob on his body right after refusing it any kind of shared pleasure. But when she tried to twist away, he stopped her.

Gently, carefully, he squeezed her tight. "Hey, it's okay."

"It's not. It's ridiculous." But she still burrowed herself deeper into his body, stealing his touch, his embrace. She was selfish on a bone-deep level, and she hated herself for it.

With a growl, she twisted away from him, her limbs aching at the loss of his hug. "I'm sorry."

When he had proposed, she hadn't been ready for any kind of intimacy with him. But even worse than that was that she still wasn't, not really, even as she wanted him—one of those complicated layers she could feel unfurling inside her, showing itself even when she didn't want to look at it.

"I know." He just sat there behind her, not moving. She could feel his presence, solid and far too understanding.

And he waited.

Tension warred inside her. Part of her wanted to flee, to hide, to ignore everything he had shared today and try to force their relationship back into the neat box it had been in just hours earlier.

But what had really changed?

He'd confessed a desire she had already seen.

He'd shown her, repeatedly, that it didn't matter if she had sex with him or not, he was still her guy. Her friend, her partner.

Her husband. He had firmly and completely disassociated the sex part from a marriage, but not because he didn't want it.

Because *she* didn't.

Hadn't.

Did she?

When he proposed, she'd tested the chemistry between them, wanting to find—and finding—a lack of a spark. Adam's kisses had always been nice. Warm, lovely, kind. He was a good kisser, to be more than fair.

But she hadn't wanted more. Hadn't let herself want more, and now, in hindsight, she was questioning everything. Had she managed to lie to herself about that chemistry? Because the other day...

So she should test it again now. It would be the transparent thing to do. Turn around, brush her mouth against his, and prove to them both that any desire he might be experiencing was one-sided and temporary.

What if she felt something more?

She was horrified to realize there wasn't much of a *what if* to the question. She knew even without kissing Adam that she would want more. There had been enough kisses already, enough glancing touches and subconscious watching of him—of his body, the shape of him moving through her life, the size of him next to her in everything they did—to know something had shifted deep inside her.

She felt so much for him already.

She wasn't ready to let that dam burst wide open. Not yet. But could she test it. A controlled experiment.

Maybe she just needed another drink first. She glanced at her glass, but it was empty. Then she twisted around and looked at Adam.

He gave her a funny look as she swayed closer. "What are you doing?"

She smiled, and it felt all warm and thick, like a stream of honey or molasses, heated up. "I'm going to kiss you."

He groaned. "No."

"What?" She leaned in closer. Clearly he'd misheard her, because he wanted her kisses. He'd told her as much. He wanted more than kisses. He wanted to lick water droplets off her naked body. "I said, I'm going to *kiss* you."

He skated his hands up her arms, his touch featherlight until he reached her shoulders. Then he tightened his grip just enough to ease her back.

Away from him.

And he shook his head, his face tight with tension. "Not tonight."

Her pulse pounded in her ears as she scrambled back. Embarrassment coursed over her in hot waves.

He followed, his gaze intent and locked on her face. "Don't run away from me. I'm not rejecting you. I want you so much it hurts. But if you're going to kiss me, especially after telling me that you aren't sure…I need us both to be sober."

"I'm—" She cut herself off. Her head spun. No, she wasn't sober anymore. She cut her attention sideways, trying to focus on the bottle of wine. "How much of that did we drink?"

He grabbed it and wiggled it in the air, showing her it was empty. "Far too much."

"Oh." She pressed her eyes shut.

He was right.

"If you still want to kiss me in the morning," he whispered, close enough she could feel his warm, wine-sweetened breath against her face. "I'll be waiting. And right now, I think we should go to bed."

She wanted to protest, but she could feel the wine in her veins, and knew he was right. She pushed herself up, and the room spun wildly in one direction. "Whoa," she whispered as she reached for the nearest thing to hold on to—which was Adam.

"I've got you," he murmured.

"Can you tuck me into bed?"

Adam groaned, and then she realized how that sounded. Sexy, like an invitation.

Would she still have the courage to say something like that to him in the morning? Would she be brave enough to be that honest in the morning?

She hoped so. She liked the noises he made when she admitted what she wanted.

CHAPTER FIFTEEN

ISLA HESITATED outside Adam's door for the second time in twelve hours. It was early, but his alarm had gone off. She'd heard it as she'd lain in bed. Heard him get up, heard the shower come on. She'd imagined him brushing his teeth and combing a bit of touchable product through his hair.

She'd expected him to come downstairs next, but he hadn't.

So here she was, trying to work up the courage to knock on her husband's bedroom door.

As she raised her hand, the panelled wood swung open, and she narrowly missed knocking on Adam's nose.

He was faster than she was, though, and dodged the unintended attack with a laugh. "Hey there," he said, catching her wrist in his hand.

Her breath whooshed out of her chest at the warm, sure contact. She opened her mouth to say something witty, and a gasp slid out instead.

Time slowed as Adam dragged his gaze up to her face, as she stepped in closer, then stepped back again, bumping against the doorframe. There wasn't enough room for both of them in the narrow space of his open bedroom door, not early enough space, or oxygen, and he was expecting her to say something.

To *do* something.

She had come upstairs to find him, because she had woken up with a startling and frightening realization: she really wanted to kiss her husband. She wanted to kiss him when nobody was watching, she wanted to kiss him for her own reasons. Hungry, confused, horny reasons. And she didn't want to lie about that anymore, to herself or to Adam. She just wanted to kiss him and she really didn't want it to be a problem.

But now that she was here, and he was looking at her with an impossibly sweet warmth, what she wanted—and how frightening it was—had her paralyzed.

Adam whispered her name, and she nodded.

He grinned. "You came up here."

Another nod.

He slowly released her wrist, letting her arm tumble to her side, and he leaned in very close, bracing his arm above her on the door frame. "Did you come up for a reason?"

Heat flooded her torso and she swayed in the tight space between his body and the wall. "I—"

His eyes glittered as he searched her face. "How'd you sleep?"

Restlessly. Tormented by dreams.

He'd told her he dreamt of her naked, and her mind had run wild with that overnight.

"I dreamed of you," she finally managed to say. "And I woke up thinking about you."

He swore under his breath, which made her laugh

weakly. It was an honest response, at least. His jaw flexed as he set his mouth back to rights and fixed his piercing gaze back on her face.

"I don't know how to do this," she admitted, her voice shaking. "Was that too much, too soon?"

"You can't do this wrong." He strangled the words, grinding them out. "It's all good. Whatever you want to say, or do, I'm here."

She raised her hand and brushed her fingertips against his face. His jaw, his cheek, and the corner of his mouth. She liked the way his eyes darkened, grew inky and stormy as she got close to his lips.

In August, she hadn't known what she was doing by kissing him in the dance club, hadn't understood the journey that would spark. Now she couldn't claim ignorance or innocence. Kissing Adam now would spin them wildly out of control, and neither of them could predict where it would take them.

Was she willing to take that chance? Risk their friendship to see what his barely restrained fervour tasted like?

"I'm scared," she finally admitted, and saying it out loud was freeing. She breathed his name next, suddenly filled with something else more powerful than fear. "Adam..."

Every muscle in his body flexed against her, his thighs hard, and when she slid her hand down to his waist, she felt his abs contract against her touch, like a bow pulled taut. She wanted to be his arrow, see how far he could send her flying. She remembered now how good it had felt to have his mouth on her skin, his hands on her body.

She wanted that again. She wanted *him*.

So she took a final, shaky breath and wound her arms around his neck.

He groaned as she softened her body, melting into him, removing the final few centimetres of space between them.

Yes, this felt good. She smiled as she brushed her lips against his, then opened her mouth and teased the seam of his with her tongue. Repeating his name, she licked at the corner, savouring the way he tasted.

The whole time, he held completely still, letting her explore without taking over.

But when she nipped at his lower lip, then fit her mouth more firmly against his, when she kissed him firmly, that was the signal he seemed to have been waiting for. With a rumble, he wrapped his arms tight around her, one hand sliding down her back to settle on the curve of her bum, the other tangling in her free flowing hair.

His mouth opened, his tongue swiped against hers, and it was game on. His embrace tightened as their kiss deepened. A push-pull, weeks of desire battling against a flood of newfound need. She wanted all of him, now. Every thrust of his tongue made her shiver, each retreat dragged an unholy moan from her throat.

Who was this man, and why were his kisses now affecting her on this intense, primal level? She'd kissed Adam before. It had been pleasant, arousing, friendly, kind, sweet, and most recently, a bit distracting.

This was all of those things jacked up to a thousand amps.

He wasn't quite ravaging her—he was still holding himself back, she could feel that tension in his body. But this kiss was undeniably sinful, with a healthy layer of fresh *Hey Friend, So Maybe My Feelings Aren't Platonic After All* poured on like molten lava.

Did her kiss taste just as different to him? Could he tell

that her feelings had changed over time, maybe even more than his had?

Her pulse was a drumbeat now, hammering inside her head. Loud enough she could swear Adam would be able to hear it, although the way he was plastered against her, he could probably feel it, too.

Bang, bang, bang.

Double bang.

With a gasp, she wrenched away from her husband's embrace. That wasn't her pulse, that was the door. Blinking away the lust fog that had descended on her, she turned her head to the stairwell and the foyer below. "Catie's here."

Adam blinked at her, his eyes glassy and unfocused. "What?"

"It's Monday. Catie's here to work out." Her legs didn't work, though, so she didn't move.

He laughed. "Fuck."

"I know."

He glanced down his body, and her attention followed to where his erection strained against his jeans. "I need a minute."

"I'll tell her to go away."

He caught her hand and lifted her wrist to his mouth. "No." He dragged in a deep inhale, then let out a shaky laugh before kissing her tender, sensitive skin. Every inch of her was on fire, and he wanted her to go work out with a friend? "We'll take our time. Yes. God, you smell good. But that's a great plan."

Like he was convincing himself, too.

Isla stepped back, her legs shaky and reluctant to move away from the warmth of Adam's body. But her friend was downstairs, and he was right. They could take their time with this.

She ignored the fluttery feeling in her chest as she wrenched the front door open. "Sorry, I was, uh…" And then she trailed off, because she didn't have a good excuse. "Come on in."

Catie slid inside, shivering, then glanced at the stairs, where Adam was now sitting wearing a sloppy grin. "Hey, Catie."

Her friend gave her a knowing raised eyebrow, and for the first time, Catie's assumption that they had a smoking hot marriage wasn't wrong. "Am I early?"

"Nope. We just lost track of time," Adam said. The fluttery feeling in Isla's belly intensified. "She's all yours—"

Another knock interrupted them.

This time it was Will on the other side.

"Shouldn't you be at the school?" she asked as she stepped back, letting him in. He hesitated a beat when he saw Catie, but then nodded in greeting to her and Adam before answering. "I should be, but our boiler stopped working in the middle of the night, so school was cancelled for the day. I went in to check on the repair progress, but I was just getting in their way. Thought I might convince my brother to come to the garage for a few hours."

"Yeah, sounds good." Adam stood and ambled down the last few stairs. He grabbed his coat, then turned back to Isla. "I'll be back for lunch."

She gave him a secret smile. "I'll see you then."

He hesitated for a split-second, not even long enough to look like a pause to anyone else, then stepped in close and brushed a quick kiss across her mouth that sent her heart soaring. "Can't wait."

As the door thunked shut behind them, Catie mock-swooned. "Jeez, you two…honeymoon heating up as the temperatures drop outside, or what? Your husband loves you so much, it's adorable and gross at the same time."

Isla laughed, because that was the appropriate response given what it looked like from her friend's point of view, but inside her chest, something soft and squishy felt a little bruised. Adam didn't love her. He didn't believe in love, and neither did she—not anymore.

Adam liked her a lot, though, more than anyone else, and he thought she smelled good. He wanted to kiss her, and was always going to be there for her.

That was all that mattered.

That was all she could ever want, really. Anything else was romantic dreams, and Isla didn't play at those anymore.

———

"I didn't know Catie and Isla were friends," Will said tightly as he headed for the harbour.

Adam shot his brother a quick glance from the passenger seat of Will's work-in-progress, an orange Duster from the seventies. "Why do you say it like that?"

"No reason."

"Do you have a problem with Catie all of a sudden?"

"Nope."

Adam should let it drop, but he wasn't the one who'd brought it up in the first place. And twenty-nine years of youngest-brother training meant it was a reflex to push his thumb into a bruise when he saw it—on his brothers, at least. "It sure seems like you might."

Will shrugged. "What were they doing?"

"Isla's helping her train for something." He changed the subject temporarily as they arrived at the garage. "What are we doing today on this beast?"

Will schooled his features, his annoyance falling away. "Josh ordered me a sway bar. Should be an easy install." He stopped the car and honked his horn. The right-hand door on the garage bay slowly rolled up, revealing an empty slot for him to pull into. "Let's get to work."

Yeah, Adam wasn't nearly as interested in that as he was getting to the bottom of whatever was going on with Will and the real estate agent.

He climbed out of the car and hollered across the bay to Josh. "Hey! Have you ever noticed Will acting funny around Catie?"

"Fuck right off," Will snapped, then pointed to Josh. "Don't answer that. He's barking up the wrong tree." But their brother's cheeks were decidedly pink, and not from the cold weather.

"Oh, no. This is too good to let lie. Man, if you're interested in her, just ask her out."

"Last I checked, Will was a grown-ass man who should know how to just ask a lady out on a date," Josh drawled. Then he squinted at his older brother. "Oh, wait, nope. Sorry, wrong brother. This one's uptight about everything and unlikely to ever get laid."

"Says the jerk who won't say boo about his own personal life," Will snapped.

"The jerk who ordered you in a custom-built sway bar?"

"That one." Will grinned. "My favourite jerk."

Adam hopped up onto a raised ledge at the back of the garage. "I think we should cover all of this in great detail. Josh, when was the last time *you* got laid?"

"None of your fucking business."

"Will?"

"I went on a few dates with someone in the summer." Will grabbed a wrench off the wall and pointed it in Adam's direction. "We know, you're all newly wedded and happy as can be. Don't rub it in."

The truth couldn't be further from that assumption, although Adam *was* pretty fucking happy right now. The sweet memory of Isla's mouth still lingered on his lips. "Hey, I'm no relationship expert. Isla and I are...still figuring out how to be good to each other." That wasn't a lie. "If either of you have suggestions for me, I'm all ears. We can start with me, and then loop back to your problems."

Will stopped joking around and gave Adam a serious look. "Is everything okay?"

"Never better." Another truthful statement, he was on a roll.

"It's not like you to ask for advice."

Josh hauled a long cardboard box from one of the cabinets on the haul. "That's a good point. Something must be wrong."

"What's wrong is that Will's interested in Catie and for no discernible reason, won't ask her out on a date."

"You have it all wrong," Will barked. "Although there would be no point in asking Catie out, because she certainly doesn't think I'm—if you must know, she was looking for volunteers for a bachelor auction to support the animal shelter. I put my name forward. She—uh, she declined my offer of participation."

He said the last six words with mechanical precision, like he was reciting them from the memory of a cold-ass email.

Yikes.

Josh set down the box, his mouth hanging open. Adam had a similar expression on his own face, he could feel it. "What?"

"She declined— You heard me." There was that pink-cheeked expression again. Will was *embarrassed*, but not because he liked Catie. Because she'd told him he wasn't an eligible bachelor?

Adam was hot under the collar now for his brother. "That's bullshit. Do you want me to talk to her?"

"Jesus Christ, not in the slightest." Will waved his hand to the car. "I'll pop the hood. Let's get this done, then you can go make your wife happy, which is the only thing you should be concerned about from this whole unnecessary conversation."

CHAPTER SIXTEEN

ISLA'S CAR was in the drive when Adam got home, but the house was quiet when he let himself in. He poked his head down the hall and saw that her bedroom door was closed. She had come upstairs to find him this morning. Could he return the overture?

With a nervous hitch in his step, he carried himself right to her door.

And hesitated.

In the quiet as he stood there, he realized the shower was running on the other side of the wall. Flashes of Isla burst in his mind like fireworks. Her wide-eyed expression as she stood outside his door that morning. The flushed abandon in her cheeks as she rolled back on a hotel bed. The way she'd moved beneath his body and the scent of her as she'd climaxed. He'd forced himself to forget, but after this morning, it was all there in his frontal cortex, like a buffet of imaginings.

And he didn't need to imagine for much longer.

He pulled out his phone.

Adam: I'm back. Came to find you, can hear that you're in the shower. I'll be playing it cool in the living room if you want to hang out.
Adam: And by hang out, I mean kiss some more.

Then he stalked back to the living room and spent the next five minutes second-guessing everything about both texts.

When he heard her bedroom door open and her foot-steps quietly pad down the hall, before she appeared in the doorway, he thought his heart might stop working. He managed to get himself to his feet just as she stepped into view. Her hair was still damp, dark blonde tendrils falling past her shoulders, and she was wearing a tank top and a worn pair of blue jeans. Nothing else, and she looked like his fantasy come to life. Better than his fantasy, because she was real. She stopped in front of him, but only for a moment, and then she leapt into his arms. He caught her with ease, the weight of her feeling so damn good after weeks of the briefest of contact. Had he known, truly, how much he wanted to hold her before now?

This time it was Isla who kissed first, her mouth eagerly finding his, and then his thoughts scrambled. Soft, sweet licks quickened, then slowed as she quested deeper into his mouth. He opened for her, letting her lead. His heart pounded with need, but he resisted the urge to rush to the next step. This was a gift in itself—but a gift with a countdown clock on it.

As her thighs tightened around his waist, and his craven desires started to spool out a feature-length film list of fantasies he wanted to turn very real with her, he knew they didn't have time for that. He needed to be in bed early tonight, and then he'd be gone for twenty-four hours.

Fucking and running away was a recipe for disaster.

Even as his blood pounded in his veins, Adam knew they couldn't get naked today. Now he just needed to stop kissing Isla long enough to explain that to her.

Maybe they should sit.

He turned and blindly carried her in the direction of the couch. When he bumped into it, Isla slid down his body, catching his hands and pulling him down on top of her in one fluid, beautiful motion.

He caught himself on his forearms as she rocked her hips against him from below, and his brain went on the fritz again.

What had he wanted to talk to her about? Was it how good she felt beneath him, how intoxicating he found the rub of her breasts against his chest, even through both of their shirts?

He'd been dreaming of her breasts, and now they were pressed against him. Bare swells in a threadbare tank top. He dragged his mouth down her neck to her collarbone, then her fingers tightened in his hair, bringing his lips back to hers.

Her kisses were like oxygen, a rush of light filling him.

He could so easily sink into her. Rub against her until she shattered for him. He remembered the first orgasm he gave her in the hotel room, even before she took off her panties, and he wanted that again.

The problem was, he wanted far too much. He could gorge himself on her right now if he wasn't careful.

Tits in his face, nipples in his mouth. The low, angsty groan she let out when he sucked her flesh into his mouth would last him all week, until he could be back in her arms. That's what he'd tell himself, that he could get drunk on her and then sleep it off. That it would keep him.

But it wouldn't.

He'd be thinking about her while he was working, race back to her at every possible turn.

So after the next long, drugging kiss, he slid down her body, just enough to disengage his hips from hers. He pressed his face into her cotton-covered chest, inhaled deeply, then forced himself to sit up.

He didn't leave her flat on her back and confused, though. He helped her up and curled her into his side. "Wow."

She smiled and kissed his neck. "We both needed that?"

"I guess so." He exhaled and laughed, then caught her fingers in his, lifting them so he could kiss her knuckles lightly. "Listen, I want to make you feel good. And I want to take my time. I want to hold on to you forever, and I know I have a twenty-four-hour shift tomorrow." He laughed again, and then immediately groaned. "When it comes to you, I'm pretty hot-blooded. I didn't realize how much you affected me after we hooked up—I swear, I didn't. But now I've spent a…healthy amount of time with those thoughts. And whatever boundaries you want, I'll understand. Hell, I think I'm asking for a few of my own right now, actually."

"Boundaries?" She whispered the word like a question, her gaze searching his face, but her expression was soft and understanding. "You want to take it slow?"

He nodded.

"To protect yourself as much as me." She blinked in surprise. "Oh. I didn't see that coming."

"I don't want to wreck what we have. Go too far, cross

a bridge we can't uncross. Let's see where kissing takes us this week, how does that sound?"

"It sounds nice." Another whisper, and she rose on her knees beside him.

He dipped his head and tasted her mouth again. A long, leisurely sip.

She arched against him and he hauled her on top of his body, spreading her legs wide around him.

Crude, wicked thoughts spiralled out of control in his mind.

"It's hard to stop," he said roughly. Between them, his erection throbbed.

She rocked her hips slowly, then came to a stop. "We'll go slow."

He fisted his hand in her hair and tugged gently. "Want to watch a movie?"

"Yep." She kissed him softly. "Let go of me and I'll grab us some cozy blankets."

Amusement tugged at the corners of his mouth. "I think we can share one now, don't you think?"

———

The next morning, Adam was in the kitchen making coffee when Isla wandered in. It was dark outside, and he didn't need to leave for his shift at the station for almost two hours.

"Couldn't sleep?" she asked as she wrapped her arms around him from behind. Her heart lightened as soon as he leaned back into her embrace.

"Slept like a king, actually." He turned around and settled his hips against the counter, spreading his legs so she could nestle right in close to him. He lifted her chin with his fingers and lowered his face so his lips brushed against hers, then again, deeper, a good morning kiss that kept going until she was flushed and breathless. "Woke up bright-eyed and damn ready to do that."

"Well." She swept her hands over his chest. "Lucky me."

He had her travel mug ready to go, too. When the coffee maker stopped burbling, he filled it for her, then poured himself a mug. "Feel free to blow up my phone with text updates all morning. I don't think we have any trainees scheduled to join us until the evening. I'm taking the truck to Will's school in the afternoon."

"That's fun." She took a sip of her coffee, not wanting to leave. But she had cinnamon bread to put in the oven, and that schedule was precise. She gave him a shy look from behind her mug. "Can I have another kiss for the road?"

He took the travel mug from her hands, set it on the counter, then pulled her hard against his body. He smelled like body wash and aftershave. She wanted to imprint the scent on herself, to carry her through the rest of her day.

"Have a safe shift," she whispered before he kissed her. *I'll miss you.* The sentiment surprised her, and yet as soon as she thought it, she knew it was true. She was proud of the work that he did, and knew the twenty-four-hour shifts were a part of it. But her heart already yearned for him to be on the other side of this shift, on the other side of the sleep that would follow. For all intents and purposes, she would see him tomorrow night for dinner, and then they would repeat that cycle for two more shifts. Six whole days consumed by mere glimpses.

This was why he wanted to go slow. They hadn't yet

tumbled into bed, and she already longed for uninterrupted time together.

But once she was at the bakery, that unexpected ache softened into a sweeter, more tender appreciation for the stolen moments they'd had that morning. The sound of Adam's voice as he'd said he slept like a king would fuel her for hours. The pride in those words reinforced they'd made the right decision to step carefully in this new direction. Maybe a little sexual frustration—properly vented through delicious, lingering kisses—would do them both some good.

All morning, she floated on that idea.

Waiting wasn't going to be hard at all. It was going to be *worth it.*

Adam was on her mind in more ways than one, she realized after she took advantage of a quiet lull to work on the chalkboard for the next day's menu, and instead of writing her usual list of treats, she gave them all names.

It started with the chocolate chip cookies, which she'd teasingly promised Adam and his brothers would be the best they had ever had. That memory slid into Adam suggesting that could be his nickname in her phone. *The Best She'd Ever Had.* He'd been teasing, but it was the truth —and that was before they'd built an entwined life together.

A week before, she wouldn't have been able to even hold that thought in her head. Today? It made her float on air. She picked up her chalk and started writing.

Best I've Ever Had (chocolate chip cookies)
Born in the Bruce (butter tarts)
Better When It's Wild (marshmallow dream bars)

The third one made her blush, and when the bell above the door dinged, she had to take a second to compose herself before heading to the front again.

Over the course of the afternoon, she thought of a few more names, and before she locked up, she put the chalkboard in place for the next day.

Then she texted a photo of it to Adam, and headed home.

She texted him again after dinner, before crawling under his favourite blanket on the couch to watch a show.

When her phone rang immediately after hitting send, she almost answered it without looking, assuming it was Adam. But at the last second her brain registered the name on the screen, and she dropped it in her lap.

So much for her ex having been scared off after his drop-in at the bakery.

She waited until the call ended, then blocked his number. She should have done that before, but she hadn't heard from him again, so she assumed wrongly that he'd lost interest in whatever his game was with her.

She'd been mistaken.

Fingers shaking, she called Catie next.

"Hey," Isla said as casually as possible.

"What's wrong?"

So much for casual. "Eh, you know. Just dodging calls from my ex and Adam is working tonight. How do you feel about staying on the line with me forever, or until I go to work tomorrow morning?"

"I'll be right over."

"No, it's—" But before Isla could pretend it was fine, that she didn't need company, the line went dead. And five minutes later, Catie's headlights flashed through the front window.

CHAPTER SEVENTEEN

THE NEXT TWO shifts were the busiest Adam had ever had. Not a single second for sleep overnight, two shifts in a row, meant the week disappeared in a blur of work, recovery, work again, and by the time they handed off to the next crew on Friday morning, he was beat. Ready for an exhausted collapse into bed. He had one more shift on Saturday to get through, and then he'd have four days off to focus on Isla.

As he headed down the stairs, he caught sight of Owen arriving for the day. He had a travel mug in one hand and a stack of files in the other.

"Morning," they said to each other at the same time.

Owen shifted his mug to the other hand and swiped his pass card to open his office door.

Adam jogged over and caught the door with his hand, pushing it open for his brother. Owen nodded in thanks as he dumped his paperwork on the desk. He sat down, yawned, and took a big gulp of coffee.

"Late night?"

"Kerry and I were in the city yesterday." Owen

scrubbed the heel of his hand into his temple. "We're seeing a fertility specialist."

Adam sank into the chair across from his oldest brother. "Babies?"

"Yeah."

"Well, that'll give Josh something to freak out about even more than farmer's markets."

Owen snickered. "Indeed. Anyway, my day is just beginning. How did the last twenty-four hours go for you? I'm surprised to see you here again this week."

"Just fine." It would have been more believable if Adam hadn't growled the answer. Had any of his shifts really been truly great? No, they were all fine, which was the truth, because he survived them and that was his goal.

Owen's eyebrows raised slowly, but he held back any retort. Like he wasn't sure what Adam wanted to hear, and that made two of them.

Adam had known that this first year in this job would be survival-mode. Sure, he'd earned his place on the team. But it was going to be a long time until he graduated out of the real probationary period. It was de facto expected of him to put in multiple years, perhaps, maybe even a decade, before they saw him as his equal. Maybe he would be the rookie forever, until someone younger or newer joined the team, and that wouldn't be until Richard retired. It was one of the downsides of working in a small town on a single crew.

He was, for all intents and purposes, once again, the baby brother. He was in the exact same position he always found himself—or never put in the time to grow out of. He had known that's what he was getting into. Maybe on some level, that was the position he wanted to seek out in his life, but why, when it frustrated him so much?

Was there some part of him that thought if he just earned approval from his crewmates, then he was finally going to earn approval from his brothers?

"It's been a long week," Adam finally said, the words grinding out of him. "One more shift to go."

"Three in one week?" Owen frowned. "Didn't you work three last week, too?"

"Don't get involved."

That didn't stop his brother. "What are they doing, hazing you? Everyone else has forty-eight hours of downtime in between shifts. Max seven in a month. You're—"

"I'm taking extra shifts with different crews, because I'll be covering extra days over the holidays. Just getting up to speed. It's fine. I get a week off after Saturday."

Owen muttered something under his breath that sounded dangerously like *that's not how I'd do it*, and Adam was damn glad he didn't work directly for his brother. Even though the fire service and the EMT crews shared a building, Owen's people worked twelve-hour shifts, so even when they did overlap, it was only for part of a shift —or, as in this moment right now, their shifts starting when the other was finishing.

Owen finally settled on a sentiment they could agree on, at least. "You need time at home with your wife."

"That's true." Adam rubbed his jaw. "Listen, about Isla… I don't want this to sound like a favour…"

"God forbid you ask your family to help with anything," Owen snarked.

"Because they're always so understanding," Adam snapped back. Then he groaned, because *fuck*, he was just as much to blame for picking a fight as any of his brothers. "You know what? I'm sorry."

"You should be."

"I am."

"Good. Asking for help is not a sign of weakness."

"Noted." Adam rolled his shoulders, then his neck. He could do this. "I'm working a double Christmas Eve and Christmas Day—"

"What the—" Owen swore. "That's not okay. Who scheduled that? Denise?"

"I agreed to it. That's not the problem. You don't need to worry about me."

"You don't get to decide when I stop worrying about you. Because that's going to be never."

"Well, can you find a way to care about me that is slightly less judgemental?" Adam shook his head. "Because the first year on the job would be tough for anyone, and I'm managing."

"I'm not judging you."

Adam got up. This had been a mistake.

"Hey, what was the favour? About Isla?"

"If I'm going to be working, can you include her in your Christmas?"

Owen looked like Adam had slapped him. "Of course. Why wouldn't we?"

"I dunno." He scrubbed a hand over his face. "I'm tired."

"Look, I was actually thinking…I might put myself on the Christmas shifts, too. Not to keep an eye on you, but to be around as a colleague. I don't mind being a safe ear if you need to vent. You're right—the first year is hard. Fucking hard, and you're doing better than I did. I hated it so much I didn't last that long before I went back to taking EMS shifts. But it's a good fit for you. You're a natural. Just like Dad was."

Aw, fuck. Adam blinked his scratchy eyes. The fatigue

was getting to him. "Thanks." Even his voice sounded rough.

"So if we're both here on Christmas, maybe I'll suggest to Will that he has Kerry and Isla over to his place? That way it's not even a favour to you, or Isla. Just a big brother looking out for the whole family type of conversation." Owen spread his hands wide. "Let me have that, at least. I love doing that shit."

Adam sagged back against the door, suddenly not ready to leave just yet. "Thanks. I appreciate it, I really do. Hey, speaking of Dad and Christmas. You remember the wine he and Mr. Minelli used to drink?"

Owen laughed out loud and nodded.

Adam grinned. "I bought a bottle. Meant to save it for Christmas, but one thing led to another with Isla and we ended up drinking it one night."

"Damn, son." Owen gave him a look that was all peer. "Nice."

That was too much of a tone shift for Adam going on twenty-seven hours without sleep. "All right, I'm going home. Time to hit the hay. See you later."

"Yep." Owen picked up his mug. "And I'll be around on Saturday if you want to stop in again. This was fun."

Adam snorted. They needed better definitions of the word fun, but it had been something, and not at all what he'd expected when he'd stomped down the stairs half an hour ago.

The fatigue caught up with him on the short drive home, and by the time he let himself in, his eyelids were heavy and hot.

He climbed the stairs, dropped his clothes on his bedroom floor, and crawled face first under his blanket.

Six hours later, he heard the front door unlock and

bolted straight up in bed. Apparently, he hadn't closed his bedroom door when he came home.

Isla typically stuck to the main floor, but if she came upstairs for any reason, she'd see his bare ass sprawled out in the least flattering way possible, and that wasn't how he wanted her first impression of his naked butt in months to go.

He listened to her move quietly through the house, and once she was in the kitchen, he leapt out of bed and grabbed a pair of grey sweatpants from his clean laundry basket. Then he went downstairs to find her.

She was putting food away in the kitchen, and glanced over at him as he entered. "Milk and butter we need to use up," she said as she straightened up.

He caught her around the waist and pulled her in close. "Pasta for dinner? Something creamy?"

"Spoken like someone who has another shift tomorrow and will do a long workout." She laughed. "But yes, definitely. Maybe with some peas and bacon?"

His stomach growled. "Want that for lunch?"

"We can. But if you're hungry right now, I brought some treats home from the bakery. Would a *Born in the Bruce* butter tart help, or maybe a Peninsula cookie?" She held up an obscenely shaped sugar cookie. "The butter in the dough made the shape a bit…different than intended. Obviously, I can't sell them."

Adam choked on his laughter. "That's a…dick."

"I tried icing it," Isla deadpanned. "It made things worse."

"White icing? You're joking."

She rolled her eyes. "Yeah, no. Definitely joking. I didn't even try to ice them. As soon as the peninsulas came out of the oven looking like penis-insulas, I knew I'd have to scrap them. I brought four home as a memento to share with you, the rest were turned into cookie crumbs for an individual birthday cake stack I'm going to try to make tomorrow."

"You brought me dicks. So thoughtful." He took a big bite. "Delicious."

"I'm happy with how they taste, for sure." She snorted. "I just heard how that sounded out loud."

He waggled his eyebrows. "Sounded just fine to me." He shoved the rest of the cookie in his mouth, then washed it down with a glass of water. "It feels like you're coming up with a new recipe idea every other day."

She took his glass and refilled it, then pressed her mouth to his jaw before giving him the water. "Maybe your kisses are good for my creative inspiration."

"God, I'm glad to hear that." He emptied the glass and shook the last bit of sleep out of his head. "Sometimes it scares me how much I think I need you."

She made a soothing sound. "You don't need me. You're more than capable."

He raised his head, knowing his gaze burned dangerously hot, and her breath audibly hitched in her throat. "Oh."

Oh was fucking right. He didn't mean he needed her to get through the day. He wasn't dependent on her.

He needed her on a different level. "I'm sorry," he rasped. "I shouldn't—"

She cut him off with her mouth. This kiss wasn't the sweetness of the last few days. It wasn't eager, either. It was both shaky and confident at the same time, two warring realities for this woman who felt so much and had been hurt even more. Her lips trembled, but she plunged ahead, and he caught her, holding her tight as she kissed him harder than ever before.

Then she broke away. "Do you still want to wait?"

"Wait for what?"

She smiled. "Sunday. Or some other point in the future?"

Taking it slow. God damn it all to hell. "I—"

No. He didn't want to wait. But should they? He needed her, yes. But he didn't *need* her to rush.

"Maybe…" She trailed her fingers down his neck and across his bare chest, making his brain short-circuit. "Have we waited long enough?"

"I don't need you to do this."

"Maybe I do." She slid her fingers over his bare shoulders. His muscles shook under her touch. "I see you, Adam. It's okay."

"I know that," he ground out.

She nodded. "You're exhausted. They're putting you through the wringer."

"That's the job."

Another nod. She stroked her hands up his neck and into his hair. He shuddered as her fingertips rubbed into his scalp.

She whispered his name, and his gaze sharpened, locking on her face.

"I want to be your comfort today. Is that okay?"

"You have to be sure." His words were rougher than a whisper, but just as quiet. The faintest growl.

"You're so restrained," she whispered back. "You don't need to hold yourself back anymore. I'm sure."

As soon as the words crossed her lips, he had her in his arms.

He believed her. She was confident, strong.

Isla had come into her own. This was the woman he'd once known and admired—and been intimidated by, in hindsight.

And then it had been his turn to be strong for her, to be her support, and he'd been so careful to not push her. But now she'd opened the floodgates for him, and his need for her flooded to the fore. A physical need, yes, but also beneath that, having her in his arms soothed that wounded part of his soul, too. He needed her in every way.

A kiss first, then his hands roamed, tugging her tight against his body. She felt like heaven, soft and warm. The shape of her felt *right*, like she fit against more than just his body.

He scooped his hands under her shirt, then shuddered as he found her bare flesh. No bra between his palm and her breasts.

Breaking their second kiss, he pressed his forehead against hers and looked down to where his hand worked beneath her shirt. She was warm, her breasts full and firm against his touch. Her nipple hardened as he stroked her skin, and he dropped his head to her collarbone, then lower. He sucked the taut peak into his mouth through her shirt first, then growled when she whimpered and went soft, pliant in his arms. He hoisted her onto the counter and tugged the cotton up, baring her breasts for his eyes and his mouth.

"Look at you," he said huskily. "You're so sexy. So soft and sweet looking, and then you make those sounds when I taste you." He pulled on her nipples with his mouth, his tongue working the underside of her breast as he swallowed more of her flesh.

Like that.

Her breathy gasps, her horny pleas for his ears only.

Those sounds made him feel ten feet tall.

He needed to get her all the way naked, and not in their ramshackle kitchen.

Rearing up, he covered the wet, pebbled skin with his hands again, and kissed her hard on the mouth. Then he said a single, potent word. "Bed."

"Where do you want to…" She glanced down the hall to her room.

It was closer, but Adam wanted to be all alone with her in every possible way. His room was the quietest room in the house, far from the front door—and the front porch, which had a window that looked into Isla's room. Curtain or no, that was too close to the potential of a friend or sibling dropping by unannounced.

"Upstairs." Another single word ripped from him, a hoarse command, and she smiled shyly, tangling her fingers in his as she led the way. Her shirt still rode high on her torso, like she didn't care that she was exposed to him, and that sent blood surging south.

They stopped at the side of his bed in silence. Time slowed as he curved over her, taking her mouth with his. Like downstairs in the kitchen, this was the start of something that he intended to last a while. He wanted her naked in his bed for the whole afternoon.

And he was prepared—as much as he'd talked about waiting, as soon as they'd crossed the kissing line last weekend, he'd stocked up on condoms.

He didn't need those yet, though. There was so much to do before they got to fucking. He tumbled them onto the bed, still kissing her as he stripped her down to her panties, his own clothes getting shoved aside too, then crawled down her body.

She tugged on his hair, then pushed on his shoulders, trying to stop him from kissing along the cotton edge of her underwear, then laughing as he lifted his head and growled up at her.

Her eyes shone with a beautiful brightness as she bit her lower lip, scraping it between her teeth before releasing it with a sexy-as-fuck pop. "I wanted this to be for you. I wanted to make you feel good."

Feasting on her *was* for him. It was a treat he had thought he might never get again, had convinced himself was not meant to be. And yet here she was, stretched out on his bed. Nearly naked, curvy, warm, and most importantly, willing.

This wasn't secret desire unlocked by booze, or a general need to cut loose.

This was Isla Petersen, his wife, wanting to be right where she was right now—in his bed.

His wife, *in his bed*.

Fucking hell, yes, he wanted to be in control. To focus on her pleasure and make it everything she had ever wanted in lovemaking.

Nothing like an impossibly high bar to reach for, but he didn't care.

"I want this to be for both of us," he murmured as he swept his hands up her sides and onto her breasts. Her skin was so soft and responsive, he could spend hours just stroking her flesh and listening to the shuddering little gasps that slid over her lips when he found a good spot.

She arched her back, giving in to his caresses.

He buried his face between her thighs, against the cotton first, and then when she ground against him, he tugged the panties to the side.

Enough for a taste. A tease. But that wasn't enough.

The last scrap of fabric between them needed to go. He groaned as she helped pull them down her legs, then dove in again. Her clit swelled against his tongue and he loved it gently. A lick, a suck, a tug. Up and down he moved, slow at first, then faster, deeper, until she grabbed his hair again—this time not to pull him away, but to hold him *just so*, there, *right there*, and he latched on, sucking her hardened clit through her first orgasm.

Then he pressed his forehead to her belly and cupped her sex, gently holding her until the aftershocks passed. When she slowly started to rub against his hand, he carefully stroked his way between her folds, testing if she was slick and ready for him. Her legs fell wide as he circled her entrance with the blunt tip of his finger.

He reared up, kneeling between her legs, panting and barely able to restrain himself. He fisted his cock.

And she grinned up at him, like she *liked* him like this, slightly feral and full of need for her. "Yes," she breathed.

This wouldn't be like their first time. This wouldn't be light and sexy and easy. But the way she smiled at him, fuck, it would still be fun.

Just fucking intense at the same time.

He grabbed a condom and rolled it, his erection twitching at the slick stroke.

Dropping forward again, he braced himself on one arm this time, his thighs pressing against the softness of her legs. She curled beneath him, her hips lifting as he fit them together.

Her warm, snug heat welcomed him with a familiar pleasure, but the look on her face—desperate wonder— was new. He recognized that in himself, too. This *was* different. The second stroke of his hips went deeper, and that wild sensation in his chest grew.

His wife.

This was so fucking different it hurt, the best kind of hurt, and he felt his gaze widen as her lips parted, their eyes locked on each other.

A third pulse of his hips seated him fully inside her, buried his cock *inside his wife*, and something new cracked in his chest. Sharp, jagged, wild. A wedding consummation two months delayed.

His. Beautiful. Wife. He said her name, a breath, a growl, and she cried out.

Her heels dug into his ass, urging him to move.

He withdrew, then thrust all the way in. They both cried out, then he surged faster, roiling need driving him into her body over and over again. The wild abandon in her pleasure threatened to take him too soon, the way she looked beneath him. Flush and wanton, pink and luscious. Her tits, her mouth, her soft, sweet eyes. His control slipped a little bit with each breathy gasp, the sounds more erotic than anything he'd ever heard before. Had she made those sounds their first night together?

He couldn't remember. Couldn't see or hear anything other than her right here, right now, open and soft for him.

With a cry, she stiffened, then rocked herself up his cock once more, her legs locking around his hips. The tight hold kept his erection rubbing against just the right spot deep inside her, her rippling climax doing the rest. His pelvis jerked hard one final time, all of his muscles contracting as one as his orgasm ripped loose from the deep.

He fell on top of her, the corners of his vision going dark. She ran her fingers through his hair, then down his neck, whispering his name over and over again.

He buried his face in her neck, breathing in the sweet

scent of her, sex-tinged and lovely, then rolled to his side. He dealt with the condom one-handed. The other arm stayed looped around her, holding her close. He never wanted to let her go.

That thought circled in his mind, a lazy loop of words. *Tell her*. He'd never been one for pillow talk before, nothing emotional, but Isla was different. This moment was different, and his chest felt tight, like it would hurt if he didn't confess just how important she was to him.

He brushed his fingers through her hair. "When I said I needed you..."

She laughed, slow and husky. "I think we both needed that."

He chuckled. "Well, yeah. But it's not just that. I want you to know..." He rolled over so he could look at her. He shoved a pillow under the side of his head and took his time studying her face.

He wanted to imprint the way she was looking at him now, all soft and sweet, on his memory forever.

"What is it?"

"You know work is tough. I knew it would be, and I'm handling it. But everything always feels like it's teetering on the edge of falling apart." He scrubbed a hand over his face. "I hate that. I'm fucking desperate to get to the point where it's not like that anymore. But you make it all... smoother. And not just the kisses. Bringing you here...I know I struggled to explain what I wanted in a partner, and why I knew this would be good for me, but I'm glad you said yes. Even before now, which was really fucking nice, too."

She smiled and traced her fingertips along his jaw. "Maybe that's a reminder that you should trust your instincts. They're on the right track."

Some of those words sparked an unexpected memory. *"You should trust your instincts.* You told me that about leaving the army. Do you remember?"

She shook her head. "I don't. When was that?"

He took a deep breath. "We were at Bagram, ready to fly home. I was done on every level, and I said something to Stevie about never wanting to go back there. I felt so fucking guilty when you overheard that, because I knew there was a planeload of guys about to arrive, and I pitied every single one of them. But you didn't get mad at me. You told me not to forget that feeling when the opportunity to get out came up. You said there was no shame in trusting my gut."

"There isn't." A shadow crossed her face. "I forget that rule myself sometimes."

"We make a good team."

She closed the small space between them, pressing her naked length against his. She kissed him softly, then with a sharp inhale, dove in deeper. Her hand found his cock between them and carefully stroked him. An unspoken question. *Again?*

Soon.

He pulled her on top of him, the warmth at the apex of her thighs settling on his lower abdomen. Very soon.

The press of her lips against his, the play of her tongue, it was something else. Not just arousing, more primal and base than that.

It came to him as she moved her mouth down his neck, and he gasped for air.

He tumbled her onto her back. "I thought your kisses were like oxygen, like a heady rush, but I was wrong." He nipped at her lower lip. "It's more like strapping on an air tank before I go into a fire. You do that, you realize how valuable each breath is. I never take the air I breathe for granted. Kissing you is as good as breathing."

Her eyes flared wide. "Is it?"

He nodded slowly and traced her perfect lips with the tip of his finger. "You know what I think? You are…" He felt a hot swell of feeling rise up inside him, pushing out words he never imagined he'd say, but they felt right. "Your mouth is an anchor in the storm, because it's attached to your heart, and your goodness. Your kisses are everything good in this world, and I want them every single day."

"Morning, noon and night?"

He rolled her on top of him, savouring her giggle of delight. "Especially at night. Sleep here with me tonight. Or I can come to your bed."

"Will we actually sleep?"

"Probably not, so we should nap this afternoon."

"Brilliant." She touched his mouth, mimicking the way he'd traced her limits. "Your kisses give me something special, too."

"I know. You already showed me. Penis cookie inspiration."

She threw her head back, her neck stretching wide as she lost it, and he kissed the glorious expanse of skin there, which lead him lower, to feast on her breasts.

He'd give her something special with his mouth, all right. Morning, noon, and night.

CHAPTER EIGHTEEN

THE PREVIOUS GRUELLING week of non-stop shifts meant that Adam had most of the following week off, and Isla was delighted when he spent much of those days at the bakery with her. Officially he was there to re-fill both of their digital calendars with the business side of things, and be a sounding board as she talked out the menu and ordering decisions.

Unofficially, he would linger as long as she wasn't busy, and return as soon as the shop closed. Neither of them could get enough of the other's presence, it seemed, and she secretly loved the attention.

When he returned to work, she missed him in a new and sharp kind of way. Even on his days off, he was often asleep until she finished for the day. So when he strolled in right after her last customer left for the day, she lit up like a midtown Manhattan electronic billboard.

"Flip the lock," she said, a happy smile on her face as she sagged against the counter. "And turn the sign? This shop is *closed*."

"Good morning?"

"Great morning." She glanced at the clock. "Did you get enough sleep? I'd expected to tiptoe into the house in an hour and hear you gently snoring."

"Do I snore?"

She laughed. "Way to change the subject."

"I grabbed an hour." He looked like he was going to say more, then slid into a charming, seductive grin instead. "I was wondering if I could convince you to have an afternoon nap with me when you were done here."

That sounded perfect. "So I shouldn't make you a shot of espresso?"

"Not today." He eyed the glass display case. "But I would take one of those cupcakes."

"Actually..." She crooked her finger. "I've been working on something new I want you to try. A different flavour of cupcake. Come on back."

He followed her, and picked up her clipboard as she pulled a piping bag from the fridge. "Hey, these new numbers look great. Right? Am I reading this correctly?"

She beamed at him. "You are. Thanks to your help last week, this week I had way less wastage than usual, and the margins reflect it. I don't want to put the cart before the horse, but I'm also getting busier. I think the ramp up to Christmas should be pretty sweet."

"That's great."

Snagging a bare vanilla cupcake, she piped a healthy swirl of the new raspberry icing on top and held it out. "A celebratory first taste of a new flavour?"

Instead of taking the treat, he moved in closer and let her feed it to him. When it was down to a few crumbs and a swipe of icing left on her finger, she slid that across his lower lip, then closed in so she could have a taste, too.

"We probably shouldn't..." He glanced around her pristine kitchen. "Right?"

She nodded. "Right. Definitely not in here." She closed her non-sticky hand around the front of his shirt and tugged him back to her office, which had a solid door and no windows. "But here," she said after closing them into the tight confines, and leaning back against the desk. "This is fair game."

He descended on her hungrily, her shirt going flying, followed by his, and then he peeled her out of her pants before dropping to his knees. "I'm still hungry."

She dropped her head back, giving herself over to the sensations. He was so good at this, thorough and enthusiastic. It didn't take long before she was lifting her hips to meet his tongue. Her body was a taut bow, and as her arousal spiked, and she curled forward, the sight of his head between her thighs, his powerful shoulders the perfect leg rest, was what put her over the edge. Shaking, trembling in every cell, she buried her hands in his hair and ground against him as he swallowed every bit of her climax.

He rested his head on her belly and exhaled. "Yeah. That. I needed that before I could sleep."

Holy fuck.

She closed her eyes and rubbed her fingers through his hair. When her heartbeat returned to normal, she pulled him up her body, giving him a long, slow kiss of thanks, then spun them around so she could return the favour.

It took them a good long while to get dressed again and stumble out into the kitchen, laughing. Isla washed her hands, then picked up the raspberry icing piping bag, thanked it for its help, and returned it to the fridge.

Adam watched her with a smirk on his face. "So what exactly happened here?"

She winked at him. "I seduced you with a very slick move. I lured you in with some sexy profit margin talk and then hit you with the raspberry buttercream frosting."

"I didn't see it coming."

"That's what makes it a very slick move."

He grinned sleepily. "You bamboozled me."

"That's what I'll call it! The cupcake. It's a Raspberry Bamboozle." She wrote that down on her clipboard, then gestured to the front. "I'll just put the leftovers into day-old boxes for tomorrow, then we can get going home."

"You don't have any more work you want to do today?"

She shook her head. "I'll work extra long tomorrow, but my only remaining to-do task today is go home and have a nap with you."

But when they climbed into his bed, they didn't go straight to sleep. Adam ran his fingers through her hair, his nails scraping her scalp just enough to make her purr, and turned the conversation back to the bakery. "As much as I really do like being your admin 2IC, have you thought about hiring someone to help? Someone who doesn't sleep during the day quite so much?"

She giggled. "First of all, you're irreplaceable for reasons I should hope are obvious by now. But...help? I was hoping to hold off on that until next summer. I'd like to have a full year of data, at least for the slower months, so I'm not making any false promises to anyone about work hours."

"But will busier periods cover the cost of employing someone in the slower months?"

"Yes. Definitely. By next summer, I should be able to

save enough money to know I can make it through next winter, even if business slows down."

"Then what do you think about taking out a line of credit—" The scalp massage stopped as Adam held up his hands, as she lifted her head and glowered gently at him. "Which I will co-sign. We can use the house as collateral."

The offer to help financially didn't lessen her glower in the least. "I can't ask you to do that."

"Which is why I'm offering instead. I believe in you, and the bakery, and I don't think you'll even dip into the loan. But it would be good to have it just in case."

"I'll think about it." She wouldn't accept the offer. She couldn't. But she knew Adam needed her to really consider it, and she'd give him that much before saying no. She'd show him she didn't need any help, that she could manage all on her own.

"Good." He tugged her back down onto the pillow. "Now let's talk about the obvious reasons you like having me around..."

———

Isla hadn't forgotten Adam's birthday, exactly. She'd put it in her phone in the summer, but then he'd spent the fall filling her calendar with reminders to order butter and do inventory and reconcile the books.

So that one blue-coloured calendar entry had slid down the list, until suddenly it was the first week of December, and her husband's thirtieth birthday was around the freaking corner.

"We have to have a party," she said as she slid onto his lap at the table.

"We do not," he replied, handing her a piece of toast. It

was a Monday, and they both had the day off. She'd moved her workout with Catie to the afternoon so they could have a lazy morning together.

"It's a big deal!"

"So was our wedding, and we celebrated that in private." He waggled his eyebrows at her. "I'm happy to have a private party just with you. Maybe you can bring home some of that bamboozle icing and I'll lick it off—"

She was not going to be deterred. "Has anyone ever made a big deal about your birthday?"

"Yeah, of course." His lips pulled together in tight concentration. "At some point. When I was a kid, my mom did, absolutely."

But his parents were gone before he hit sixteen, eighteen, twenty-one.

"This is a milestone," she said firmly. "And I want to make a big-ass deal about it, in a way you will be comfortable. Dinner party, backyard shindig, or a meet up at the pub?"

He looked around the faded kitchen. "Not a dinner party. And it's a bit cold for a…" His lips twitched as he repeated her words. "Backyard shindig."

"A fire pit would solve that."

"Let's go to the Green Hedgehog," he said. "That's a great idea."

She hadn't been yet, but he'd talked enough about the pub that she knew it was where he used to hang out. Before her, before the all-consuming new job.

She called and left a message at the bar, asking if they had any private rooms available for booking, and if she could bring in her own cake. When she didn't hear back by later afternoon, after she finished working out at Catie's house, she drove across the highway and into Lion's Head.

The Green Hedgehog was bigger than she expected, more of a sprawling restaurant than a cozy pub, although it had all the character of exactly that. A series of rooms in an old Victorian mansion, it was dead quiet in the pre-dinner lull.

Isla idly wondered if they wanted to order pies like she was making weekly for Mac's Diner.

There wasn't anyone at the bar, so she kept going, finding a back room full of pool tables and lined with dart boards that would be perfect for a party.

Just as she went to turn back, she heard Adam's name mentioned clear as a bell, and in the context of her own voice mail.

"So apparently Adam Kincaid's *wife* left a message? She wants to book a party room."

She froze.

"The baker?"

"Yeah. Have you met her?"

Isla wished she knew people around here better. She didn't recognize either of the voices. Two women were standing just around the corner, clearly familiar with her husband and his family, but who were they?

"Oh yes, a few times. The bakery's..." The last bit of that sentence dropped off to being incomprehensible, and Isla leaned in further.

"What is she like?"

The answer to that was also mumbled, and Isla told herself to make her presence known before she heard something she'd regret, but she was frozen.

"I guess we'll see them in here next week if she wants to have a party for him. Can you imagine? Adam blowing out birthday candles?"

They both laughed.

Isla frowned. Why the hell not?

"People ask about him, you know. What the deal is with her, why Mr. Player suddenly got hitched. How long it's going to be before he reverts to his old ways?"

That didn't feel good to hear. *It's also not true.*

"Maybe he's really changed."

And then they laughed again.

Laughed. At the thought of Adam being a good husband.

Isla saw red and stepped around the corner. She didn't recognize the taller blonde woman, but the shorter, curvier one was Bailey Patel, whose eyes went wide in recognition.

"Isla, I'm..." Isla raised her eyebrows and Bailey visibly cringed. "Lore, this is..." And then she swore under her breath.

Isla laughed, because while it was hella awkward, that was also kind of funny. She held out her hand. "I'm Adam's wife. I left a message earlier?"

And then Lore swore too, not at all under her breath. "Fuck, I'm sorry. We shouldn't have been talking about you."

"You weren't talking about me as much as you were my husband," she said dryly. A decade of knowing troops would talk about her behind her back—and much of it in the *very not good* category—had inured her to the brunt force of gossip. It had taught her a few tricks for correcting the narrative, too.

To Lore's credit, she didn't look away. "We shouldn't have been doing that, either."

"No, you shouldn't have." She wanted to set them straight, tell them that she had known Adam for years, and the perception of the community was only one side of who he was. She wanted to tell them that Adam knew exactly what he wanted, but it wasn't any of their business. All that mattered was that *she* knew how committed he was to her and their relationship. It still rattled her more than she liked that anyone might question their relationship.

It hit a little too close to the truth of how their marriage started, for one thing.

But for all intents and purposes, they had a real marriage now. Unconventional, but…

Adam only wanted her. She had to stay focused on that part.

CHAPTER NINETEEN

THE PARKING LOT at the Hedgehog was jammed full of vehicles Adam recognized, so it was hardly a surprise when they walked into the back room to find his brothers and neighbours there. He liked the way everyone turned and cheered as he stepped into view, and he loved the way Isla leaned into him, pleased with the party she'd put together in his honour.

He scanned the room, grinning, then did a double-take, because one of the guests actually *was* unexpected.

Leaning against the wall, holding a bottle of beer, was Stevie. Adam grabbed Isla's hand and tugged her through the crowd, waving at everyone as they went, then pulled his friend in for a bear hug. "Hey, man."

"Happy birthday." Stevie thumped him on the back, then turned to Isla and gave her a nod.

She wrapped her arms around him, too. "Thanks for coming," she said. Then she turned to Adam. "Surprise!"

"How did you…?"

"The internet can be used to search for people and then reach out to them." She winked. "Stevie said he'd been thinking of coming home, but couldn't swing the Christmas break, so a visit now made more sense. We made sure to line the party up with when he could be home."

Adam tapped his chest. "Wow. You guys." He turned back to Stevie. "How are your folks? Good?"

Stevie nodded.

"Awesome. We'll catch up later, yeah?" Another nod, and Adam wanted to just stand there and lean against the wall with his buddy. "I'll be back soon. I'll do a quick loop and then—"

"Go." His friend grinned. "I've got my drink. I'm good."

But when Adam moved on, Isla hung back, and as he greeted everyone, he noticed her quietly talking to Stevie for some length. She didn't leave his friend's side until he returned, in fact, and when he got back, Stevie was actually grinning.

Adam caught Isla around the waist, pulling her in for a hug. It felt good to hold her in public and not worry about accidentally crossing a line with her. She wiggled against him, and he kissed the side of her head, then her mouth when she tipped her face up to look at him.

"My turn to make the rounds," she whispered. "Let you guys catch up."

Stevie watched her walk away for a second, and Adam did, too, for a lot longer than a second. She was wearing a dark purple sweater tonight that made her eyes pop, and the world's tightest jeans that made his mouth water.

When he looked back at his friend, Stevie had a knowing look in his eye. "Captain Petersen, eh?"

Adam felt a hard tug in his chest. "Yep."

"She's great."

"You don't know the half of it, man. I really lucked out."

"I go out west, and you stumble into a real relationship with her? I'd call that some fucking luck."

Stumble was the right word for it, too. A real relationship by way of a fake one, although that was Adam's dirty secret he'd bury forever. "Wait until you taste her baking. Do you want to come over tomorrow? Isla has to work, but we can visit the bakery. It's really great. You remember the cafe? She's totally re-done it."

He spent the next five minutes raving about Isla, and when he finally came to a proud, grinning halt, he looked around for his wife.

He found her on the other side of the room, half-listening to something Kerry and Owen were talking about. But her attention was focused in his direction, and the soft smile on her face made him feel like a king.

Thank you, he mouthed, and her cheeks went pink as she quickly nodded.

Best birthday ever? Without a doubt. It would only get better when he got to tumble into his bed with her at the end of the night.

"Go over there," Stevie said, nudging him. "I'm going to grab another drink."

"You sure?"

"Yeah. I know other people here." His friend gave him a lopsided grin. "I'll be fine. And you look like you're desperate to get her in your arms again, so…go on. Do it."

He wasn't wrong.

As he rounded the far pool table, Kerry and Owen moved away, and he had a moment alone with Isla. "This is amazing," he whispered. "Thank you."

"There's still more fun to come. I made you a cake. And

Josh said something about you really wanting everyone to loudly sing you Happy Birthday?"

He winced, then grinned. "Sure."

"I'm teasing."

The way she laughed made him downright giddy. "Honestly, it's all good. I really—"

Before he could finish his thought, Will bumped into him from behind, then Josh slammed in for a group hug. Adam barely had a chance to brace Isla against him before a couple of ex-army guys joined in, and then he was lofted up onto their shoulders.

She waved at him as he was carried to the centre of the room, and someone—good Lord, it was Josh, the fucker—loudly announced the birthday boy needed thirty swats.

"I will fucking kill you," he roared, and everyone cheered.

"Time for cake, then," Isla called out, rescuing him, and the crowd turned. "I'll get it while everyone sings for the birthday boy."

———

The worst part of owning a bakery that was open all weekend?

Having to wake up at four in the morning after a very good party.

The best part would be closing at twelve noon, precisely, and coming home for a nap in Adam's bed, which was rapidly becoming Isla's preferred bed.

She dragged herself out from under his heavy arm and tiptoed downstairs to get ready in her room. The birthday boy didn't move when she kissed his cheek goodbye, either.

Grinning, she headed off to the bakery, and went through her pre-dawn routine with a satisfied lightness in her step.

That happiness was disrupted briefly when she realized who her first customer was, waiting five minutes before the top of the hour when Isla stepped into the front shop to unlock.

Bailey Patel.

"I want to apologize again for last week," she said as soon as she stepped inside.

"That's not necessary."

"Oh, but it is. Because I've been wanting to come in and talk to you about something, and then I made the absolute worst impression, and I regret that so much."

That was not what Isla expected to hear at all. "Uh, well...come in." She circled back behind the counter. "Did you want anything this morning, or were you only looking to speak to me?"

Bailey pulled out a twenty. "Could I get a latte? With an extra espresso shot, please. And I'll take one of the *Snowbirds* lemon bars, and a *Born in the Bruce* butter tarts. I really like the new names, by the way. Very catchy."

"Thanks." Isla rang that up, then carefully made the latte. "You said there was something else you wanted to discuss with me?"

Bailey's expression turned wistful. "In a way, it's related to what you overheard. Which wasn't judgement, I should tell you—or wasn't intended to be. It was jealousy. I want..." She trailed off.

Isla swallowed a burst of jealousy and reached for some understanding inside herself instead. "Do you have a crush on Adam?"

"Oh! No. Goodness. Uh, no." Bailey laughed nervously.

"Wow, that would make this very weird, and it's already hard enough. No, I'm not jealous of you, although you seem lovely and this bakery is amazing. I'm jealous of *Adam*. You were right last night. Nobody in this town sees how much he's changed, and how he did that for himself. I want that, too. I'm a bit lost, and I've been admiring what you're doing here—from a distance, because I didn't know how to broach it all."

It was a startling admission from a near-stranger. "Wow. That's…very honest." Isla frowned and leaned forward on the counter. "You must have a reason for coming in and sharing all of that with me."

"I have a business proposition for you."

Isla's elbow slipped as she did a double-take. She caught herself and stood up, slowly. "Pardon?"

"I'm twenty-three. I have a university degree, and probably a decade of experience in the local retail market."

Isla trying to do the math on that must have showed on her face.

Bailey grimaced. "My parents own the hardware store in Lion's Head, and a larger one in Wiarton. I grew up working there, and I like the business side of things. Not just like it, I'm quite good at it. So much so that they want me to go to business school, but I want to find my own way. I noticed that you had a stall at the farmer's market for a few weeks before you opened up, but you haven't been back there since…" Isla went from confused to stunned to impressed as Bailey outlined a very sound plan for Isla to hire part-time staff to work at the store and at the farmer's market. "You have a great business idea here and an incredible product, but your entire marketing plan is posting to Instagram, and that's not enough."

It wasn't, and Isla knew it. She just hated that someone

else knew it, too. "I have ideas for more layered marketing plans."

"But you don't have time to implement them. Of course you don't, it's a full-time job."

"Maybe I've given you the wrong impression, but the bakery isn't making enough money to pay for a full-time marketing specialist."

Bailey smiled confidently. "Not yet. But if I did my job correctly, it would more than pay for itself. And I'd be willing to work on commission to prove that to you."

Isla thanked Bailey for her earnest and very good proposal, and then turned her down firmly. Not this year. Maybe next.

But she didn't stop thinking about it across the rest of the morning, and some of the things Bailey had suggested niggled at her, sharp and pointy, because they were things Isla leaned on Adam for, and other things she wanted to do but knew she didn't have time for.

She wanted to talk about it out loud, but when she got home, Stevie was visiting, and ended up staying for the whole afternoon. She went upstairs to Adam's room for that nap, and when she woke up again, it was dark, dinner was on the table, and they had acquired a couple more guests as well.

Talking out her business plans with her husband would have to wait.

CHAPTER TWENTY

THE COLD SNAP roared in late Monday night, long after they were asleep. They'd gone to bed early—in bed by eight, mutual orgasms by nine, and lights out at nine-forty-five, snuggled in together in Adam's room—and when they woke up just before five, the temperature had dropped significantly.

Adam was thrilled when Isla agreed it was too cold to walk the five blocks to the bakery.

She still protested that it took longer for her car to warm up than it did to drive there, but at least she wasn't exposed to the biting wind at five-thirty in the morning for longer than she needed to be.

By mid-day, the weather had worsened.

Adam: Text me when you get home.

Isla: I'm already cozy under a blanket, working on my business plan for Q1. I forgot to tell you Bailey Patel had an interesting idea.

Adam: I'll call you after our training meeting this afternoon.

But he didn't get a chance to call her, because there were two calls back to back before dinner, a car accident that needed fire support and then a carbon monoxide alarm that wouldn't stop going off in one of Pine Harbour's few low-slung apartment buildings.

"Shitty evening to need to evacuate," Richard said.

It was the first thing they'd agreed on in days. Adam silently nodded. The volunteer fire brigade was called out to manage the residents, who were temporarily sheltered in the United Church basement. By the time they had cleared every apartment, it was nearly ten at night.

Adam didn't even try to call Isla, he didn't want to risk waking her up if she was already asleep.

None of them felt like cooking when they got back, so they all fended for whatever leftovers were easiest to grab. Then Richard and Stan took the recliners, Denise crashed on the couch, and Adam headed downstairs in search of his brother because Owen was working the night shift.

He'd just hit the bottom of the stairs when the alarm sounded. Busy night, he thought as he headed to the garage. Shoes off, step into the boots. Pants up, suspenders over his shoulder. He turned up the radio strapped across his chest, then pulled on his protective hood, then his coat.

By the time he was dressed, the others were in their positions, too. Richard vaulted into the driver seat, no sign of the tired old man who'd wanted to rack out on the recliner just ten minutes earlier.

For all the grief his team gave him, Adam had to acknowledge they were relentlessly professional when it mattered.

And when Richard pulled into the frigid night and asked dispatch for the address, Adam was damn glad for that professionalism.

"Pumper 2, this is a retail location. 139 Main Street. General alarm sounding inside a store. Name of the store is Bake Sale. I repeat, 139—"

Adam's blood ran cold. He shot a quick look at Denise, who nodded back at him, then hit her radio button. "Dispatch, this is Pumper 2's team lead. One of our firefighters is married to the owner of that building. We may need additional support. ETA in—"

She paused and Richard cut in. "Ninety seconds."

"Understood, Pumper 2."

The longest ninety seconds of Adam's life. It was a general alarm, triggered by the updated system he'd installed for Isla when she bought the place. It could be nothing, but if it wasn't, she would be devastated.

He would be, too.

Riding backwards in the truck, he couldn't see the store as they approached, but as soon as Richard stopped, Stan was on the ground. "I'll circle around to the back."

Denise nodded, then approached the front door. "Dispatch, this is Pumper 2. We've arrived on site at 139 Main. No signs visible, can you relay more details?"

Adam held himself back from racing through the front door, knowing there was a procedure to follow and the best way to help Isla would be to follow it.

And he was damn glad his brother was on the radio frequency, too.

"Pumper 2, EMT supervisor is en route to the store owner's residence and will notify, provide transport. Over."

"Roger." Denise nodded at Adam. "Owen's on it."

From the back of the building, Stan checked in. "No sign of smoke or heat. Possible false alarm. Should we wait for the owner?"

Denise looked at Adam. "Your call."

"Wait," he said without hesitation.

It was the right call, he knew, but he still watched the storefront intently for any sign of fire for the five minutes it took for Owen's supervisor vehicle to pull up, lights on.

Isla scrambled out of the passenger seat and ran to Adam, who led her to Denise at the front door.

"I'll open up, then we'll take a look. If it's safe for you to enter, Adam will let you in." Denise unlocked, then stepped inside.

Adam's role was often this point of scene control at the front of a call, but it flexed differently when it was his wife he was holding back. She looked sleep-rumpled and terrified, but at a first glance inside, the store looked fine.

First glances were often wrong.

"All right, send her in," Denise called out.

As soon as Isla stepped into the kitchen, a string of swear words rip out of her mouth.

"Dispatch this is Pumper 2. Broken water pipe has flooded the back of the retail location and shorted out the electrical panel. We'll need…"

Adam listened to the rest of the report, then Stan returned from the back of the store. "I've got this if you want to go in."

He didn't need to be told twice. Owen followed him inside, and Isla met them at the front counter. Her eyes were big, her face taut. "So the fridge and freezer are both out. The panel may need to be replaced, and it will take at least a day?" She glanced behind her to Denise. "Right?"

The senior firefighter nodded. "I'd say. We'll get the inspector here in a few hours and know better then. I've opened the back door to let the water pour out. Do you have a mop you can use to clear a path to the fridge?"

"Yeah." Isla disappeared again, muttering a string of

filth under her breath that would make any army guy proud.

Adam repeated Isla's most colourful curse as he looked at Owen. At least they had the alarm. This way she knew about the fridge and freezer tonight, and it wasn't a sad, soggy discovery in the morning. He pointed to his brother, who already had his phone out. "We need to find her twenty, maybe thirty cubic feet of freezer space. See who has room in their deep freeze. She tends to keep things in boxes, so if people could make room for a few..." He did the mental math. "Twelve by twelve by eighteen-inch boxes? That's the size she usually has."

"On it."

"Maybe we need ten people who could take two of those. Or five people who could take four. That would be better."

"Got it."

"And—"

Owen said his name, cutting him off. "I hear you. We'll help her."

"Thanks."

———

"What a mess." Catie was the third person to arrive at the bakery and state the absolute obvious, but Isla just took a deep breath and nodded. It hadn't seemed so bad when she'd first stepped into the back, but now that the foot of water by the back door had drained out, and battery-powered lights had been hung up, it was clear there was a lot of damage to the walls.

The kitchen would need work before a health and safety inspector would allow her to prepare food in it. But that was getting way ahead of herself, because she had a frozen-food brigade to supervise first.

It was midnight, and help kept rolling in.

"Have you taken video yet for insurance?"

Isla shook her head, and Catie pulled out her phone. "I can do that."

"Can you use my phone?" Isla cast her attention around. "It's…"

Adam appeared at her shoulder. He'd taken off his coat and helmet. "Here."

"Thanks." She passed it to Catie, but her attention stayed on Adam. "This is a huge drama, isn't it?"

He squeezed her shoulder. "That's not a problem."

"I don't want—" The back door swung open, bringing with it an unwelcome gust of icy air.

"We're ready," Owen said.

Adam's brother had been nothing but professional to her the entire time, but she wasn't sure she agreed with Adam's assessment that this massive drain on her new town was *not a problem*. It seemed like a major inconvenience, and Isla was just waiting for someone to snap at her. She really didn't want it to be Owen. "Great, thank you." She rushed over to the freezer, nearly slipping on a new slick of water that had come from somewhere. "I'll pass the boxes out. They're all clearly labelled."

Adam stopped her. "I can do this."

"It's— I—" She swallowed around a razor blade in her throat.

"Let's work together." He held out his hands and gave her a warm look. As long as he was right by her side, she was fine. This would be…they'd be quick, and everyone could get to bed soon.

When she slipped again, Adam firmly asked her in his

best firefighter voice to move away from the freezer, so she swapped spots in the chain with Owen.

That was when she realized just how many people had turned up, winter gear from head to toe, to take her supplies to their home freezers.

Owen's wife Kerry. Olivia Minelli, whose car was running because she had a sleeping baby inside it. "We were up anyway," she said cheerfully. "Teething. I saw the text and was grateful for the excuse to go for a drive. Rafe will help me unload the boxes at home. We've got you, Isla."

Jake Foster and Tom Minelli both had trucks, and Tom took a double amount of boxes because there was extra space in the freezer at the park office, too.

Catie joined the line of people accepting boxes, too, and tucked Isla's phone into her coat pocket. "I took some video of the sexy firefighter unloading your freezer, too. For the Insta."

Isla's laugh had a tinge of hysteria in it. When would she remember to post that? She'd have to try to make light of this. Spin it somehow. Not tonight, though. Her little Instagram account was the least important thing to her right now, although it was thoughtful of her friend to think of that.

She ducked inside to grab the next box from Owen, and ran straight into Josh and Will.

"All hands on deck," the school principal said. "What can we do?"

CHAPTER TWENTY-ONE

BY THE TIME dawn rolled around, everyone had cleared out. Isla wasn't allowed to turn the power or water back on for forty-eight hours and then another inspection, but she didn't want to leave her bakery.

Owen offered to drive her home, but she decided to wait until Adam was done with his shift. She sat down at the table under the window and listened to the hum of the electric heater in the kitchen, and the faint growl of the loaned generator powering it from just outside the back door.

As far as catastrophes went, this was a manageable one. She hadn't expected to make an insurance claim so soon after opening, but shit happened, and nothing had been so badly damaged that she wouldn't be able to re-open in a week. Adam's offer of securing a line of credit crawled around at the back of her mind, a gremlin she couldn't quite evict no matter how hard she tried not to think about it.

She wanted to find her own way through this. She needed to know she could do it on her own. But there was now a hollow hole in the middle of her chest where certainty and security had started to take up residence. Once upon a time, stressful events hadn't been a problem for her. She'd done four tours overseas and sailed through all of them without any mental health issues.

One awful marriage later, and she felt fragile as fuck over a bit of water damage.

She'd started to think the one very happy marriage— deliberately constructed to protect her!—would counter-balance the toxic past, but here she sat feeling shattered, so apparently it wasn't that easy.

A knock at the front door startled her out of her thoughts. She got up, prepared to apologize for not being open, but on the other side of the glass she saw Bailey Patel, who looked sympathetic enough that Isla had no need to provide explanation.

Apparently, word was spreading.

She opened the door and stepped back. "You heard?"

"I think everyone already awake in Pine Harbour has heard," Bailey said regretfully. "Catie said you were waiting here for Adam. I thought I'd see if you needed any help. I heard about the freezer brigade last night, that's great. But if you need help on the business side of things..."

"I can't think about your proposal right now, I'm sorry."

"No, of course not." Bailey glanced around. "Can I speak freely?"

Isla laughed weakly. "Sure."

"My parents have built a solid business they would love to hand over to me some day soon. I have all the work I could ever need with them. They want to send me to a fancy business school, for the prestige more than anything, although I'm sure I'd learn a few things. Bluntly, I'm not poking around in your business because I need to make money. I know we don't know each other, but I've been following you on Instagram since the first time I came in here, and there's something special about this shop. *You* are special."

Tears welled in Isla's eyes, much to her horror. "Oh."

"Shit, did I say the wrong thing?"

"No." Isla swiped furiously at her face. "I think you might be the only person in town who notices my Instagram account, though. You and Adam, anyway. Last night Catie took some video for me to post and I just…can't…" She threw herself back into the chair, tipped her head back so she was staring at the ceiling, and she howled in frustration. Then she swore a blue streak.

When she righted her head, Bailey was sitting across from her. "Feel better?"

"Hardly." She paused. "A little. Yes."

"What needs to happen?"

"Insurance claim. A plan to re-open. A plan to make that re-open profitable enough to cover the days we're closed, and a new budget plan to cover the fact that my insurance premiums will go up."

A plan to not have to lean on her husband.

"What are the first steps?"

"I see what you're doing."

Bailey gave her an innocent look. "What am I doing?"

She was helping, and Isla was being suspicious for no good reason. She cocked her head to the side. "You really want to help me talk out my next steps?"

"Yep."

"I'll be right back." Her joints protested as she slowly got up and walked back to her office. A few boxes on the floor had been damaged, but everything on the desk survived. She grabbed her clipboard, a couple of sheets of blank paper, and a pen.

Time to make a to-do list.

When she returned, another person was at the door. Catie waved, and Bailey got up to answer it this time.

Catie had three takeaway coffee cups in a paper tray, and Isla pointed her finger back and forth between the two of them. "This is starting to feel organized."

Instead of answering, Catie shoved a cup of coffee in her hand. "Decaf, so you can sleep in a bit. I come bearing a message from Frank."

Isla groaned. "It's pie day. I forgot all about it."

Her friend gave her a funny look. "Well, yeah. But he doesn't care about that. If he doesn't have any pie, he just tells people to eat more fries. He wants you to know you can use his kitchen if you have any urgent baking to do."

"His pies are the only external order I have." Isla took a long, restorative inhale, breathing in the perfect scent of diner coffee. "But I should probably think about taking him up on it, if only to make stuff to sell at the farmer's market this weekend. If I can get a—"

"You can," Bailey interjected. "I know, you didn't want to think about the plan until next year, but I'd done my preliminary research anyway. They haven't been booking all the tables out over the winter, you've got a spot there if you need it."

Isla glanced at Catie. "Did you know about her scheme?"

"Only in the broadest of strokes."

"Is that how the two of you wound up here at six in the morning?"

"Who can sleep with all this excitement? We'd much rather be here so you can tell us all about your next steps."

"It's really boring." Isla stopped, hearing herself. Bailey was angling for a job, so her interest was at least related to that. But Catie had been here most of the night, and had a business of her own to open in a few hours. The only reason she would have come back with coffee, the only reason she would have reached out to Bailey and made all of this happen, was out of friendship. "You're really interested, too?"

Catie pulled up a chair. "You know, I really hope your ex wanders back into town at some point so I can punch him in the face for whatever he taught you about asking people in your life for things. Or just, you know, talking shit out. Yes, I'm here to just listen to you talk about whatever you want to talk about. That's what friends do."

Isla squished up her face, forcing hot tears to stay the hell back. She had work to do. "We're brainstorming how to take over the world, isn't that right, Bailey?"

"It sure is."

They were still working when Adam arrived an hour and a half later.

He looked sweaty, dishevelled, and tired. He also looked so good it made Isla's chest ache, which only reminded her that every part of her body hurt.

"I'm not interrupting anything, am I?" he asked as he stepped inside.

Catie and Bailey immediately stood up, put on their parkas, grabbed their coffees, and made their goodbyes.

"I'm ready to go home," Isla said, leaning into Adam's warmth.

"Hot shower and bed for us both," he murmured into her hair. "Together."

On the short drive, she told him about leaning on Bailey. "And then Catie showed up, just to listen, and I felt really stupid for questioning them."

"It's not a sign of weakness to ask for help," Adam said. "Owen reminded me of that, and it's true. Sometimes it's really hard—which makes it a sign of strength."

"I'm scared of relying on others."

"You've been hurt before. That makes sense." He squeezed her hand through her gloves. "But you're one of us now. And Pine Harbour loves nothing more than an opportunity to pitch in and help one of our own."

"I'm trying to be soft and open to that."

He winked at her. "I'd like to help you in the shower, for example. Can you be soft and open there, too?"

Heat swirled through her belly at the downright filthy way he said *soft* and *open*. She nodded wordlessly as he pulled into the driveway. She sure could.

Whatever he wanted, however he wanted it.

———

The next four days were an emotional rollercoaster on steroids, but at every turn, Adam and her new friends and even the broader community were there for moral support. She went to Mac's to bake Frank some pies, and in the three hours she was in his kitchen in the lull between lunch and dinner, no fewer than fifteen people stopped to say hi through the pass-through window. When she left, the waitress gave her a mason jar stuffed with cash—a spontaneous collection from diners.

"I don't need this," Isla whispered, her throat tight.

"Oh, honey. We all need a pick-me-up, and nobody else is currently dealing with what I'm sure is quite the paperwork nightmare. Buy yourself something pretty with it."

She went straight to Catie's salon.

"It's been months since I've done anything other than pull it back into a bun or a ponytail," she said when it was her turn in the chair.

"Do you want to add any colour or highlights?"

Isla looked at the reflection of a very tired woman in the mirror. "Maybe something around the face?"

"Bold or subtle?"

That was easy. "Let's go big. It's time for a change."

Two hours later, she headed home with a shorter set of waves, perfectly cropped just above her shoulders, and a thick shock of pale blond sweeping over her eyes. She couldn't wait to try out a really smoky eye look with it, maybe pale pink lip gloss. If she squinted in the right light, she might look like Charlize Theron, and that would be a fun surprise for Adam. He was at work for the first time since the bakery flooded, but maybe she could swing by with some takeout from Mac's.

Just to say hi.

Just to show off her new do.

Just to see him.

That was the most honest answer. She was so consumed with her plan, she almost missed noticing that the mailbox at the end of their lane had its flag up, indicating new mail. Backtracking, she opened the door on the box. Inside was a single letter.

She grabbed it, put down the flag, then continued to the house, her thoughts still consumed with the idea of surprising Adam at work. Maybe she should call him first, make sure he wasn't busy. But would it be weird to make up a reason to drop by, when she really just wanted it to be a sweet, short surprise? *Look at me, I'm pretty!*

Once inside, she dropped the letter on the coffee table, then headed to her bedroom. She got halfway down the hall before something dragged her back, something awful and gross, something she had recognized about the letter but not really processed.

The letter wasn't postmarked.

It was addressed to Adam, but it wasn't postmarked, and as soon as she took a second look at it, she recognized the handwriting. Adam's name and their address was written in her ex-husband's sharp, angular pen.

There was no return address, no external proof she was right about who had written it, but she dropped the envelope like it burned her skin.

He had been here, again. In her town, on her property.

And he'd written *Adam* a letter? This was his new game?

He'd found a new way to get under her skin, even after she had blocked him. He needed to leave her alone, and he really needed to leave Adam alone.

Part of her was terrified to see what was inside the envelope. Another part of her did not care. *It's not up to you*, she reminded herself.

She could destroy it. Adam would never need to know. But what if Brett sent another one? What if he somehow found Adam's phone number, or worse, called the fire department looking for him?

Pretending this hadn't happened wasn't an option.

She called Adam.

"I'm sorry to bother you at work." Her voice shook, and she counted slowly in her head to try and stay calm as Adam excused himself from his co-workers.

"It's fine," he said when he found a quiet corner. "Do you need something?"

"Brett was here. He left a letter in the mailbox. It doesn't have a stamp on it, so it was delivered in person."

"What did it say?"

"It's not addressed to me. I'm sure it's his handwriting, though. It's…he wrote it to you."

"Do you want to open it?"

"I don't want to touch it." Even though Adam couldn't see her, she took another step back from where the envelope lay on the floor. "I thought about destroying it, but whatever he wants, he could escalate this and contact you at work."

Adam swore.

She swallowed hard. "At what point does it cross the line to stalking? This is unwanted attention, right? I want him to leave us alone."

"I'm going to come home. Hold tight, okay? I'll be right there. And if he shows up in the next five minutes, call 911."

"I don't need—"

"Maybe I need to see you," he said urgently. "I'll drive one of the station vehicles so I've got a radio and a siren. It's okay."

The next ten minutes crawled by as Isla paced back and forth in the living room, watching the laneway through the window. Hot, wild relief flooded over her as soon as the red support SUV pulled in.

Adam jogged up to the porch, burst through the door, and came to a sudden halt as she stepped into the foyer.

"Hey, your hair." He grinned widely and touched the swoop over her eyes. "This is new. You look great. Wow, I like it."

"Thanks." She heard the wobble in her voice and *hated* it. "I was going to put on makeup and all that jazz, but then this happened."

"You're beautiful." He raked his gaze over her hair once more, then cupped her face in his hands and kissed her. "Okay, show me this letter."

She pointed to where it still lay on the floor.

"You really weren't kidding about not wanting to touch it." Adam picked it up and turned it over. "You're sure it's his handwriting?"

"Yes."

He nodded tightly, his jaw like granite. "All right." He ripped into the envelope, then extracted a single piece of paper. It didn't take him long to read it. His expression didn't change as he glanced it over again, then folded it up. "Well, that's bullshit. I don't know if this crosses a legal line, but I think it's worth reporting to the OPP."

Her stomach sank. "What does it say?"

He shook his head. "It doesn't matter. None of it is true."

She pressed her hand to her chest, like that might actually keep her heart intact, but it had been fractured for a long time already. "None of what? What does he say?"

"Lies. He wrote a bunch of lies about you, to try and wound you and to get a rise out of me. Don't ask me to show you. I don't want to be a part of the pain he causes you."

His radio squawked and he turned it down.

"Do you have to…"

He shook his head. "That wasn't for me."

"I don't know what he wants. I dodged his calls for a while, and then he showed up, and I really thought that was the end of it."

Adam crossed to the couch and sat down. He looked ferocious and oversized in his firefighting pants and boots. Isla crawled onto the cushion next to him and leaned her face against the back of the sofa.

"I'm sorry," she whispered.

He jerked back. "You have nothing to apologize for."

"I…" She trailed off. "No, I guess I don't. But I *feel* sorry. I feel like this is all my fault."

"Any chance that comes from him?"

She laughed hollowly. "Every chance, yeah."

"What did he do to you?" Adam leaned back in and stroked her cheek.

She puffed out her cheeks. "In hindsight? A lot of gaslighting. Manipulation. Belitting. Nothing I did was ever good enough, and everything I did was criticized. His expectations…Whew. They were a lot."

"What did he expect of you?"

"Nothing I could ever deliver." The words sounded hollow and insufficient, but the truth was barbed, heavy, and ugly. She'd buried it deep.

"Whatever it is," Adam said with a firm intensity that quieted the worst of the voices in her head. "I don't expect that of you. Whatever he wanted, I don't want that. Tell me, and I won't make the same mistake."

"You've never…" She trailed off, because her voice was shaking, and she wouldn't let fear dominate her. Swallowing hard, she pressed her hands firmly to her thighs, grounding herself, and tried again. "It's ironic that I did this today." She gestured at her hair. "I was never sexy enough. He wanted me to always wear makeup, as in, get dolled up after work, when I just wanted to put on jammies and veg on the couch. But not just be pretty."

She could feel that she had all of Adam's attention, and

for the first time, the door on the lock box deep inside her swung open.

"He expected me to be seductive, instantly responsive. He didn't want a wife, he wanted a sex doll. If I wasn't in the mood, he would get mad."

"How mad?" Two quiet words. But they reverberated with furious anger, none of it directed at her. Adam managed to keep his face gentle even as his voice sounded like he could rampage when he got outside.

"He never hit me. I told myself if he did, I would leave."

"And he crossed the line one day?"

She gasped, that Adam thought her that brave. "No." Her voice cracked as she admitted her biggest shame. "He left me. I didn't leave him. I found out he was having an affair, that it wasn't his first one, and instead of feeling shame or regret, he was annoyed that I made it a big drama. He moved out."

Adam growled an apology and tugged her in for a hug. "I'll never do any of that."

"I know."

"You didn't deserve any of that. You deserved so much more." He kissed her hair. "I'm going to talk to a cop I know. He's never going to bother you again."

"Should I have talked to him?" She winced at the idea. "He cut me out of his life completely for more than a year. I just assumed that he was being needy because I'd moved on."

"That's probably exactly why he reappeared. That he moved across the province to be closer to you, though… that's suspect. And now this? He's trying to control you."

"You're right." She hugged Adam tight. "Thank you. You're the best."

In an alternate lifetime, maybe she would have fallen for Adam when they first met, and avoided all this heartache. It was hard for her to look back at the last five years and realize that the man she had loved so much had only barely tolerated her adoration. The memory of it had blurred and faded, but was still enough to make her stomach roil. Because she'd accepted that imbalance.

Never again.

The friendship she had with Adam was as far as she would ever let herself feel for a man. Even one who actually liked her, and made her feel sexy, and thought a new haircut was a really big deal.

CHAPTER TWENTY-TWO

AFTER ENSURING Isla was okay on her own—with the doors locked, and her having a plan to sleep securely tucked into his bed upstairs—Adam went back to work.

"Personal issue dealt with?" Richard asked when Adam walked back into the upstairs kitchen at the station.

"Yep."

"Good."

Adam's phone vibrated. He glanced at it. It was a text back from Rafe Minelli.

> **Rafe: I'm around tonight. You want me to come to the station?**
> **Adam: Yeah, if you don't mind.**
> **Rafe: Can it wait until after I put my kids to bed?**
> **Adam: Sure thing. Thanks. I want to keep this quiet.**

Richard watched him the whole time, but didn't ask again.

The letter burned in Adam's pocket. He was grateful

they had a patient transfer callout shortly after he got back. It gave him something else to focus on until the dinner hour passed. At seven, his brother showed up for a night shift, and Owen must have smelled something in the air—did freaked-out younger brother have a specific scent?—because the first thing he did when he entered the building was come upstairs.

"Everything okay?"

He asked it in front of Adam's team, which made Adam count to ten in his head before grabbing his brother's arm and pulling him down the hall to the quiet room. "Who told you?"

Owen gave up the snitch immediately. "Richard."

"What the fuck?" Adam made a fist and bounced it lightly off the wall.

"He said you had to go home and deal with something. Wanted to make sure I knew."

"Why?"

"Because you don't share shit!"

"They're called boundaries!" And in this case, it wasn't even his own privacy he was protecting. "I'll come and find you if I need you. Until then, eyes on your own paper."

"All right."

"And don't interfere when I go back out there and tell Richard to keep team shit to himself, either."

Owen raised his hands. "Far be it from me to get between you and Richard if you want to give him an excuse to kick your ass."

"He could never."

"Not physically." Owen propped his hands on his hips. "A few years ago, maybe when you were overseas, there was a guy here who wasn't a great fit on the team. Turned out, he had some shit going on at home. Ended up getting let go, and it was messy. I'd put good money on Richard being worried about you *for your own good*, and if you go beaking off to him to mind his own business, you'll get a lesson in what happens when a team turns a blind eye to trouble. I've seen it myself in paramedics, too. PTSD—"

"It's not that." Adam scraped his hand along his jaw. "Fuck, sorry. I take that shit seriously, too. It's Isla's ex-husband. He's stuck back into her, and he dropped off a letter at the house today—addressed to me, but designed to get to her. It was full of lies about her, shit that makes him sound obsessed, to be honest. I don't like it. I've already put a call in to Rafe. We'll handle it." He gestured in the direction of the kitchen. "I don't want them to know, because it's not about *me*."

Owen's face darkened with every word. "Where is he?"

"I'm going to let Rafe find the answer to that question." Adam swallowed hard. "He's in the Forces. A major, attached to the base in Meaford now."

"Quite the coincidence. Didn't they live in Pet before?" Eight hours away.

Adam nodded. "Yep."

"Fuck. I'm sorry for her. Where is she now?"

"At home. She's okay. She'll call 911 at the first sign of a problem, and I'm hoping Rafe can locate him for me before she goes to sleep tonight. At least she doesn't need to open the bakery early tomorrow."

Owen's radio burst to life on his chest, and they both paused so he could listen to the call. Then he pulled open the door. "Keep me posted," he growled. "And sorry about the rest of it."

In the grand scheme of everything, the small town lack

of privacy was Adam's least concern right now. "Yeah. Thanks."

Then it was his radio that went off, Dispatch sending them as backup to a motor vehicle accident.

When they returned to the station, Rafe Minelli was waiting for him. "Is there a place we can talk?"

Adam turned to his team to explain *something*, but Richard waved him off. "Go. We'll clean up the truck."

The winter slush and road salt made that a harder task than in the summer, and as the rookie it was often Adam's job. "I can—"

"We got this," Denise said firmly. She caught his attention and held it. Then she nodded. "Go."

He led Rafe upstairs to the quiet room, then pulled out the letter. But he didn't hand it over right away. "First of all, I need you to know that what is in this letter is not true. I'm willing to answer any questions you have about it, but Isla did not read it, and I would prefer that she never know what her ex wrote in it. It's meant to hurt her, and I would do anything to avoid that pain."

"That's understandable." Rafe frowns. "What does he say?"

"It's full of accusations about Isla, none of which align with who she really is." *She was your commanding officer. She's had inappropriate affairs with others.* That one had to be projection. *You must have been on her radar for a long time.* If only. Their lives might have been very different if Isla had looked at him as anything other than someone in her command. On the other hand, she wouldn't be Isla Petersen if she had, so that wasn't even an option. "It reads like he's stuck in time, two years ago, like they just broke up. She had to provide her divorce certificate for us to get married, Rafe. It's been over for a long time. He's unhinged."

He handed the letter over and waited while Rafe read it. As the cop turned to the second page, his eyebrows hit the roof. He looked up. *"You're co-conspirators who will be outed?"*

Adam hated that the idiot had included that line. Nothing else in the letter referred to the bakery, and he was pretty confident Jackson had no proof of it, but he didn't want to have to explain it to Rafe, either. The less said on that topic, the better. "Unhinged," he repeated. "But I'm happy to go on the record about my relationship with Isla. We never had an affair when she was my officer."

"Just to be clear, when did your relationship start?"

"In the summer. I ran into her at a market, we had a couple of dates, and then our relationship continued long distance when I moved home to start this job. She came to visit, fell in love with your mother's cafe, and we decided to get married." The truth was an exceptionally good cover story.

"And you're not..." Rafe rolled his eyes as he read another line from the letter. *"Two frauds faking a relationship?"*

Adam doubled down on the truth. "There's nothing fake about my marriage. Look, we're private people. I hope you can appreciate that, but between us, when Isla bounded back into my life, it was...profound. An old friend who I suddenly saw through a new and different lens. He is clearly obsessed with the choices she has made since their divorce, and cannot process them in an appropriate way. I know you'll want to talk to Isla, too. And at the end of the day, this is her decision to make, not mine. I'm just trying to lighten the load for her, figure out what her next steps could be so she can take them without having to jump over the hurdle of figuring out what her options *are*. But more than anything, I just want to protect her."

"That makes sense. You love your wife." Rafe gave him a sympathetic smile, not knowing his words sliced through Adam's chest.

He cared for Isla more than he ever imagined. Their bond was special. How much worse would it be if they were in love? How different would it be if she had a real marriage?

He shoved both questions away. "He came to the bakery, and then to our house. Two separate occasions, and he doesn't live nearby. He doesn't seem to have a clear reason for making contact, and this letter to me…"

"It's disturbing."

"Yes."

It was written like a warning to Adam, that he didn't know who he had married. It listed what would happen in his marriage, and the way Adam read it, it was a twisted re-telling of what *had* happened, with Isla being cast in the role of the villain in Brett Jackson's mind.

She will drive you away and make you doubt yourself as a man. What fucking nonsense. But also, potentially danger-ous. "Can he be charged with stalking her? Can we get a restraining order?"

"Those are two separate questions. I don't know if we can charge him, that will require an investigation. A restraining order is separate. That's done through Family Court, and they'll want to see compelling evidence. That could come up during our investigation, if she doesn't already have it collected."

"He hasn't threatened her." Not yet. Not explicitly.

"I can have a talk with him. Suggest it would be in his best interest to steer clear of her. Sometimes that's sufficient."

"Any chance I could ask you to help me figure out where he is tonight? He claims to live in Owen Sound. I don't like the idea of Isla being at home alone tonight while I'm here, but she doesn't want me to overreact, either."

"Tell you what; I'll find out what vehicles he has registered, and can make sure the detachment is aware of them. For tonight, we can try to get some eyes on a license plate, make sure it's in front of his house and not yours. And then tomorrow I'll go pay him a visit in uniform."

"Thanks."

Rafe handed the letter back. "Hang on to that. I may want to take a copy of it for the file."

———

Isla didn't sleep a wink that night, not even after Adam called and told her Olivia's husband had looked into Brett's whereabouts. Her phone was gripped tight in her hand when she woke at dawn, to a text message from her husband.

Adam: Coming home. Don't want to scare you when I unlocked the door.

Fuck. She hated that Brett had gotten into her head like this. Since she was awake, she got up and made some French toast with a leftover loaf of brioche she'd tested two days earlier.

When she heard the door, she went to the hallway and met Adam in the foyer. He caught her tight, his arms strong, but she didn't think she imagined that they both trembled for a second before exhaling as one.

He tangled his hands in her hair as he kissed her, then rubbed them down her back. "How'd you sleep?"

"You know. Shitty. But it's morning now." She pressed her mouth to his. Not quite a kiss. More than a kiss. "I'm glad you're home."

"Me, too."

"I cooked."

He squeezed her tight and ushered her back to the kitchen. "I was thinking we could tackle this room next? For renovations?" He kissed her temple as she tried to plate up the French toast. "What would your dream kitchen look like? Dream kitchen on a fireman's budget, of course."

Her breath caught in her throat.

He turned her in his arms, then cupped her chin in his hand, lifting her face. "I'm serious."

"That's...whatever..." She glanced up at the hole in the ceiling he'd patched before she moved in. "I love this house. Whatever you want is wonderful."

"I want a kitchen you can bake in. If we had that, maybe you wouldn't need to go to Mac's this week."

"I can't sell food I make in our kitchen," she muttered, but she was smiling. It was a thoughtful idea.

"More for me, then."

She pushed him gently out of the way and plated up the food. Then, as they ate, she let him draw her into a real conversation about what they might want.

An island, for sure. A butcher block top would be cheaper than stone. Extra deep counters, too. And lots of drawers instead of cupboards. "I'm not picky about the cabinet finish or anything like that. Just lots of rolling and prep space."

"Then I know what I'm going to do with my vacation time in the new year." Adam yawned. "And now, bed. Want to join me?"

"I'm meeting Jake Foster at the bakery at nine," she said regretfully. "I'm hoping we can get the floor and walls repaired quickly."

"You want me to come with?"

"You just said you wanted to go to bed."

"That was before I knew there was renovation talk happening."

"The man is a professional. I'm going to give him keys to the bakery and then stay out of his way, and I want you to do the same." She gave him a slow, lingering kiss. "And then I'll crawl back into bed with you, so when you wake up…"

"Yeah?"

"Yeah."

The satisfied, rumbling groan he let out was almost enough to make her forget the drama of the night before. But as soon as she was outside, she felt exposed all over again. She burrowed deeper into her parka and hurried to her car. She wasn't going to walk, not today.

At the bakery, she let herself in and held her breath as she checked the kitchen and the front of shop, but everything was as it should be.

Five minutes later, the local contractor arrived, and she gave him the paperwork she'd received from the insurance company. They would pay the hardware store directly for materials, and Jake was happy to bill them for his labour and miscellaneous supplies he already had as well. "We can get this kitchen back up and running in three days," he promised. "Can I start today?"

"Absolutely." She let out a painful breath. "Oh, wow. I was worried you might not have time before Christmas and Adam would want to try and do this ourselves, and he's capable, but..." She was babbling. She stopped and nodded. "Thank you so much."

"My pleasure." He leaned in. "My wife is eager for you to be back in business."

"Tell her I'll be at the farmer's market this weekend," she said. "And if you don't mind me making some things at home, I can drop whatever she wants on your porch."

"Butter tarts?"

"Consider it done."

He grinned. "I'll be back in two hours to get started."

After he left, Isla texted Bailey with the update. As she was turning off the lights in the kitchen, a knock sounded at the front door.

Carefully, cautiously, she moved to a position where she could see who it was while still staying in the shadows.

It wasn't her ex.

It was Rafe Minelli, in uniform.

Isla hadn't met Olivia's husband properly, but she had heard good things from Catie and from Adam, who trusted him. She hurried forward and unlocked the door, letting him step inside.

"Isla?"

She nodded.

He introduced himself, which wasn't necessary. He explained in broad strokes the conversation that he'd had with Adam the night before, and she nodded along. "He told me you talked. Thank you."

Rafe hesitated. Then he pulled a familiar-looking envelope from an inner pocket in his parka.

Isla frowned. "Did Adam give that to you?"

"No." Rafe's mouth tightened, and the bottom of Isla's stomach dropped. "This letter was left at my mother's house yesterday."

"Oh my God." Isla's knees threatened to buckle. Anne Minelli knew. Brett told her that her marriage was a lie, a fraud so she could steal this bakery from the other woman, and… She stumbled backwards, and Rafe followed.

Officer Minelli.

Fuck.

Isla found a chair through dumb luck and sank onto it. The OPP officer reached for another chair. "May I?"

"Sure." They might as well be comfortable while she faced the music.

"The thing is, Ms. Petersen… My mother is out of the country. Most people don't know that, because my parents aren't big fans of anyone knowing their business." A faint smile teased at his mouth. "They're in Italy, visiting my father's family, and won't be home until Christmas. My sister found this letter this morning."

His sister. Dani, wife of the contractor who was just here. What were the chances she would still want Isla's butter tarts? "Did she read it?"

"Yep. And then she called me. Thought I should read it, too. The charges in it are…significant. Do you have any idea what it might say?"

She didn't want to answer that question. "Yes," she whispered.

Mortified, afraid, and beneath all of that, filled with a profound guilt that she'd brought this one. What had she done to show their hand to Brett? His repeated phone calls, his appearance in the shop, the way he'd crept around town dropping letters full of lies…all of it replayed in her mind in jagged, awful chunks.

"I'd like to hear about it from your perspective," he said. "If you don't mind."

"I—" Isla wanted to tell him everything. But would doing that implicate Adam in a crime? Was getting married so she could buy the bakery something he could actually get in trouble for? "I—" She couldn't do it. "I probably need an attorney," she finally said. She dropped her gaze to the floor. Oh, how the mighty had fallen. From being an officer in the military to a person of interest in the most petty of small town crimes.

Across from her, the big black boots shifted on the hardwood floor, the uniformed legs they were attached to moving forward. She lifted her head enough to see he was leaning his elbows on his legs now, trying to make eye contact with her.

She didn't want that. She didn't want that *at all*.

The letter came into view in his outstretched hand. "Do you want to read it?"

"I'd rather not," she muttered.

"You know what my sister said when she called me about this? She said, and I quote, 'Someone really has it out for the new baker in town. Someone who is not well.' And I knew immediately what she was talking about, because I'd already read one of his letters. The one he wrote Adam."

"I didn't read that one, either."

"Adam doesn't want you to."

She jerked her head up. "Oh?"

The officer's face was soft and full of kindness. *Maybe it's a trap.* "Your ex-husband says a lot of nonsense in both letters, but none of it is anything you need to be sorry for." He glanced around. "I like what you've done with the place, by the way."

"Is this some kind of entrapment? A sting?" She laughed weakly. "And now who sounds like she's not well?"

"You've been put through a lot by someone who you thought was firmly in your past." Rafe shrugged. "You're entitled to a bit of a meltdown. Have at it. This is no sting, I promise you that."

"He thinks he knows some things about me. About my relationship with Adam." The words soured on her tongue. "Whatever he thinks, it's not exactly true. But you should know, because it might come out some other way, that it's not entirely *not* true, either."

"What are you saying?"

She took a deep breath. Fuck it. She wasn't going to lie to Anne's son, not while she stood in her former cafe. "When Adam and I got married, it was in part so I could buy this cafe from your mother for a dollar. That was a factor. I can't deny it, and if Brett is going to expose that, I'd rather it come from me. But Adam—you need to know—"

Rafe grinned. "Look, there's no question in the minds of anyone in town about how your husband feels about you. I promise you, anyone who claims otherwise will get laughed out of the village."

Isla said a small prayer of thanks that Adam was so good at playing the doting husband. "Right. Exactly."

"The only question remains, what do you want done about your ex? Two letters left in one day, clearly intended to intimidate you…that's cause for him to be arrested. I'm not sure what charges would stick, but a conversation in an interview room can go a long way."

"You're really not upset that I schemed a bit to get this place?" *A bit* was doing a lot of heavy lifting in that question, too. Isla's chest hurt as she waited for the answer.

Rafe looked around one more time. "I love my mother very much," he finally said. "But she has a stubborn streak a mile wide. This vacation to Italy? My father's been waiting to take her on it for five years. She needed to let go of the cafe, and finding a local buyer to practically give it away to was the only thing that worked in the end. You did us all a favour. My lips are sealed, and so are Dani's. Plus, we all like your butter tarts better, but don't ever tell my mom that."

"Oh my God," Isla said, her body shaking in relief. "No, that's just between us."

"Good. And about Brett?"

She took a deep breath. "I'd rather try to deal with him myself? Safely, I promise. I have some unfinished business with him and the military. I want to file a complaint with the military police."

Her initial strategy when she'd left Brett had been to starve the narcissist of attention. She thought it had worked, but as part of her life was online, he'd been able to spin a story that kept him centred in his version of her life.

No more of that.

There would be no big showdown with him. He wouldn't get the satisfaction of seeing how angry she was with him. She would deal with this in the most savage way she could imagine—by blading him in the back to the army.

CHAPTER TWENTY-THREE

ADAM SLOUCHED in the driver's seat of his pickup truck, glowering at the low slung building just inside the gates of the base.

It had been a few years since he'd been here as a soldier, but it hadn't changed much.

His role here today was strictly that of driver, and when Isla finished inside, being whatever kind of emotional support person she needed, even though he was starting to doubt he was the right guy for that job.

Two days had passed since Isla came home and woke him up, apologetic, but knowing he would want to hear as soon as possible that Brett—that *Jackass*, which was a better name for the guy—had left Anne Minelli a letter, too.

He held her hand as she placed a call to the military police on the base and set up this appointment to make a formal complaint.

The military had let her down two years earlier when she tried to be re-located away from a man she knew was emotionally abusive. Their failure at that point had led directly to the events of this week, with an officer stalking his ex-wife, a veteran, and she wasn't going to let that go this time.

It would start with this complaint. If it didn't end with Brett Jackson being moved across the country, away from her, then she would pursue other legal options.

Or Adam would rearrange the guy's body parts to the point of dysfunction.

Ideally, it wouldn't get to that point, although Adam had run through that interaction in his head many times. How he'd make the guy see that his twisted point of view was all wrong. But that was a fantasy. That wasn't how grown-ups dealt with their problems.

And Isla being harassed by her ex wasn't the only thing on Adam's mind. Now that he knew the full depth of how much Jackson had betrayed her, the weight of Adam's own decisions grew each time he thought about the choices he'd made, casually, without enough consideration of what he was asking her to give up.

He'd seduced her. Talked her into marriage.

Tricked her into another relationship where she wasn't getting what she deserved—and Adam wanted to fix that, but it was harder than he thought to figure out how to take the next step. And that they were sleeping together again only made it that much more complicated.

Because while Isla had said at the outset that she no longer believed in love, that she no longer could see herself marrying for love, deep down Adam knew she was more than capable of loving. She *was* love. Love emanated from everything she did. In her generous spirit, in her friendships, in the way that she cared for him. Even the way she worried about her ex-husband, wanting him simply *gone*, and not punished brutally. The thoughtfulness with which she carried out everything, how she made decisions. She was a loving human being.

No matter how unconventional their relationship was, it was a marriage Adam took seriously. And yet it wasn't just that he couldn't bring himself to say the l-word—he couldn't bring himself to even consider it.

That had been fine until he read the letter from Brett.

He had thought it was enough to be a good partner.

Now his guilt ate at him from the inside. And every soft gesture from his wife, every caring kiss, and even her playful banter made him feel like a fraud.

When she came out, her step lighter than when she'd entered the building, he pushed himself out of the truck and went around to open her door.

"I think it went well," she whispered before climbing into the passenger seat. "Thank you."

For what?

They stopped in Owen Sound to do some fancy food shopping, then headed home. He thought he was hiding his dark self-doubt from her.

He was wrong.

"What is on your mind?" Isla finally asked over dinner.

He didn't want to lie to her, and he didn't know how to say any of the shit in his head out loud, so he shrugged.

She rolled her eyes. "Okay."

"Maybe it's work stuff."

"Is it?"

He made a face. "No."

"Then…"

"There's a part of me that worries I'll never be good enough for you."

"You're very good for me."

"That's not the same thing." It came out like a bark, not at all how he wanted to speak to her.

Her soft gaze didn't waver. "How is it different?"

"You deserve…" *Love.* Fuck, he could *not* say that he didn't love her out loud. It wasn't true. It just wasn't… "I regret how we started. That's part of it."

"I don't." She wrapped her hand around his, but it felt like she was leaning across a chasm to hold on to him. "We needed time."

The unspoken next sentence was that she'd taken that time and come to a place of being ready for a relationship again. One she already knew how to do, because she'd give all that love to her ex, and he'd squandered it.

Like Adam was squandering it, just in a different way.

"I told you before. I'm broken inside."

She took a deep breath. "You don't feel broken to me. No more than anyone else. When I'm with you, I feel how good you are. You're nothing like him."

"Am I not?"

"No." Her eyes shimmered. "Who told you that you aren't enough?"

Everyone. "Who hasn't?"

"Me."

That smacked the words out of his mouth better than if she'd taken her hand to his face.

"I'm so sorry." His voice cracked and he didn't even care. "You're right. You are the best part of my day. You are my favourite person in the entire world."

It wasn't enough. He should tell her he loved her, but the words couldn't form. He wasn't sure, and he wouldn't say something that wasn't true. *How could he not be sure?* Because he was broken.

He pushed to stand, and she caught him by the wrist. She dragged him to stand in front of her, and she wrapped her arms around his hips, and pressed her face into his waist.

"I should get some rest. I was thinking I might sleep by myself tonight."

"Oh." She lifted her head, her expression searching and guarded. "Okay."

"The shifts are getting busier," he said, a weak excuse she saw right through. Her gaze cooled even as she nodded.

He'd just lied to her face.

If he hadn't felt like a monster before, that would be enough to put him in that category.

Slowly, she stood and pressed her palm to his cheek. "All right." She blinked, slowly, her eyelashes dusting her cheeks. When she blinked her eyes open again, tears clung to the sooty ends like diamonds. "Just remember that I know what this is, between us, and what it isn't. You don't need to beat yourself up for not being something I never asked you to be."

A painful shudder tore through him, and he deserved every bit of it.

"Good night," she said softly, then disappeared into her room.

<hr>

He didn't hear her alarm go off the next morning.

When he finally padded downstairs to see if she'd slept through it, he found her bedroom dark and empty.

She'd gotten up and slipped out to the bakery before their paths would cross in the morning.

He sank onto the side of her bed and buried his head in his hands.

————

He was still sitting in his truck at the station when Owen pulled in beside him. Richard's truck was next to arrive, and if he didn't make it inside in the next five minutes, he'd be officially late for the unofficial start time of an hour before his shift.

And still he sat there.

Owen tapped on the passenger door window, and Adam gestured for him to hop in.

"Work, wife, or life?"

"Wife," Adam muttered. "We had a fight last night."

"It happens."

"It feels like it shouldn't?"

Owen made a face. "Yeah. But it does. Just tell her you're sorry."

"I will." Tomorrow. Fuck, these twenty-four-hour shifts got in the way of doing the right thing quickly.

"Doesn't hurt to start with a text."

"Yeah." But he didn't pull out his phone.

"What did you do?"

It was what he didn't do. "I pushed her away. I think I've done something unforgivable."

"Nothing is unforgivable if you own it."

Adam shook his head. "This is."

"Try me."

"We— I— I don't feel love. Inside. I feel other things, but not that. And I thought it was fine, but it's not."

"That's what you did to Isla? You told her you don't love her?"

For once, Adam knew he deserved every bit of judgement Owen would throw at him for that failure. "Pretty much."

"Did she tell you that you were lying to yourself? Because it's pretty fucking obvious that you love her."

Adam jerked his head up, confused, because his brother didn't sound mad. He was laughing—and that made Adam see red. "I didn't lie to her."

Owen rolled his eyes. "Okay."

"Fuck you."

"No, fuck you. What is this fucking bullshit? What the fuck do you think love is, if not how you treat your wife like she's the most precious thing in the entire world?"

Adam thought his head might explode. "You don't think I want to love her? Of course she's precious. But..."

Owen raised his eyebrows. "But *what*?"

Doubt clogged Adam's throat. He didn't know. He just felt it, a dark yawning hole in his chest where love was supposed to be. Where confidence and surety were supposed to be. "I don't know how," he finally muttered. "I've never wanted it, never seen it. It's abstract."

"But you're sure you're incapable, and so this thing that walks like a duck and talks like a duck can't be a duck? Look, maybe you're not *ready* to fully embrace what love is with your wife...I can't say I haven't experienced resistance to it myself. But a time will come when you know, and then it will seem like the simplest thing in the world."

"I don't know."

"But you will. And right up until the moment that you *do* know, you don't, and it feels like you never will."

"Gee, thanks."

"I've been there. But it will click into place. And I know

this is the worst fucking timing. I get that. So text your wife, tell her that you're sorry, and tell her that you'll talk when you get home tomorrow. And then actually fucking talk to your wife. Tell her about the doubt, and the darkness. Let her hold you."

Jesus. "Just like that."

"Yes. Just like—" Owen swore under his breath. "Look, we were all just doing our best back then, but I think we could have done better. Will and me. Maybe we should have talked more about what Mom and Dad had. How much they loved each other. I dunno. But fuck, I'm sorry. You know?"

Adam screwed up his face. Yeah, he knew. He nodded wordlessly, then exhaled. "Yeah."

"If you need to go home sooner…"

"I'll be fine. Thanks."

He pulled out his phone.

Adam: I'm sorry for last night. That was shitty of me.

Isla: Yeah. It was.

Well, he had walked right into that one.

Adam: I miss you.

She didn't reply.

———

The last person Isla expected to walk through the doors of her bakery mid-morning was Owen Kincaid. And from the stormy look on his face, and the fact he was in uniform, she had a good idea he knew she'd fought with Adam. Those brothers didn't keep many secrets from each other.

"Owen," she said carefully. "What can I get for you?"

"I was hoping you might have time to talk."

The Kincaids were nothing if not direct when they wanted to be. "Sure." She gestured at the espresso machine. "Can I make you coffee?"

"Sure." He frowned at it. "Does it make regular black coffee?"

She stifled a laugh. "Nope."

"Surprise me, then. Listen, I wanted to give you this." He handed her a heavy cream envelope with a gold emblem in the corner. "It's an invitation to a New Year's Eve gala in support of the Military Family Resource Centre. It's what passes as a fancy event around here."

She slid the card out of the envelope. It looked like it would pass as a fancy event anywhere. *Black tie or formal wear.* "What do I owe you for the tickets?"

"Nothing. Bring my brother, talk him into wearing a suit."

She couldn't accept tickets she might not even use. "I don't know—"

"I do." He made a face. "Look, I don't want to get in his way. He needs to talk to you in his own time. But you are the most important part of my brother's life. More important than his career, more important than us. Watching him with you has been... I spent a long time worrying I was going to fuck that kid up."

"He's not a kid," she whispered.

"I know that now. Ah, hell, I've known that for a long time, but I wasn't ready to let go, because then my job would be done, and I didn't do it very well."

"He thinks the world of you, you know." She lifted her

chin, full of pride for her husband. "When he talks about his childhood and the years after your parents died, he's fiercely protective of your choices and how you put him and Josh first."

"He told you that?"

"More than once."

Owen grimaced, then looked down at the ground. When he looked up, his eyes were damp. "I underestimate him sometimes."

"Tell him that."

"I will." He pointed to the invite. "You get him in a suit. It'll be a good night."

"Thank you."

She was touched, she really was, but she wasn't going to push Adam on this front. If he wanted to retreat, she wasn't going to fight him. She knew exactly what the deal was. Their relationship was a friendship. A kinship, she had thought once, and that word reverberated inside her now. More than a friendship, but not what other people thought.

And she didn't expect any more of him than he was willing to give her.

On the other hand, she wasn't going to give him more of herself than he gave in return. That was the mistake she had made in her first marriage, and she would not repeat it, no matter how much she loved Adam.

And she did love him, she had realized along the way, in small incremental chunks of evidence.

She was fine with that new feeling. It was for her, and a relief of sorts, to realize she could hold love in her heart again. It did not need to be reciprocated.

Actions, investment of energy…those needed to be reciprocated. She wouldn't give him more than she got back, but she could hold in her heart more feelings than he felt for her. She could see that for months he had held an attraction to her which she hadn't reciprocated and he had been generous of spirit in waiting for her to be ready. So she could return that same favour with love.

Maybe he would fall in love with her. Maybe he wouldn't. It didn't matter as long as he was being a good husband to her.

She pulled out her phone and looked at his last text message.

Isla: I miss you, too.

***

The next morning, as Adam had a few other times after a shift, he swung by the bakery to say good morning to his wife.

This time, though, she wasn't alone behind the counter.

Bailey Patel was practicing her barista skills.

Since they weren't alone, he had to rely on his expression to privately convey everything he wanted to say. *I'm sorry. I really did miss you. It's hard to spend twenty-four hours away from you. When can we talk?*

"Do you want a decaf flat white?" Isla asked, her expression pointedly neutral.

So, not now. "Yes, please." He leaned against the counter and watched as she showed Bailey how to steam the milk. "Where did you learn how to do that?"

Bailey gave him a surprised look, like why didn't he already know that about his wife?

Well, there was a lot he didn't know about her. And even more she didn't know about him. They were at the start of the marriage, not the end of it—*never the end of it*—and they were a work in progress.

Just like him as an individual.

"Culinary school," Isla finally said. "It was a good way to get out of knife skills practice. Most instructors appreciate a perfectly poured latte."

She glanced to the side, as if a funny memory had just occurred to her.

He leaned further over the counter. "What?"

She gave him a faint smile. "I almost moved to Australia. It was a passing fancy—like, I thought about it for a week—but I heard they have amazing coffee shops there, and thought maybe I could just backpack my way around their beaches. Did you know they have ten thousand beaches? It would take twenty years to hit all of them, even if you kept moving to a new beach each day."

Adam straightened up and came around the counter. Fuck distance. Fuck expressions he couldn't read. He grabbed her in his arms and smooshed her against his chest. "I'm fucking glad you didn't," he growled in her hair.

She squeezed her arms around his waist. "Me, too."

When Bailey finished his coffee, Isla told her to make her boss one, too. "I'm going to head out with Adam for a little bit, okay? I know covering the counter isn't in your still-to-be-written job description, but..."

"Go." Bailey practically shouted the instruction. "I'm drunk on power, leave me to it."

When they got in his truck, he started it, but didn't put

it into drive right away. He had to apologize properly first. "I'm sorry about the other night."

Isla curled up on the passenger seat, bringing her knees around so she was facing him. "What happened?"

"Complicated feelings. I'm not great with them, clearly."

"You said some nice things about me, but you pulled away at the same time. That's a mindfuck."

"I know. I see that. It won't happen again." He squeezed the steering wheel. "I want to take you somewhere."

"Okay." She didn't ask where. And when he reached across the console, she let him hold her hand.

He drove them to the school. And as they sat in the parking lot of the building where his brother was now principal, he told her what it was like to be a teenage boy walking those halls like a ghost. An orphan with four older brothers who found small faults in everything he did. "When I went here, it was just the high school." He pointed to the sign. "Now it's a community school, with the elementary grades in one wing and the high school in the other."

"Wow, really?"

"Cutbacks. And this school was always too big as the high school. I think they expected a population boom that never happened when they built it." He took a long sip of his coffee, then threaded his fingers through Isla's again. "So when I started here, I was living with Owen. We'd just moved into the house he lives in now. That little bunga-low. Josh and I were sharing a room, although most nights he slept in the living room. Things were tense, but we were all surviving. And there was this girl who liked me. We were both in grade nine, and she'd already had a boyfriend. She wanted to kiss me, and I freaked out. Not my finest hour."

Isla's gaze burned against his skin, but he liked the feeling. He wanted her to peel back his outer layer and figure him out, because he was struggling with that himself, and he trusted her to dig around in his messy bits.

But he couldn't outsource this. He had to look at who he was, and where he came from. "I don't remember what I said to her, exactly. I probably blacked out a little, that's how much the kiss rocked me. But a few days later, she found me and told me it didn't have to mean anything. I… I don't think that was supposed to have a lifelong impact on me, but it did. Layer in there some shit about knowing that my brother knocked up his girlfriend, and not seeing my parents' relationship—not through any kind of growing-up eyes, anyway, and here I am. A thirty-year-old man who believes a little too strongly that none of it has to mean anything. But with you, it does. I need you to know that. You mean everything to me. I want to show you I mean that. I'm not going to ask you to take me at my word, because words are cheap."

She crawled over the console and kissed him. "Not from you. I hear you. And you mean everything to me, too."

He shoved his hands in her hair and held her close so he could kiss her back. From the slot where he kept his phone in the dashboard, a ringtone interrupted them.

Isla laughed and passed him his phone.

"It's Will." Adam felt his cheeks heat up as he glanced ahead to the school, where his brother's office was visible —which meant they were visible to the principal, too. He hit the answer button. "Yep."

"Please stop making out in my parking lot. Kids will be arriving soon."

"They aren't here yet," Adam protested. Then he covered the speaker. "Will says we need to take this home."

Isla took the phone from him, said a breathless goodbye to Will, then pointed at the road. "Let's go, then."

CHAPTER TWENTY-FOUR

THE NEXT DAY, Isla brought up the New Year's Eve Gala. "Would you like to go?"

"Take you dancing? Absolutely."

"It's formal. And will be full of army people."

"Are you expecting me to be reluctant?"

"Maybe?"

"I'm not. I think it's a great plan. We can treat New Year's Eve like our very own Christmas. What do you think about that? I'm not going to assume you got me any presents..."

"I got you presents."

"Do you want to wait until the Gala to exchange them?"

She thought about the extra warm socks she bought him and the new power tools for the kitchen renovation. "If you can wait, I can wait."

"Oh, I can wait." He tugged her into his lap. "Have you talked to Kerry yet about Christmas Eve?"

"We texted."

"Will has volunteered to drive." Adam's brothers were

taking her and Kerry to the pub for their grown-up family tradition of darts and egg nog.

"That's nice of him."

"He pulled a search and rescue pager shift on Christmas Day—"

"What is it with your family and volunteering your holidays away?" She meant it as a light tease, but Adam's face pulled tight, like he was really considering the question.

"I dunno. We grew up with our dad doing the same thing, I guess. And then the holidays just sucked after Mom died. For us, I mean. We made it good for Becca."

Isla's heart cracked for the twelve-year-old boy who had always had to share his father with the community on Christmas, and then lost even that fragmented holiday tradition, too. "What are some good Christmas memories?"

"The party my parents would throw, for sure. I think that's why they hosted a party early in the month, because my dad often worked on the actual holiday. Life of a first responder," Adam warned. "That's not likely to change for me."

"I know. I like the alternate day, don't worry." She nuzzled into him, hoping her attempts to gain intel weren't too obvious. "What was your favourite present growing up?"

He didn't miss a beat. "Lego."

She made a mental note to order him some. "Nice."

"How about you?"

"Science kits were always fun. And one year I got a camera, which was amazing. I went through a real photography phase in my early teens."

"What kind of pictures did little Isla Petersen take?"

She blushed. "I took it to school and documented the sports teams. It was a good tool for spying on my crushes."

"Have you always been shy?"

"I'm not—" She cut herself off, letting Adam look at her. The way he studied her felt soft, like a caress. "Am I shy?"

His smile started as a crooked, surprised notch at the corner of his mouth, then softened and widened. "Yeah. Secretly, maybe, but yes."

Damn. "I've never thought about it like that, but..." She tried to grab the swirling thoughts twisting around in her mind. "What you said about your first kiss not going well. You know, I didn't have my first kiss until I was seventeen. And it was lacking in a certain sizzle. I didn't really date at all until I went to university."

"Are we a couple of misfits?"

"It turns out that we are." She touched his face. "I didn't see that coming for you, I gotta say. You were so sexy and cocky when I met you."

If she wasn't looking at him closely, she might have missed the twitch at the corner of his eye. "What is it?"

"You thought I was sexy?"

"Well, yeah. Objectively speaking."

"And subjectively? Are you saying that five years ago, twenty-five-year-old me could have scored your number?"

She frowned. "You had my number." She gave him her sternest officer look. "For work reasons."

His face relaxed. "I knew it."

"Knew what?"

"I've said too much."

"Or not enough."

"Not to put a damper on the moment, but it's something…"

"Brett said?" White hot rage sparked inside her. "What? Did he accuse us of having an affair?"

"It made no sense."

"But you thought you'd just double-check that I wasn't exactly who he described?"

"I know you aren't!" He pushed himself up to sit forward as she scrambled off his lap and started pacing. "I never, for a second, not even a nanosecond, believed anything he said about you. I read that letter as the deranged, biased perspective of someone who didn't value you when he had you, and maybe didn't realize he'd lost you until it was far too late. It was desperate and nonsensical."

"But it's all living in your head now. And if I say something benign, it triggers doubt."

"No."

"Yes."

"Fuck."

"Yeah." She clenched her fists, then shook her hands out to release that tension. "Tell me everything he said."

"I don't want to."

"Why not?"

"I don't want you to hear it."

"I've already heard some variation of it, Adam. I lived with him. I think it's probably more likely that *you* don't want to have to say it out loud, to me."

"Okay. Yeah. That."

"So."

"So?"

"Out with it." She waved her hands, urging him to

unload it all. "It doesn't have as much power if you just say it." That was her hope, anyway.

"He said you manipulated men. You had affairs with subordinates. He suggested we had an affair six years ago, and alluded to knowing that we got married for…" He trailed off. "Which when you think about it, it makes no sense. Which is it? Either something improper happened when you were my commanding officer, or we have a sham marriage."

Brett couldn't even be consistent with his poison pen. And neither was true, at least not anymore. No, it had never been true. Adam had gone out of his way to make sure they both entered this relationship eyes open. They'd even been pretty honest with his brothers about why they got married.

Was pretty honest enough to stop feeling guilty?

As if Adam read her mind, he shook his head. Then muttered something that sounded like *nothing to feel bad about*, before leaning back on the couch and giving her a long, hooded glare that somehow felt…good. A bit rough and a lot raw, but he wasn't looking away, and he wasn't running away.

Finally, he sighed. "Owen says I should tell you about my darkness."

A laugh slipped out before Isla could stop herself, and she dropped to her knees in front of him as he gave her a startled look. "I'm sorry," she whispered, leaning in. "But you don't have any darkness. It's just not who you are."

"I don't know about that. Sometimes I feel a heavy weight of not being *enough*."

She sighed and leaned in further, wanting to be as close to him as possible. He urged her up and into his lap again, and she wrapped her arms around him. "You know what I think? The people who really need to deal with the darkness inside them don't feel that weight at all. Guilt and conscience are wrapped together pretty tightly. I worry that I'm being selfish, but I know intellectually that I'm not."

His brow furrowed. "You're not selfish at all."

"That's a matter of debate."

"It's not." He cupped her face, his fingers solid and warm. "Why do you say that?"

"Because I..." She frowned. Because she wouldn't settle? Because she held out for what she really wanted in life? Because she wouldn't give too much of herself?

"You're not," he whispered. Then he brushed his fingertip gently at the corner of her eye. It smeared a wet tear across her temple, and he turned her face, kissing it away. "You're not selfish," he murmured again. "I promise you."

"And you aren't dark." Her words were husky as she clung to him. "Tell me you see that. We're both doing the best we can."

"I'll get there. I'm a—"

She kissed him. "Work in progress. I know." *I love you.* It was right on the tip of her tongue, but she swallowed the words back. In time, maybe. And until it was a shared feeling, she wasn't going to get carried away.

"Can we go for a walk? Get out of the house for a bit."

"It's freezing tonight."

"We'll bundle up." He urged her to her feet, and they silently dressed for outside. Their little lane was dark and quiet, but as they turned down the street, everyone had Christmas lights up. They didn't talk, just strolled together.

Isla didn't push Adam further. And as they moved, a

bittersweet peace settled into her bones. She'd thought she couldn't handle the risk inherent in a relationship. But then she'd gone and tumbled into the most important relationship of her life anyway—one that was imperfect and limited, but wonderful, too.

And in these moments where they bumped into their limits, but didn't run scared, it felt right and good. Almost whole, and they would get better at filling the gaps created by wishes and unrealistic dreams.

When they returned home, she pulled him into her shower. She cupped his face, those tense muscles flexing beneath her touch. He didn't say it, but there was a wordless question in his gaze. How was she able to stay soft to him when he was being uncharacteristically brittle? He wouldn't push her away, though, not that he was trying that hard. She wouldn't deprive them both of touch that fed their souls.

She ghosted her lips against his, and the contact sparked—for a brief moment—that old fear of being selfish and burning herself for it. She craved him, had for longer than she wanted to admit, and that could get so messy.

But tonight, that worry faded to nothing in comparison to how good it felt to be with him, and a new desire to show him that what they had was perfect in its imperfection.

Eyes wide open.

One day they would be more fluent in the language that matched their connection. Until then, they could cling to each other, exhaust each other, and satisfy each other's endless appetite for pleasure.

She kissed her way down his chest, then sank to her knees as steam swirled around them.

The way Adam breathed her name as she put her mouth to him, the way his hands cupped her head and guided her to take more of him down the length of her tongue.

Endless. Appetite.

His scent swirled around her and her thighs began to tremble as he whispered he was close.

She broke away only long enough to smile at him, and ask him to finish in her mouth.

"Fuck," he whispered as he braced one hand against the tiled wall.

She ran the thick, flared head of his erection over her lips. Yes, exactly.

CHAPTER TWENTY-FIVE

CHRISTMAS IN PINE Harbour was magical, even without much time with her husband.

The week before the holiday, Isla poured herself into work. Bailey confidently worked the front of house and trained a part-timer who would be running the *Bake Sale!* stall at the market in the new year, which left Isla free to develop a savoury take-and-go lunch menu. The most popular limited run test recipes included a seasonal duck and mushroom hand pie, and a leek and apple tart she liked so much she made extra to take home for dinner.

It was a similar burst of creativity as had happened after she started being intimate with Adam, and as much as her soft, squishy heart was sad to discover it wasn't his magical kisses after all, it was a relief on another level to know that this inspiration really came from inside herself. When Isla was happy, when she was settled and content, then she could do her best work.

It helped, too, that she received an unexpected phone call three days before Christmas from her former commanding officer. He apologized for not advocating for her transfer when she requested it, and let her know that Jackass had been recalled to Petawawa. Knowing her ex was once again eight hours away instead of just an hour made the holiday period all the more festive.

She spent the morning of Christmas Eve in the bakery, where she sold out of every last treat before noon. Every last treat except those she had already set aside.

When she arrived at the station, the fire truck was gone, on a call, but one of the volunteers directed her to Owen's office.

"Merry Christmas," he said when she knocked on the door. "What brings you by?"

She lifted a white cardboard box in the air. "A little something for those who are working today."

He pressed a button on his radio. "Pumper 2, there's a special delivery of…"

"Peppermint mocha Nanaimo bars and candy cane cupcakes," she filled in.

"Lucky Adam." Owen cleared his throat and pressed the radio button again. "Sorry Pump 2, let's try that again. There is a special delivery of Nanaimo bars and cupcakes for your team when you get back to the station. Unless, of course, you'd like to donate it to the EMS team. Spirit of Christmas and all that."

"EMS Supervisor, this is Pumper 2," Adam said over the radio, his voice cool and professional. "We are returning to station. ETA five minutes. Touch a cupcake and lose a hand. Merry Christmas."

Isla chuckled as she pulled another box from the tote. "Those are actually for your team," she said. "The fire-fighters never need to know."

She met the truck in the bay and gave Adam a quick kiss in front of everyone before leaving them to their work.

That night, Will picked her up, then swung over to get Kerry, and chauffeured them to the annual "this is how grown-ups do Christmas Eve" party at the Green Hedgehog in Lion's Head. There was an egg nog fuelled darts competition, and Isla held her own, coming in second behind Josh.

The next morning she had a leisurely sleep in, followed by a brunch with all of Adam's family who weren't working.

A few days after Christmas, Isla came home from the bakery and found a large box waiting on the porch with Adam's name on the shipping label. She took a picture of it and texted it to him.

Isla: You have a big package
Adam: Why thank you
Adam: Oh, it took a minute for the photo to load
Adam: My acceptance of the compliment still stands
Isla: It's heavy, too

Then she added an innocent angel emoji to know that she'd meant the double entendre that time.

When he got home, he carried the box upstairs to the workout room, but not before lifting her onto the kitchen counter and rubbing his other big package right up against her until she got all steamed up from the inside out.

And then the day before New Year's Eve, Adam went out for an hour, and returned with Christmas lights of their own, which he strung up through the entire house.

"Tomorrow night," he said when he showed her the master switch. "When we get home from the gala, you'll flip this switch and it'll be *our* Christmas Eve."

CHAPTER TWENTY-SIX

ISLA TURNED as Adam knocked on her bedroom door, which she'd left ajar. They had split up to get ready for the gala, and now her heart climbed into her throat at the first sight of him all dressed up.

He wore the suit they got married in, but he had a very different expression on his face than he had that morning in August. Tonight he had a gleam in his eye that made her pulse quicken, and when he crossed the room to her, she caught a whiff of a new scent.

"That cologne," she murmured, swaying into him. "What is that?"

"I used to wear this to go clubbing."

She inhaled, and the sharp, heady aroma of clove, black pepper, and a sweet kiss of jasmine dragged her back to their first dinner together. "You haven't worn it since coming home." She wanted to climb inside his shirt. "Why not?"

He tucked a strand of her hair behind her ear, his fingers lingering on her neck. "I can't wear scents...at work..."

She jerked her face up, surprised to hear the distraction in his voice. When she met his gaze, she found the gleam had been replaced by naked desire. "Hi," she whispered. "You smell really good."

"As do you." He glanced down her body, lingering on her cleavage before meeting her eyes again. "And you look incredible. The dress is a surprise."

It was a black velvet piece that clung to her curves. She had bought it after her divorce, for an event she went to without a date. It had a cowl neckline that swooped wide across her cleavage, hiding the tops of her breasts from anyone except someone standing right up against her, so his particular vantage point at the moment had never been experienced before by anyone, and it gave her a thrill that he was the first to appreciate her in it. "I'm glad you like it."

"It's very…touchable." He traced his fingertips along the edge of the fabric, skating across her skin and raising goosebumps as he went.

She covered his hand with hers and drew his touch under the fabric, gasping when he grazed her nipple.

"We're going to be late." He gave her a rakish grin that promised he didn't care.

Neither did she. "Is it a fixed arrival time?"

"Nope." He dropped his head, his mouth following the trail of his fingers. He tugged the dress down and revealed the barely there demi-cups of her bra. His lips closed over one tight peak, through the fabric, and she made an unholy sound.

He grabbed her hips and bunched her dress up in tight, jerky motions. But as soon as his hands were on her bare skin, his gestures smoothed. Just as rushed, but gentler.

Adam was always endlessly gentle with her. Even when need overtook them.

He lifted her up enough to perch her bottom on the edge of the bed. Then they worked together to undo his fly. He was hard for her already. She was ready, too, and as she clung to his shoulders, he thrust inside her. He took her quickly, each pump of his hips driving her whole body against the edge of the bed. With each surge, she breathed in more of his cologne, a scent she hadn't smelled in months. *This* was the man she had first connected with, a man Adam had hidden from her for months, because she hadn't been ready for this side of him. But she was ready now.

"Harder," she whispered. "Faster." Her words came out in bursts now, desperate, eager pleading. No, not pleas. Commands, because there was nothing shy about how much she wanted her husband. All night she would bear the flush of his effect on her. It would feel obscene, even after she tidied up.

She would be his secret, wanton woman beneath a formal gown and behind a rack of medals.

Pleasure built in her body, a tight stack that marched upwards inside her and then started to wobble, and just before it toppled, exploded instead. Throwing her head back, she groaned through her orgasm, then Adam pulled out with his own cry.

As the after effects made her twitch, his mouth found hers for a soft, seemingly endless kiss. *Thank you*, it said. *No, thank you*, her lips pressed back.

When she finally pulled away, she knew she'd have to go and fix her makeup all over again, and she didn't care at all.

"I should..." she trailed off. She didn't care about moving.

"Yeah. I need to find a different handkerchief," he said wryly.

She followed his gaze to the cloth in his hand.

"I didn't want you to be all messy for the evening." And then he blushed.

That took her breath away. The sweetness had never been an act for Adam. They could be dirty and lovely to each other at the same time. She leaned back on her hands, relinquishing her grip on his shoulders, and he stepped back. His gaze dropped to her splayed legs, and she had to force herself not to slam her thighs shut.

Not for him, but for herself—she wanted him to look his fill, wanted to soak up the warmth of his hungry gaze. She liked the way he looked at her. She rarely compared him to her past relationship now, but this moment was starkly different from how she'd been seen in the past, and the comparison didn't have the same sharp edge this time.

It was softer, like a new memory was being formed that would dull her experiences.

This is what she would remember when she thought about trying to be beautiful for her partner. With Adam, there was no need to try. She simply was beautiful in his eyes, always, and *that* was sexy.

***

The gala was held in a converted barn, which sounded more rustic than elegant, but as soon as Isla saw the sparkle of silver and gold in the lobby, she knew the invitation hadn't lied about the event's formal note.

They found Owen and Kerry at a table, but Adam didn't want to sit. After greeting them, he wrapped his arms around Isla from behind and swayed her back and forth. "May I have your first dance?"

"You can have all of them." She spotted Catie on the other side of the room, wrapped in red satin, and waved.

Adam tugged her onto the dance floor.

She relaxed into his arms. He was good at this kind of dancing, too. "Last time we were on a dance floor, we got carried away."

He spun them around, then pulled her close enough for him to whisper in her ear. "We already got carried away tonight. Burned off that filthy energy so we could remain respectable in mixed company here."

She buried her face in his neck, her body shaking with silent laughter, but that just gave her a nice dose of his cologne all over again. If being respectable meant not inhaling her husband's scent, well, she didn't want any part of that.

He pressed his hand into the small of her back, then spun them again. Oh, if he wanted to really dance, she was game for that, too.

They stayed on the dance floor for three songs, then made their way back to the table, where Josh had just arrived—and a bottle of champagne had, too.

Adam snagged his brother to help him grab food from the buffet and Isla waved Catie over to join her for a glass of wine.

"You look stunning," she said as her friend sat down beside her.

"Thank you. You do, too. I didn't know you owned anything quite this luxurious."

"It's an exception in my wardrobe. If we come to this next year, I'll be wearing the same thing. Unless there are other formal events I should know about?"

"The Pine Harbour social calendar trends more heavily towards blue jeans and plaid shirts than black velvet dresses, but maybe that should change." Catie looked like she was going to say more, but Will slid into the chair next to her. She gave him a quick smile, but seemed flustered by his arrival. "Hey."

He reached for the bottle of champagne. "What are we talking about?"

"Fashion," Isla offered.

"Nothing," Catie said at the same time. Then she stood up. "Oh look, the buffet."

Will watched her leave, then glowered in Isla's direction. "Was that about the bachelor auction?"

"I genuinely don't know what you're talking about, so nope." She tipped back her glass, then extended it. "Top me up and tell me what the bachelor auction is."

"It's nothing."

Isla sincerely doubted that, but she wasn't going to pry if the school principal didn't feel like elaborating. They were both saved from further conversation when Adam and Josh returned with plates laden down with appetizers.

Adam slung his arm around her, his fingertips playing against the skin revealed by the swoop of her neckline. He wasn't looking at her, but she could feel his attention anyway. Warmth bloomed everywhere he touched, just as it had before they left home, when she'd guided his hand further along that same path.

After eating, they hit the dance floor again. There was a

pause in the dancing an hour before midnight for a raffle, and they had another plate of food from the buffet at that point. Then it was dancing again until the countdown to the new year.

As Auld Lang Syne played out over the speakers, Adam swept Isla back into a dip and kissed her until she was breathless.

"Happy New Year's." His eyes twinkled as he righted her. After weeks of big feelings, this felt like she had old Adam back again, and she loved it.

She kissed him back, then led him to the table where Kerry was pouring one last round of champagne.

"Any New Year's resolutions?" Owen asked after they all leaned in for a toast.

Kerry elbowed Josh. "To get this one to join the co-ed soccer team."

Will grinned. "I'm going to start two new clubs at school."

"All work and no play makes Will a dull boy," Josh griped.

Adam took Isla's hand in his. "Take my wife on a belated honeymoon."

She did a double-take. "What?"

He winked at her. "We'll talk later."

Kerry made a swooning sound. "That's right, you didn't get a honeymoon."

Adam's hand swept up and down Isla's arm, his touch distracting. But she didn't miss what he said next. "When I fell for her last summer, it was perfect timing at the absolute worst time. We didn't even have a chance to talk about it, and then we were both diving into new jobs. It's time to rectify that."

When I fell for her last summer.

Something about the way he said it tugged at her inside.

"Honeymoons are overrated." Josh shrugged when everyone at the table turned as one to give him A Look. "What? They are."

"And how would you know?" Owen asked, laughing.

Josh tipped his flute back and drained the last of his champagne. Then he set it down on the table and sighed. "Because I spent mine in Bali. And the wedding was annulled when we landed back in the States. All right?"

The din of the party surrounding them faded out to white noise. Isla felt her mouth drop open, then, as if moving in slow motion, she dragged her gaze to Adam—shock—and Will—horror—then Owen—confusion.

"You what?" Kerry asked faintly.

"Excuse me?" That was Owen.

The party sounds roared back to life around them. Josh shrugged. "Not my finest hour. Didn't feel like sharing it before."

"Who was she?"

"Someone on the racing circuit. A mistake." He waved it off. "This was not the best moment to dump that news, I guess."

"Not sure there is ever a good time," Will muttered. "Was there a wedding we weren't invited to?"

"No."

"That's it? No? That's all we get?"

"Maybe I'll share a little more of the story next year." He shrugged.

Beside Isla, Adam took a deep breath. "Well, on that note, I think I'm going to take my wife home. It's been a long day. This was fun. Weird, but fun."

Isla mouthed *thank you* to Owen, who was laughing at

his brothers, and he nodded in acknowledgement. It had been fun, a lot of fun, and only a little weird. Weird in a good, close family kind of way.

After they got their coats from the coat check, Isla thought about what Adam had said. "Hey," she whispered, taking his hand in hers. "So…last summer?"

He slid her a glance. "Oh. That."

"Yeah. That."

"Let's go home," he murmured. "We can talk all about it there."

What was there to talk about, besides maybe everything?

They drove home in silence. The only thing that kept Isla from completely falling apart was the tight grip Adam had on her hand—not letting go even for a second after he put his truck into drive—and the echo of his words.

When I fell for her last summer.

She believed him.

She loved him.

And yet it felt like they still had a mountain in front of them to climb, to get over, because she hadn't known. There was still so much they didn't know about each other.

When they got home, Adam let go of her hand to put the truck in park and turn the key. Then he exhaled roughly, twisted in his seat, and reached for her as she was launching herself across the console.

He shuddered and kissed his way past her lips. Urgent, demanding. She wanted to crawl into his lap, get inside his coat with him, and never let go.

But the sharp wintery cold outside was starting to seep into the truck cab already, and Adam's breath puffed in clouds between them as he pulled back.

"I need—"

"Let's go in—"

They both stopped, and then he gestured for her to go ahead.

"Let's go inside," she repeated.

He squeezed her hands, his gaze hot and mesmerizing even in shadow. "Stay right where you are."

He was around the truck in a flash to help her down, then kept his body shielding her from the wind and snow all the way to the front door.

Inside, he guided her into the living room without turning on any lights.

He kissed her in the dark for a long, urgent moment. Then he shuddered and stepped back. "I want to show you something," he whispered. "Stay here. Stay here and be beautiful, just exactly as you are. I'll be right back."

She shook as he left the room, as he climbed the stairs. He returned quickly, carrying something.

"I had a plan for these," he said as he set down the large box that had arrived earlier in the week. "I was going to…well, it doesn't matter. Now is perfect."

He cupped her face in his hands, kissing her again, then asked her to close her eyes.

She pressed her eyelids shut.

———

Adam had spent the last week planning an absolutely perfect "Christmas morning" to act out on New Year's Day, and now none of that mattered.

He already had the hooks in place, so it didn't take long to open the box and hang the frames. His hands shook the whole time, desperate to get back to Isla, eager to show her what he had done. What he had finally figured out.

It had taken him too long to realize what Owen had tried to tell him—what had already happened long ago.

He couldn't be vulnerable with Isla until he was vulnerable with himself.

Taking a deep breath, he returned to the living room and took her hand. He guided her to stand, and she laughed lightly, softly. Perfectly. "Where are we going?"

"You need to turn on the lights." He led her to the switch for the Christmas lights, then turned her so she couldn't see the hallway. "Open your eyes."

She blinked her eyes open, then gave him a wide, beaming grin. "Now what?"

He gestured to the switch. "Turn the lights on, and turn around."

She kissed him first, then did as he instructed.

The gasp she let out when she saw the first framed photograph was the best sound he'd ever heard. It trumped any orgasm he'd ever wrung from her body, and every sweet laugh. It was a sound that said she knew how he felt.

He had finally shown her what he needed to say out loud—and he would, as soon as he dealt with the lump in his throat.

She moved closer to the frame and lifted her hand, ghosting her fingers over the image. It was a still from their wedding day video which Adam had never shown anyone, but looked at many times himself. He'd had it professionally printed in black and white on archival paper, framed for posterity. For the rest of their lives, they'd be able to look at this photo and remember the moment they exchanged vows in the most earnest, special way.

He hadn't known yet that he loved her, but in hindsight, there was no doubt in his heart that he did at that moment.

In the photo, her head was cocked to the side, listening to him give his vows, and the way her gaze was locked on his face gave him life. More than once in their marriage she had made him feel like a king. Now it was his turn, quite overdue, to ensure she knew she was his queen.

"There's more," he whispered, his voice gravelly.

Three more pictures, all from his phone. One of just Isla, working in the kitchen at the bakery. He loved the way the light hit the side of her face. Another photo was of her wedding bouquet on the night she moved in. And the final picture was from the bathroom renovation, a selfie he'd taken of himself in his tool belt, but in the shot was the mirror he'd just installed, and captured on that reflection was Isla laughing at him.

Her beautiful, loving laugh. With him, never *at* him.

"For a long time, I thought I couldn't love, because I didn't want to love. And I never had to look closely at that until I fell in love with you." It was better that she was still looking at the last photo, that he could say this while holding her, but not looking at her. "And I think I realized, terrifyingly, deep down, that if I love you, I can lose you. And I never want to lose you."

"You won't lose me." Her voice cracked as she spun in his arms and hugged him as tight as humanly possible. She squeezed him with all her might. "Where did these photos come from?"

"I have a collection on my phone. When I'm at the station and I have some down time, I look through them. I never get enough of looking at you. You're my queen." He tipped her chin up. He'd got through the hardest part. It didn't matter if his voice broke now, if he teared up and couldn't say much else. "You're my wife. And I love you."

Her eyes widened and her lips parted into a silent O.

"I'm your husband," he said huskily.

She nodded.

"Say it."

"You're my husband."

That felt majestic. "Say it again."

She grinned. "My husband."

Damn straight. "You're my wife, Isla. Forever. And I love you with all of my heart. I want to race home to you after every shift, and hold you every night that I'm able. Wake up to you every morning. I need you in my arms, and when you aren't there, something's just wrong."

"I know." She dazzled him with another smile. "I feel the same way, because I love you, too."

He had spent eighteen years convincing himself he didn't need to hear those words.

Had thought the biggest hurdle would be saying them.

But hearing them?

From Isla?

A shudder rolled through him, an unexpected earthquake of feeling, and his grip on Isla tightened, plastering her to his chest.

"Let's go to bed," she murmured into his neck. "I want you again."

The downstairs bed was closer, so he picked her up and swept her in that direction. At her closet, they undressed together, him helping her out of the velvet dress, her working at his shirt buttons.

The bedding was still rumpled from the fast fuck

they'd had earlier on the edge of the bed. Now, Isla swept it back and tugged Adam under the duvet.

He sprawled out on his back and she climbed on top of him, straddling his already hard cock with the sweet spread of her thighs, but made no rush to rub against him or take him into her body. Instead, she leaned forward, tugging the blanket up over her back, cocooning them in together.

Naked, entwined, just the two of them.

She gave him the happiest smile. "The photographs are the best present ever. I need you to know that I got you socks."

He laughed out loud, and kept laughing for a good long while. "That's amazing."

"But I have something else that might be a good present." She looked a little bashful, just for a second, then her expression turned sensual, lusty, and it was a direct hit to that primal part of his brain that wanted his wife. "It's a secret."

He groaned happily. "Yes. Tell me."

"I always want you." She swayed her breasts back and forth, trailing her nipples against his chest. "Do you remember when we redid the bathroom, and you used my shower? I was in the kitchen. When you came out in just a towel, my knees went weak. I think that's when I knew, deep down. I watched you disappear into the darkness of the hallway, and you were just the most beautiful body I had ever seen. I'd been able to resist you once, to lock it down, but after that day, something changed for me. It took me a long time to feel worthy of that desire."

"And now?"

"Now?" She planted her hands on either side of his head and brought one nipple to rest on his open mouth.

He slowly swirled his tongue around that perfect tip.

She inhaled sharply, then sank lower, giving him more of her flesh to suck on. "Ah, yes. That. Oh, Adam."

But he wanted more of what she was saying. He replaced his mouth with his hand, squeezing her skin gently as he pushed for the rest of that sentiment. "And how do you feel about your desire for me now?"

"It's unquenchable," she whispered, bringing herself down to lie on top of him. She kissed him then, her lips questing against his, her tongue sure and naughty.

From beneath her, he stroked her hips and breasts, urging her to move against him until she was ready, and then, as he watched her pulse flutter at the base of her neck, he thrust into his wife, bringing her to sit fully on his cock.

She rose again, the blanket tumbling to pool around her hips, and slowly they began to move. He guided her with lust-filled words, his voice thick with unrestrained adoration, telling her how beautiful she was, how much he wanted her. And he asked her questions, too. What she wanted him to do, where she needed his touch.

They took their time.

When he thought she might be close, she slowed down and slid off him, crawling down his body to lick the taste of herself off his erection. Her flicking tongue, distracting and perfect and tormenting, gave him the wickedest of ideas, and he tumbled them around until she was on all fours at the edge of the bed and he loomed behind her.

First, he teased her with his erection, making her rock her wet, swollen sex back against him. But then he dropped to his knees, surprising her with his tongue, his whole mouth, and the scent of her drove him wild.

When he rose again, this time filling her from behind, it

was *her* words that drove them both to the edge. "I need you," she gasped. "Yes, just like that. Right there. Don't stop."

He would never stop. Never stop loving her, never stop needing her.

As her climax rippled through her, her pussy clenching around him, he roared and thrust deep one last time, barreling forward and collapsing on top of her.

And then, as her gasps turned laughter, happy, out of control giggles, he dragged himself to the head of the bed and pulled her with him.

"My wife," he murmured.

"I love you," she whispered back.

CHAPTER TWENTY-SEVEN

JANUARY BROUGHT two major storms to the peninsula, closing roads and causing "snow days" for the school more than once, but one advantage of living within walking distance of the bakery—and having a husband with a truck that went through anything—meant *Bake Sale!* could open no matter what.

On snow days, she ran hot chocolate sales, so kids could have a cookie and a hot chocolate for twenty-five cents each, and grateful parents rewarded themselves with the fancier treats on sale that day.

With Bailey's encouragement, she also tried some themed days. For Australia Day at the end of the month, she featured bake sale items inspired by the bakeries in Melbourne she'd once thought about going to work in. Lamingtons, mini Pavlovas, vanilla slice, and for the savoury set, Vegemite scrolls.

At the end of the day, she reported to Adam that the Vegemite scrolls hadn't sold well, but everything else was a hit.

She brought the jar of Vegemite home, because she

wasn't likely to use it again at the bakery, and *she* quite liked it on toast with a slice of cheese. As she opened the pantry door to put it away, a scurrying shadow made her jump back.

"Adam!"

He came running.

"The fucking mouse is back."

"Makes me want to run you a bath." His lips twitched. "I'd like to hear that shriek again. Run in and see you all…"

"All what?"

"Soapy."

She liked the way his eyes twinkled, but this was serious. "We need to talk about the kitchen renovation. When is your vacation time next month? And what can I do to help make this house mouse proof?"

"I'll check my calendar." He set his hands on her shoulders and turned her away from the kitchen. "I was serious about that bath, by the way. I'll run you one."

"You're so good to me."

"And then I have a favour to ask."

"What is it?"

"Let me wash your back first." He urged her upstairs.

One change they'd made over the last month was they had switched the workout room and her bedroom. Now the weights and treadmill were in the room downstairs, with the adjacent big shower, and all of her clothes and personal belongings were upstairs with Adam's. The second room upstairs was essentially a walk-in closet with natural light, and the bedroom at the back was just for sleeping.

And sex.

She stripped out of her work clothes, then wandered

naked into the bathroom, where Adam had left the tub filling. She stepped into the hot water and sank into it, letting the heat soak into her muscles.

When he returned, he had a cup of tea for her, and an innocent look on his face.

She narrowed her eyes at him. "What's the favour?"

"I want to go on vacation."

She jerked upright and the water sloshed dangerously close to the lip of the tub. "What?"

"I want to go lie on a beach somewhere hot. Drink fruity rum beverages out of coconuts and float on ocean waves. I'm tired, you're tired. We've both worked hard, and if we can find enough days off between the two of us —if you're willing to close the bakery, or stock it with easy things that Bailey can put in the oven or pull out of the freezer—if you—"

She frowned. "That's your favour? You want to go on vacation?"

"I'll pay for everything. You just need to pack a bathing suit or three. And sunscreen. But I'll take care of that. The buying of it, and the rubbing it into your flesh." He gave her his best boyish grin. "Come on, Isla. Wouldn't it be nice to sleep in every morning, with the warm Caribbean air finally coaxing us to the beach for a late brunch…"

She shook her head, laughed, then slid under the water. When she came back up for air, water streaming down her face, she was laughing harder still.

"What's so funny?"

"How on earth is that a *favour for you?* I know you're the world's best husband, but come on. You want to take me to a beach and you're pretending like that isn't the world's greatest gift to *me?*"

"I thought you might not want to close the bakery," he

mumbled. Then his eyebrows shot up as what she'd just said sank in. He grinned like he'd never grinned before. "You think I'm the world's best husband?"

She flicked water at him as she nodded happily. "Not the most modest, though."

"Is that a yes?"

"It's a hell yes. Take me away from the sleet and the snow." She crawled onto her knees, braced her hands on the side of the tub, and leaned up to kiss him. "You said your new year's resolution was a honeymoon. Who am I to stand in the way of a goal like that?"

"I did, didn't I?" His gaze darkened as he glanced down her body. "Oh, hello bubbles, my old friends."

She slid back into the tub, and waved her foot at him. "Come join me."

He stood and peeled off his t-shirt. "Don't have to ask me twice."

EPILOGUE

ISLA BAKED her own wedding cake—a year late.

Adam woke her up on their first anniversary with slow, lingering kisses, then hauled her out of bed so they could go to the shop.

"It's my day off," she mock protested, but she was grinning from ear to ear.

Adam had flowers waiting for her, a close replica of the flowers she'd carried in her bouquet, and a beautiful card. Isla gave him her anniversary gift after they got dressed. It was a long, flat box that weighed nothing, and she loved the look of confusion on his face as he tried to guess what it was.

The look of delight on his face when he opened it up and found matching aprons was something she would never forget.

They were both blue, like her favourite aprons at work, but these were special because they were monogrammed *Mr. Bake Sale!* and *Mrs. Bake Sale!*

"You have been my rock this past year, and I wanted to acknowledge how special this day is, not just because I love you, but because of what you gave me last year. And I think we should wear them to bake our wedding cake together."

"Technically, you baked it yesterday," he reminded her.

"Right. We should wear them to *decorate* the cake together."

They drove over in Adam's truck, so they could transport the cake home, and he parked behind the bakery. After he parked, he hustled around to open her door, then jogged ahead to unlock the bakery, too.

"You're being extra chivalrous today," she teased, looking back at him as she stepped into the bakery kitchen.

The transition from bright light outside to the dim shadows of the kitchen meant it took her a minute to notice it was full of people. All their friends, Adam's brothers. Even her brother, she realized, who she wasn't close to, but apparently Adam had found him online. And Stevie, too. She stopped, shocked at all the faces, and then Catie popped the cork out of a bottle of champagne. "Surprise!"

Adam wrapped his arms around her from behind, and she leaned back against her husband. "Happy anniversary," he whispered against her temple. "We're having a champagne brunch after a group effort to decorate the cake."

She took a glass of champagne Kerry offered, then hugged every last person in the place before returning to the kitchen. Adam had his apron on, and she donned hers, too.

Adam had insisted on a three-tier cake.

She'd joked that there was no way even Josh and Will could eat that much, and it would go to waste. Now she was glad she'd also made cake pops from the excess cake she'd cut off the rounds the day before.

The bottom tier was vanilla cake with bourbon buttercream filling. The middle tier was lime sponge with a curd. And the top tier was raspberry, with the raspberry bamboozle icing she'd made for Adam.

After they decorated it, Adam carried it into the front of the shop, and then he thanked everyone for coming, and Will and Josh for helping him arrange the surprise. "There's one more thing I wanted to do before we cut the cake." He nodded at Josh, who popped a Bluetooth speaker from out of nowhere and set it on top of the display case. "Owen remembers our parents dancing to this song when we were kids. It was my mother's favourite. And since we didn't get a first dance last year…" A song started playing that Isla recognized from her childhood, *Could I Have This Dance* by Anne Murray. "What do you think?"

She slid her hand into his and let him twirl her into his arms. "For the rest of our lives."

———

———

For more information about Pine Harbour, visit the series website at www.pineharbour.ca. Discover a town map, try Isla's baking recipes, and read about all the books set in this town… including Will's book, coming next: Wild at Heart.

ACKNOWLEDGEMENTS

First and foremost, I need to thank every firefighter who ever allowed a ride along to be filmed, because I think I've watched YouTube's entire catalogue in that category at this point. Writing a book without being able to do any hands on research is a challenge, especially in this series, where I usually am able to go up north and do some in-person scouting around.

I also owe an endless amount of gratitude to Jessica Alcazar, who puts up with panicky messages about literally everything, but mostly about covers. The last minute switcharoo on this series was facilitated by her wise counsel!

It was a joy to work on this book with Kristi Yanta, an exceptional editor who always reminds me to put more of what matters on the page, and strip out what doesn't.

Elizabeth, Monica, Cecly Ann, and Becky, thank you for the keen typo and grammar notes!

And finally, a thank you to someone named Dora who posted a chocolate chip cookie recipe to AllRecipes.com more than a decade ago. I've been making those one-bowl

cookies ever since, and it was while munching on a batch
early in the pandemic, in March of 2020, that I had the idea
for this book. In her honour, Isla makes those cookies too.
(The recipe is on the town website, www.pineharbour.ca!)

~ Zoe

ABOUT THE AUTHOR

Thirteen-time USA Today bestselling romance author Zoe York lives in London, Ontario with her young family. She's currently chugging Americanos, wiping sticky fingers, and dreaming of heroes in and out of uniform.

www.zoeyork.com

facebook.com/zoeyorkwrites

twitter.com/zoeyorkwrites

instagram.com/zoeyorkwrites

youtube.com/zoeyorkwrites

pinterest.com/zoeyorkwrites